致敬译界巨匠许渊冲先生

许渊冲译
桃花扇

PEACH BLOOMS PAINTED WITH BLOOD

（舞台本）

〔清〕孔尚任 著

译

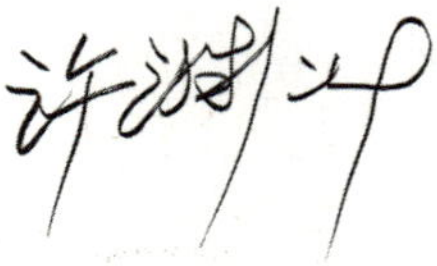

许明

中国出版集团
中译出版社

译序

我国清代最著名的戏剧是洪昇的《长生殿》和孔尚任的《桃花扇》。《长生殿》是写唐玄宗和杨贵妃的爱情故事，陈寅恪认为那是唐朝由盛转衰的关键;《桃花扇》是写侯方域和李香君的爱情故事，反映的却是明末清初的历史。

侯方域是明末的爱国名士，李香君是金陵八艳之一，郎才女貌，一见钟情，互赠信物，以定终身。方域赠香君一个扇坠，扇子后来画上桃花，就是桃花扇了。方域远道而来，钱囊羞涩。阮大铖要联络名士，代马士英为侯送上妆奁财物，香君因为马阮是魏忠贤的奸党，拒绝接受，这一下就得罪了马阮二人。明朝末代皇帝崇祯自尽之后，福王即位，马阮因为拥戴有功，马被任为首相。侯方域却因为指出福王有谋害太子、篡位夺权、贪敛钱财、强纳民女几大罪状，被关入狱中。阮大铖还强迫香君改嫁，香君不从，撞头倒地，血溅扇上，画成桃花，所以桃花扇成了爱情忠贞的象征。阮大铖一计不成，又生一计，强迫香君入宫为福王歌舞。直到农民起义军攻破京城，香君才得以离宫，方域也逃出牢狱，两人看破红尘，分别去山中修道。这就是一对乱世情人的遭遇。这对情人的离合，反映了明朝末年的形势——君主昏庸，贪恋酒色，小人当道，迫害异己，结果内外交困，国破身亡。

《长生殿》写的却是盛世的君王和贵妃，也因为任用了杨国忠为首相，引起了安禄山的叛乱，唐玄宗逃离京城，路上六军哗变，要求处死杨国忠和杨贵妃，结果造成了一对情人的死别。

无论《桃花扇》的生离或还是《长生殿》的死别，写的基本上是真人真事，反映了中国古典文学现实主义求真的要求。剧中歌颂了坚贞的爱情，批评了以权谋私的小人，反映了道德上求善的原则。《长生殿》在情人死别之后，又像《牡丹亭》一样加上了还魂的一段，这反映了作者浪漫主义求美的思想；而在《桃花扇》中，即使如李香君〈骂筵〉时说的：

> 妾的心中事，乱似蓬，几番要向君王控。
> 拆散夫妻惊魂迸，割开母子鲜血涌，
> 比那流贼还猛，作哑装聋，骂着不知惶恐。

也可以看出辞藻的华丽。

侯方域和李香君的爱情故事是全剧的主题，在〈访翠〉中，方域送了香君一个扇坠，并在扇上题了受到赞美的诗句：

> 南国佳人佩，休教袖里藏。

随郎团扇影，摇动一身香。

又如香君不肯改嫁，撞头倒地，血染诗扇时，连鲜血也美化了：

你看疏疏密密，浓浓淡淡，鲜血乱蘸，不是杜鹃抛，是脸上桃花做红雨儿飞落，一点点溅上冰绡。

《桃花扇》的结局有三个版本：一是侯方域和李香君在分飞之后，终于团圆；二是他们分后重聚，聚后再分，各自到南山北山去修道（孔尚任本），表示对明朝的忠贞，对清朝的抗议；三是侯方域投降清朝，做了大官，到修道院去找香君，受到香君责备（电影舞台本），这三个版本都反映了国破家亡的痛苦。第一个是苦中作乐，因为古代喜欢大团圆的结局；第二个是消极对抗，反映了道家的出世思想；第三个是抗日战争时期的作品，反映了当时的爱国主义精神，以及对投降主义的批评。

这种通过爱情故事来反映国家兴衰的剧本，在西方有没有类似的文学作品呢？在莎士比亚的戏剧中，《李尔王》有国破家亡的故事，但写的是父女的感情；《麦克白》有弑君夺位的故事，但那是个人野心的发展，都与爱情没有什么关系。和爱情有关的是小说，如司各特的《昆廷·杜沃德》。昆廷是法国国王路易十一的卫士，爱上了贵族小姐伊莎白，这个少年英雄作战勇敢，赢得了小姐的爱情。小说反映了国王知人善任，老谋深算的一面，但国王并不是小说的主角，主角是少年英雄昆廷。司各特通过昆廷来写路易十一，这和《桃花扇》通过侯方域和李香君来写福王、马士英、阮大铖等，都是从一个侧面来写历史，从一件小事中看出国家大事。不过侯李马阮都是真人真事，小说中却只有国王公爵等是历史人物，英雄美人都是虚构的主角。俄国批评家别林斯基说，司各特用历史为媒介使艺术和生活的统一达到了完善的境地，在这一点上，他可以说是莎士比亚第二。这就是说，孔尚任把《桃花扇》当历史来写，重的是真；司各特把《昆廷》当艺术来写，重的是美。因为重真，《桃花扇》中对反面人物只有批评；因为重美，司各特对路易十一是既有褒又有贬的。由此可见中国文学重善。这是因为中西传统不同，中国最古老的《诗经》中歌颂的就是圣君贤臣和劳动人民的和平生活；而西方同时的荷马史诗描写的多是英雄勇士的非凡力量。这就是说，西方更重强人，征服自然，征服世界；中国更重好人，顺应自然，天人合一。这是中西文化不同的一点。把《桃花扇》译成英文，可以增加西方对中国文化的了解，对建立和谐的世界，也可以算是一砖一瓦罢。

Translators' Preface

There are four important Chinese dramatic works written in rhyme from the 13th to the 19th century, namely, *Romance of Western Bower, Dream in Peony Pavilion, Love in Long Life Palace,* and *Peach Blooms Painted with Blood.* All these four works tell us love stories which reflect the times from Tang to Qing dynasties. *Love in Long Life Palace* is said to reflect the strife between love and power, *Romance of Western Bower* between love and honor, *Dream in Peony Pavilion* shows that love can revive the dead, and *Peach Blooms Painted with Blood* that political power can separate living lovers.

The hero of *Peach Blooms Painted with Blood* is Master Hou, patriotic intellectual of Ming Dynasty, and the heroine is Fragrant Lee, one of the eight famed songstresses in Jinling. They fell in love at first sight and he presented her a fan as token of love, on which he wrote the following poem:

The beauty of the Southern land
Holds you not in sleeves but in hand.

You follow her as summer fan
Brings her fragrant breeze when you can.

They were soon married. The last Ming emperor died as a result of the troubles within and without, a new emperor succeeded to the throne. As Hou did not support the new ruler, he was put in prison and Lee was forced to remarry another lord. She would prefer death to remarriage, so she dashed her head against the ground and her blood stained the fan, on which a peach blossom was painted, and that is why the fan was called peach blossom fan. When she sent him the blood-stained fan, she sang:

You see the blood in deep or light red
Densely or sparsely spread.
It is not cuckoo's tears fallen in showers
But my own blood blent with peach flowers.
It pours out of my heart and from my face,
And leaves on icy silk its trace.

This story tells us the strife between love and power, and ends in the separation of the lovers.

Is there any love story in the West which reflects the rise or fall of an empire? In drama we have Shakespeare's *Antony and*

Cleopatra and in novel Scott's *Quentin Durward*. Shakespeare's play may be compared with *Love in Long Life Palace*, while Scott's novel reflecting the times of Louis XI, may remind us of *Peach Blooms Painted with Blood*. But in the Chinese drama almost all the characters are historic figures while in Scott all the heroes but Louis XI are created by imagination. Here we see realism in Chinese literature and romanticism in Western fiction. In Chinese works the heroes are glorified and the corrupt officials blamed, which shows Chinese idea of morality, while in the West, Louis XI may not be a good king, but he is not criticized. This shows another difference between the East and the West. But the love of beauty is common in the West as in the East, so Fragant Lee may rival Isabelle in Scott's *Quentin Durward*. This tradition comes from *the Book of Poetry* in China and Homer's epics in Greece. In the former more common people than heroes are glorified, which is also a difference between the East and the West. For instance, we may read *A Home-coming Soldier after the War* in the *Book of Poetry* composed about six centuries BC:

When I left here,
Willows shed tear.
I come back now,
Snow bends the bough.
Long, long the way,

Hard, hard the day.
My grief overflows.
Who knows? who knows?

In Homer's *Iliad*, when Hector left his wife for the front, he said:

Where heroes war, the foremost place I claim,
The first in danger as the first in fame.

This shows the difference between realism in the East and romanticism in the West.

目录

Contents

译序 I
Translators' Preface

第一本　一见钟情结良缘
ACT I　Beauty and Duty

第一出　访翠 /002
Scene 1　Visit to a Beauty /003

第二出　眠香 /032
Scene 2　Wedding Night /033

第三出　却奁 /054
Scene 3　Dowry Rejected /055

第二本　一封书信阻刀兵
ACT II　Word and Sword

第一出　抚兵 /076
Scene 1　The Army /077

第二出　修札 /088
Scene 2　The Message /089

第三出　投辕 /104
Scene 3　The Camp Gate /105

第三本　三罪阻立继位人
ACT III　Crime and Succession

第一出　辞院 /130
Scene 1　Parting /131

第二出　哭主　/150
Scene 2　The Emperor's Death　/151

第三出　阻奸　/172
Scene 3　Succession to the Throne　/173

第四本　三番两次逼香君
ACT IV　Persecution on Persecution

第一出　拒媒　/194
Scene 1　Refusal　/195

第二出　守楼　/218
Scene 2　Fragrant in Her Bower　/219

第三出　寄扇　/236
Scene 3　The Fan　/237

第五本　歌舞声中花泣血
ACT V　Songs and Tears

第一出　骂筵　/258
Scene 1　The Banquet　/259

第二出　选优　/282
Scene 2　Selection of Songstresses　/283

第三出　题画　/304
Scene 3　Lee's Bower Revisited　/305

第四出　余韵　/318
Scene 4　Epilogue　/319

第一本　一见钟情结良缘

·
·
·

ACT I　Beauty and Duty

第一出　访翠

【缑山月】〔生丽服上〕

金粉未消亡，
闻得六朝香[1]，
满天涯烟草断人肠。
怕催花信紧[2]，
风风雨雨，
误了春光。

小生侯方域，书剑飘零，归家无日。对三月艳阳[3]之节，住六朝佳丽之场，虽是客况不堪，却也春情难按。昨日会着杨龙友，盛夸李香君妙龄绝色，平康[4]第一。现在苏昆生教他吹歌，也来劝俺梳栊；争奈萧索奚囊[5]，难成好事。今日清明佳节，独坐无聊，不免借步踏青[6]，竟到旧院一访，有何不可。〔行介〕

Scene 1 Visit to a Beauty

(Enter Hou Fangyu in elegant dress.)

Hou (singing to the tune of ***the Moon over the Mountain***):

The powdered face in golden dress not passed away
Reminds me of the splendor of the bygone days.
Seeing the misty grassland would break my heart,
For it announces spring in bloom will soon depart.
How could I not complain
Of spring gone unenjoyed in wind and rain?

I am Hou Fangyu, a scholar roaming for long with my books and sword. Now on a bright sunny day of the third moon and in a magnificent place inhabited by so many beauties, how can I not enjoy spring to the full, at least as much as a roaming poet can? Yesterday I met Yang Longyou, who told me about a young courtesan named Fragrant Lee, whose beauty is beyond compare in the capital of the Six Dynasties. Now she is learning from Su Kunsheng how to sing songs and how to play on the flute and the lute. And I was told not to miss the chance of paying her a visit. But what can I do with a lean purse

【锦缠道】

望平康，

凤城[7]东，

千门绿杨。

一路紫丝缰，

引游郎，

谁家乳燕双双。

〔丑扮柳敬亭上〕

黄莺惊晓梦，

白发动春愁。

〔唤介〕侯相公何处闲游？

〔生回头见介〕

原来是敬亭，来的好也；

俺去城东踏青，正苦无伴哩。

〔丑〕老汉无事，便好奉陪。

〔同行介〕

〔丑指介〕

那是秦淮水榭。

〔生〕隔春波，

碧烟染窗；

倚晴天，红杏窥墙[8]。

as mine? As today is the festival for ancestor-worship, how can I pass such a festive day by sitting lonely in the hotel and not going out to tread on the green in the countryside? I will take the chance to visit the famed delightful resort. (walking)

(Singing to the tune of ***Silk-Paved Way***):

I look up and down
East of Phoenix Town,
From door to door stand willow trees.
I flip my violet whip
All the way in my trip,
Swallows in pair fly in the breeze.

(Enter Liu Jingting, an old friend of Hou's)

Liu (Singing): I wake to hear the oriole's song;
Vernal grief whitens my hair long.
(Calling): Master Hou, where are you going?

Hou (Turning back): Ah! It is Master Liu. You are welcome. I am just in need of a friend to go to the eastern suburbs to tread on the green.

Liu: I am rich in leisure and would be glad to be in your company. (They walk together.) (Pointing to the riverside) See there stand the well-known western bowers!

Hou (Singing): *With vernal waves as screen,*
Windows are dyed in green.
Leaning on a fine day, apricot red
Peeps over the way with its head.

〔丑指介〕这是长桥，
我们慢慢的走。
〔生〕一带板桥长，
闲指点茶寮酒舫。
〔丑〕不觉来到旧院了。
〔生〕听声声卖花忙，
穿过了条条深巷。
〔丑指介〕这一条巷里，
都是有名姊妹家。
〔生〕果然不同，
你看黑漆双门之上，
插一枝带露柳娇黄。
〔丑指介〕这个高门儿，
便是李贞丽家。
〔生〕我问你，李香君住在那个门里？
〔丑〕香君就是贞丽的女儿。
〔生〕妙，妙，俺正要访他，恰好到此。

〔丑〕待我敲门。〔敲介〕
〔内问介〕那个？
〔丑〕常来走动的老柳，
陪着贵客来拜。
〔内〕贞娘、香姐，都不在家。
〔丑〕那里去了？

Liu (Pointing to the bridge): Behold the Long Bridge! Let us go there with ease.

Hou (Singing): *The wooden bridge is long*

With teashops and wineshops along.

Liu: Here we are in the famed delightful resort.

Hou (Singing): *I hear the cry of selling flowers*

Come through deep lanes of bowers.

Liu (Pointing to a lane): You know this is the lane of the famed sisters.

Hou (Singing): It is distinguished in view:

On the burnished door painted anew

Hangs a golden willow branch pregnant with dew.

Liu (Pointing to a house with high doorsteps): This is the house of Mother Lee.

Hou: I want to know where Fragrant Lee lives.

Liu: You do not know Fragrant is the daughter of Mother Lee?

Hou: What a surprise! I want to pay her a visit without knowing her address. What good luck! Now I come to her bower without knowing it is hers.

Liu: Let us knock at the door. (Knocking)

Voice within: Who is it?

Liu: I am the frequent visitor Liu Jingting. Today I have a distinguished friend with me.

Voice within: Mother Lee and Fragrant Lee are not at home.

Liu: Will you please tell us where they are?

〔内〕在卞姨娘家做盒子会哩。

〔丑〕正是，我竟忘了，今日是盛会。

〔生〕为何今日做会？

〔丑拍腿介〕老腿走乏了，
且在这石磴上略歇一歇，
从容告你。〔同坐介〕

〔丑〕相公不知，这院中名妓，
结为手帕姊妹[9]，就象香火兄弟[10]一般，
每遇时节，便做盛会。

【朱奴剔银灯】

结罗帕，
烟花雁行[11]；
逢令节，
齐门新妆。

〔生〕是了，今日清明佳节，故此皆去赴会，
但不知怎么叫作盒子会。

〔丑〕赴会之日，
各携一副盒儿，都是鲜物异品，
有海错、江瑶、玉液浆[12]。

〔生〕会期做些甚么？

〔丑〕大家比较技艺，
拨琴阮[13]，笙箫嘹亮。

〔生〕这样有趣，也许子弟[14]入会么？

〔丑摇手介〕不许不许！最怕的是子弟混闹，
深深锁住楼门，只许楼下赏鉴。

Voice within: They are joining the box party at Jade Bian's bower.

Liu: How could I forget it! They have a festive party today.

Hou: What festive party?

Liu (Flapping on his thigh): My old legs are tired. Let us sit down on the stone bench for a rest, and I will tell you what. (They sit down.)

Liu: My dear Master Hou, do you not know the famed courtesans are vowed sisters? They would give a party on each festive day, and today is the festival for mourning the dead.

(Singing to the tune of ***Silver Candlelight***):

Kerchiefs in breeze

Fly like wild geese.

On festive day

Dress on display.

Hou: Oh yes, today is the Ancestor-Worship Day. People will go to their parties. Why is it called "box party" today?

Liu: All courtesans of the party should bring a set of boxes carrying different delicious food such as sea fowls or aquatic food or jade-white juice, etc.

Hou: What will they do when they gather together?

Liu: They may vie in their skill in music, play on the lute or on the flute.

Hou: How interesting! Is man allowed to join their party?

Liu (Waving his hand): No man is allowed to join them upstairs, but he may stay downstairs to appreciate their art.

〔生〕赏鉴中意的如何会面?

〔丑〕若中了意，便把物事抛上楼头，

他楼上也便抛下果子来。

相当，竟飞来捧觞，

密约在芙蓉锦帐。

〔生〕既然如此，小生也好走走了。

〔丑〕走走何妨。

〔生〕只不知卞家住在那厢?

〔丑〕住在暖翠楼，离此不远，

即便同行。

〔行介〕

〔生〕扫墓家家柳。

〔丑〕吹饧处处箫[15]。

〔生〕莺花三里巷。

〔丑〕烟水两条桥。

〔指介〕此间便是，相公请进。

〔同入介〕

〔末扮杨文骢、净扮苏昆生迎上〕

〔末〕闲陪簇簇莺花队，

〔净〕同望迢迢粉黛围。〔见介〕

〔末〕侯世兄怎肯到此，难得难得!

〔生〕闻杨兄今日去看阮胡子，不想这里遇着。

〔净〕特为侯相公喜事而来。

Hou: Could a man meet the artist he appreciates?

Liu: If he appreciates her, he should send a present upstairs and fruit will then be sent down in return. (Singing):

Like wine-cups passing from hand to hand.

Lovers may meet in their dreamland.

Hou: If such is the case, I will go and try my luck.

Liu: A try will risk nothing.

Hou: But I do not know where Jade Bian's bower is.

Liu: She lives in the Warm Emerald Bower not far from here, and I will show you the way.

(They walk together and sing.)

Hou: Green windows weep on Mourning Day.

Liu: Flutes heard here and there swing and sway.

Hou: Flowers won't wake the lane in dreams.

Liu: Two bridges lie on the misty streams.

(Pointing to Bian's bower): Here we are before the Warm Emerald Bower. Will you please go in, Master Hou? (They walk in together.) (Enter Yang Wencong [Longyou] and Su Kunsheng.)

Yang: I come with courtesans in bloom.

Su: Afar powdered faces and penciled brows loom. (They salute Hou and Liu.)

Yang: It is sheer luck to meet Master Hou here.

Hou: Nor did I expect to meet you here for I was told that Master Yang was together with the bearded Ruan.

Su: I come here to announce happy news for Master Hou.

〔丑〕请坐。

〔俱坐〕

〔生望介〕好个暖翠楼!

【雁过声】

端详,窗明院敞,
早来到温柔睡乡。

〔问介〕李香君为何不见?

〔末〕现在楼头。

〔净指介〕你看,楼头奏技了。

〔内吹笙、笛介〕

〔生听介〕鸾笙凤管云中响,

〔内弹琵琶、筝介〕

〔生听介〕弦悠扬,

〔内打云锣[16]介〕

〔生听介〕玉玎珰,一声声乱我柔肠。

〔内吹箫介〕

〔生听介〕翱翔双凤凰。

〔大叫介〕这几声箫,
吹的我消魂,
小生忍不住要打采了。

〔取扇坠抛上楼介〕

海南异品[17]风飘荡,
要打着美人心上痒!

〔内将白汗巾包樱桃抛下介〕

Liu: Will you please sit down?

Hou (Gazing at the bower): What a warm green bower!

(Singing to the tune of ***Passing Wild Geese***):

I gaze at open court and windows bright.

It is the dreamland for a tender night.

(Asking) Why has Fragrant not yet appeared?

Yang: They are still upstairs.

Su (Pointing upstairs): They begin to play music now.

(The flute is played upstairs.)

Hou (Listening): *The phoenix flute asks clouds to undulate.*

(The *pipa* is played upstairs.)

Hou (Listening): *The pipa's strings vibrate.*

(The gong is struck upstairs.)

Hou (Listening): *I hear ringing jade start*

To stir my heart.

(The lyre is played upstairs.)

Hou (Listening): *Music wafts here and there*

Like phoenixes in pair.

The music of the lyre

Makes my heart fly higher.

How can I send my present up?

(Sending his fan pendant upstairs and singing):

The tassels of my pendant fly apart

To strike the beauty straight into her heart.

(A plate of red cherries wrapped in a white silk towel is sent

〔丑〕有趣有趣！掷下果子来了。

〔净解汗巾，倾樱桃盘内介〕

好奇怪，如今竟有樱桃了。

〔生〕不知是那个掷来的，

若是香君，岂不可喜。

〔末取汗巾看介〕看这一条冰绡[18]汗巾，

有九分是他了。

〔小旦扮李贞丽捧茶壶，领香君捧花瓶上〕

〔小旦〕香草偏随蝴蝶扇[19]，

美人又下凤凰台。

〔净惊指介〕都看天人下界了。

〔丑合掌介〕阿弥陀佛。

〔众起介〕

〔末拉生介〕世兄认认，

这是贞丽，这是香君。

〔生见小旦介〕小生河南侯朝宗，

一向渴慕，今才遂愿。

〔见旦介〕

果然妙龄绝色，

龙老赏鉴，

真是法眼[20]。

〔坐介〕

〔小旦〕虎邱[21]新茶，

down from upstairs.)

Liu: How interesting! The fruit is sent down.

(Su unties the towel and takes out red cherries from the plate.)

Su: It is curious. How can we have red cherries now?

Hou: Do you know who the sender is? What a wonder and joy if it is a gift of Fragrant Lee?

Yang (Examining the towel): Judging by the silk towel, I think the sender must be she.

(Enter Mother Lee holding a teapot, followed by Fragrant, a vase of flowers in hand)

Mother Lee (Singing): *Fragrant grass sweetens butterfly's wing;*
The beauty comes down from Phoenix Terrace.

Su (Startled): Behold! The Fairy Queen descends from the Paradise.

Liu (Clapping his hands): Buddha is blessed!

(All rise to the feet.)

Yang (Introducing the two courtesans): Dear Master Hou, here come Mother Lee and her daughter Fragrant.

Hou (To Mother Lee): Your humble servant is named Hou Chaozong (Fangyu). I have long considered it an honor to make your acquaintance. Now my hearty wish is satisfied.

(To Fragrant) Your beauty outshines the fairy queen and would win the admiration of the dragon king.

(They all sit down.)

Mother Lee: The tea is new, with its leaves just gathered from

泡来奉敬。

〔斟茶〕〔众饮介〕

〔旦〕绿杨红杏，

点缀新节。

〔众赞介〕有趣有趣！

煮茗看花，可称雅集矣。

〔末〕如此雅集，不可无酒。

〔小旦〕酒已备下，玉京主会，

不得下楼奉陪，贱妾代东[22]罢。

〔唤介〕保儿[23]烫酒来！

〔杂提酒上〕

〔小旦〕何不行个令儿，大家欢饮？

〔丑〕敬候主人发挥。

〔小旦〕怎敢僭越[24]。

〔净〕这是院中旧例。

〔小旦取骰盆介〕得罪了。

〔唤介〕香君把盏，待我掷色[25]奉敬。

〔众〕遵令。

〔小旦宣令介〕酒要依次流饮[26]，每一杯干，

各献所长，便是酒底。幺为樱桃，

二为茶，三为柳，

四为杏花，五为香扇坠，

六为冰绡汗巾。

〔唤介〕香君敬侯相公酒。

〔旦斟，生饮介〕

Mount Tiger, and here the new brew is presented for your appreciation. (Pouring tea out from cup to cup)

Fragrant (Singing): Green willow and red apricot in view
Adorn the festive new.

All (In praise): What more felicity can fall on us than drinking tea in company with flowers!

Yang: How can there be no wine in such a felicitous party!

Mother: Wine is prepared and Jade Bian should preside at the party. But as she is hostess upstairs, she cannot come down, so I preside in her place. (Calling) Let wine be served!

(Wine is served.)

Mother: Why not make merry and play games?

Liu: We shall do what our hostess tells us to.

Mother: How can I take Jade's place to lead the game?

Su: Why not since such is the rule of the green mansions?

Mother (Taking out the die): Then I shall do in Jade's place. (Calling) Now, dear Masters, hold your cup, please!

All: Your order shall be obeyed.

Mother: Wine should be drunk in turn. When one cup is dry, the drinker should answer the riddle by showing his best. Now I shall cast the die: one means cherry, two means tea, three is willow, four is apricot, five means fan pendant, six means silk towel. Is it clear?

(Calling) Fragrant, fill the cup of Master Hou!

(Fragrant fills Hou's cup and Hou drinks.)

〔小旦掷色介〕是香扇坠。

〔让介〕侯相公速干此杯，请说酒底。

〔生告干介〕小生做首诗罢。

〔吟介〕

南国佳人佩，
休教袖里藏；
随郎团扇影，
摇动一身香。

〔末〕好诗！好诗！

〔丑〕好个香扇坠，
只怕摇摆坏了。

〔小旦〕该奉杨老爷酒了。

〔旦斟，末饮介〕

〔小旦掷介〕是冰绡汗巾。

〔末〕我也做诗了。

〔小旦〕不许雷同[27]。

〔末〕也罢，下官做个破承题[28]罢。

〔念介〕睹拭汗之物，而春色撩人矣。

夫汗之沾巾，
必由于春之生面也。
伊何人之面，而以冰绡拭之；
红素相著之际，
不亦深可爱也耶？

〔生〕绝妙佳章。

〔丑〕这样好文彩，

Mother (Casting the die): Five, it is the fan pendant. (Offering wine to Hou) Please drink this cup and answer the riddle.

Hou (Drinking his cup): I will croon a poem to the fan pendant. (Singing)

The beauty of the Southern land

Holds you not in sleeves but in hand.

You follow her as summer fan

Brings her fragrant breeze when you can.

Yang: What a nice poem! What a nice poem!

Liu: What a fragrant pendant! I am afraid it would be damaged by too much fanning.

Mother: Fragrant, now it is Master Yang's turn to fill his cup.

(Fragrant fills Yang's cup and Yang drinks.)

Mother (Casting the die): Six, it is the silk towel.

Yang: I will also croon a poem.

Mother: Do not do what others have done.

Yang: Then I will compose something in prose.

(Reading): A towel is used to wipe sweat off the face. Sweat on the face is the fruit of love's labor in the heart. When it is wiped away, lover's charming heart will be revealed. How beautiful is the lover's face caressed by a silk towel! Will it not reveal the rosy cheek impearled with sweat, fruit of love's labor?

Hou: Excellent exposition!

Liu: Such good exposition should win honor in civil service examinations.

还该中两榜[29]才是。

〔旦斟丑酒介〕柳师父请酒。

〔小旦掷色介〕是茶。

〔丑饮酒介〕我道恁薄。

〔小旦笑介〕非也，

你的酒底是茶。

〔丑〕待我说个张三郎吃茶[30]罢。

〔小旦〕说书太长，说个笑话更好。

〔丑〕就说笑话。

〔说介〕苏东坡同黄山谷访佛印禅师[31]，东坡送了一把定瓷壶，山谷送了一斤阳羡茶[32]。三人松下品茶，佛印说："黄秀才茶癖天下闻名，但不知苏胡子的茶量何如；今日何不斗一斗，分个谁大谁小。"东坡说："如何斗来？"佛印说："你问一机锋[33]，叫黄秀才答。他若答不来，吃你一棒，我便记一笔：胡子打了秀才了。你若答不来，也吃黄秀才一棒，我便记一笔：秀才打了胡子了。末后总算，打一下吃一碗。"东坡说："就依你说。"东坡先问："没鼻针如何穿线？"山谷答："把针尖磨去。"佛印说："答得好。"山谷问："没把葫芦怎生拿？"东坡答："抛在水中。"佛印说："答得也不错。"东坡又问："虱在裤中，有见无见？"山谷未及答，东坡持棒就打。山谷正拿壶子斟茶，失手落地，打个粉碎。东坡大叫道："和尚记着，胡子打了秀才了。"佛印笑道："你听兵唧一声，胡子没打着秀才，秀才倒打了壶子了。"〔众笑介〕

〔丑〕众位休笑，秀才利害多着哩。

Fragrant (Filling the cup of Liu): Master Liu, will you please drink your cup?

Mother (Casting the die): Two, the tea.

Liu (Drinking): Is it the tea I am drinking? Now I know why I am not drunken.

Mother (Smiling): It is not the tea you are drinking, but the tea you should say something about.

Liu: Then I shall tell a story about the drinker of the tea.

Mother: A story would be too long. How about a joke?

Liu: All right. I will tell a repartee between two Song poets Su Dongpo and Huang Tingjian. Su asked Huang how to pass a thread through a needle without an eye. Huang said that Su should sharpen his eye to pierce through the needle. Su said the answer was good and he drank his cup of tea. Then Huang asked Su how to carry a gourd without a handle. Su answered that he might throw the gourd on water. Huang disagreed, saying water could not replace the hand. Then Su asked him why tea could replace wine ...

〔弹壶介〕这样硬壶子都打坏，何况软壶子[34]。

〔生〕敬老妙人，随口诙谐，都是机锋。

〔小旦〕香君，敬你师父。

〔旦斟，净饮介〕

〔小旦掷介〕是杏花。

〔净唱介〕“晚妆楼上杏花残，

犹自怯衣单[35]。”

〔旦向小旦介〕孩儿敬妈妈酒了。

〔小旦饮干，掷介〕是樱桃。

〔净〕让我代唱罢。

〔唱介〕“樱桃红绽，玉粳白露[36]，半晌恰方言。”

〔丑〕昆生该罚了，唱的唇上樱桃，不是盘中樱桃。

〔净〕领罚。〔自斟，饮介〕

〔小旦〕香君该自斟自饮了。

〔生〕待小生奉敬。

〔生斟，旦饮介〕

〔小旦掷介〕不消猜，是柳了，香君唱来。

〔旦羞介〕

〔小旦〕孩儿腼腆，请个代笔相公罢。

〔掷介〕三点，是柳师父。

〔净〕好好！今日是他当值之日。

〔丑〕我老汉姓柳，飘零半世，最怕的是“柳”字。

今日清明佳节，

Hou: Your eyes and your tongue are as sharp as theirs.

Mother: Fragrant, now fill the cup of your Master Su!

(Fragrant fills Su's cup and Su drinks.)

Mother (Casting the dice): Four, it is apricot.

Su (Singing): *At dusk she sees apricot flowers fade.*

Shivering with cold, she is afraid.

Fragrant: Dear Mom, now it is your turn to drink your cup.

Mother (Drinking and casting the dice): one, it is the cherry.

Su: Will you please let me sing for you?

(Singing) *Lips cherry-red and teeth snow-white,*

She will not speak as if in fright.

Liu: You should be punished for you take the cherry-red lips for the red cherry in the plate.

Su: You are right and I will drink another cup. (Pouring himself a cup and drinking)

Mother: Now Fragrant, it is your turn to drink and sing.

Hou: Will you please let me fill your cup?

(Hou fills the cup for Fragrant to drink.)

Mother (Casting the die): I need not tell you what is left for you to sing is the willow. (Fragrant feels shy.) Fragrant is timid. Will another Master sing for her?

(Casting the die): It falls on Master Liu.

Su: "Liu" means willow and willow is "Liu".

Liu: Today is Master Liu's day.

(Singing) *I roam like willow down*

偏把个柳圈儿[37]套住我老狗头。

〔众大笑介〕

〔净〕算了你的笑话罢。

〔生〕酒已有了，大家别过。

〔丑〕才子佳人，难得聚会。

〔拉生、旦介〕

你们一对儿，

吃个交心酒何如。

〔旦羞，遮袖下〕

〔净〕香君面嫩，当面不好讲得；

前日所订梳栊之事，

相公意下允否？

〔生笑介〕秀才中状元，有甚么不肯处。

〔小旦〕既蒙不弃，择定吉期，贱妾就要奉攀了。

〔末〕这三月十五日，花月良辰，便好成亲。

〔生〕只是一件，

客囊羞涩，

恐难备礼。

〔末〕这不须愁，妆奁酒席，

待小弟备来。

〔生〕怎好相累。

〔末〕当得效力。

Far away from the town.

Today we mourn the dead

With a willow wreath on a dog's head.

All (Laughing): A dog's head or yours?

Su: All right. Let this serve as your joke.

Hou: Now wine is served. Do not leave your cup undried!

Liu: It is not easy for a talent to meet with a beauty.

(Putting Fragrant's hand into Hou's)

Would you drink the betrothal cup of lovers?

(Exit Fragrant with her shy face covered with one of her sleeves.)

Su: Fragrant is too shy to reveal her love. How about the dowry you ordered the other day, Master Hou? Do you still like it?

Hou (Laughing): I am like the winner of the laurel crown. How could there be anything I do not like?

Mother: If you would condescend to accept my daughter, we should choose an auspicious day for the ceremony.

Su: The fifteenth day of the third lunar month is a happy day for wedding.

Hou: But I am sorry to beg your pardon, for I have only a lean purse on journey, and I am afraid I cannot afford the expenditure.

Yang: You need not worry about that, I will be responsible for the dowry and the feast.

Hou: How could I repay you for your generosity!

Yang: I would be happy to be at your service.

〔生〕多谢了。

【小桃红】

误走到巫峰[38]上，
添了些行云想，
匆匆忘却仙模样。
春宵花月休成谎，
良缘到手难推让，
准备着身赴高唐。

〔作辞介〕

〔小旦〕也不再留了。
择定十五日，请下清客，
邀下姊妹，奏乐迎亲罢。

〔小旦下〕

〔丑向净介〕阿呀！忘了，忘了，
咱两个不得奉陪了。

〔末〕为何？

〔净〕黄将军船泊水西门[39]，
也是十五日祭旗，
约下我们吃酒的。

〔生〕这等怎处？

〔末〕还有丁继之、沈公宪、张燕筑[40]，
都是大清客，借重他们陪陪罢。

Hou: Then a thousand hearty thanks!

(Singing to the tune of ***Peach Blossoms Red***):

Coming by chance atop Witch Mountain proud,
I fancy to be a floating cloud
Bringing fresh shower,
Forgetting the thirsting fairy flower.
O vernal night and moonlit bower,
Do not tell lie!
How could I say to a happy tryst goodbye,
Ready to go to Paradise on high?

(Bidding goodbye.)

Mother: I will not detain you any longer. Please come early on the fifteenth day with the invited guests and fairy sisters and happy musicians to take your bride!

(Exit)

Liu (To Su)**:** How could I have forgotten our appointment with General Huang!

Yang: What is the matter?

Su: General Huang invited Liu and me to join his drinking party in the Western Gate on the fifteenth day. So I am afraid we cannot come to celebrate this happy wedding.

Hou: What then is to be done?

Yang: Do not worry! We may invite other friends.

〔净〕暖翠楼前粉黛香，

〔末〕门六朝风致说平康；

〔丑〕踏青归去春犹浅，

〔生〕明日重来花满床。

〔众下〕

【注释】

[1]“金粉未消亡”二句意说当时的南都，还有南朝君臣追逐豪华的习气。

[2]催花信紧：催花风紧。

[3]艳阳：指风和日丽的春天。

[4]平康：唐朝长安的一个地名，是妓女聚居的地方。后用来泛指妓院。

[5]萧索奚囊：据说唐诗人李贺经常带着背锦囊的小奚奴（僮仆）出游，每写好了诗，就投入囊中，后人称作奚囊。这里是手头拮据的意思。

[6]踏青：中国过去风俗，每逢清明节，大家都出郊外扫墓或游玩，称踏青。

[7]凤城：禁城。南京曾一度是明朝的都城，因此称它凤城。

[8]“隔春波”四句：形容秦淮水榭景色。碧烟指水气。宋朝叶绍翁《游园不值》诗：“春色满园关不住，一枝红杏出墙来。”红杏窥墙，暗用此诗意。

[9]手帕姊妹：结拜姊妹。

[10]香火兄弟：古人盟誓多用香火，因此用来指称香火兄弟。

[11]烟花雁行：烟花指妓女。烟花雁行这里指结成姊妹的妓女们。

[12]海错、江瑶、玉液浆：海错指各种海味；江瑶是一种海蚌，它的肉柱是一种名贵的食品，称作江瑶柱；玉液浆，指酒。

[13]阮：阮咸，乐器名，和琵琶很相近，相传是晋朝阮咸创制的。

The Epilogue of the Scene

Su: *In Warm Green Bower beauties in display*

Yang: *Remind of splendor of the bygone days.*

Liu: *Treading on green will cast in spring no gloom.*

Hou: *Tomorrow flowers will be in full bloom.* (Exeunt.)

[14] 子弟：宋元俗语，指嫖客。

[15] 吹饧（xíng）处处箫：饧即饴糖，如麦芽糖。本句是说处处都听到卖饧人吹的箫声。

[16] 云锣：乐器名，是用十面大小相同、厚薄不同的小铜锣挂在一个木器上，敲打时能发出清浊不同的声音。

[17] 海南异品：指扇坠，用海南檀香制成。

[18] 冰绡：绡是一种用生丝织的绸，冰绡，形容绡的洁白。

[19] 香草偏随蝴蝶扇：蝴蝶偏随香草扇，为了跟下句对得工整，把句子倒装过来的。

[20] 法眼：佛家有五眼，是肉眼、天眼、慧眼、法眼、佛眼。这里借指有高度鉴别能力的眼光。

[21] 虎邱：地名，在江苏吴县西北七里，是苏州的名胜。

[22] 代东：代作主人。

[23] 保儿：妓院里供使唤的男子。

[24] 僭越：在礼数上超过了个人的本分。

[25] 掷色：掷骰子。

[26] 流饮：轮流饮。

[27] 雷同：抄袭、摹仿的意思。

[28] 破承题：破题与承题。

[29] 两榜：古时乡试叫乙榜，会试叫甲榜，合称两榜。

[30] 张三郎吃茶：阎婆惜留张三郎吃茶，见《水浒传》第二十回。

[31] 佛印禅师：宋代名僧，名了元，能诗。黄庭坚，字鲁直，号山谷道人，宋代著名诗人，为江西诗派的创始人。

[32] 定瓷：是中国一种著名的瓷器，在定州出产。阳羡茶，阳羡在今江苏宜兴县南五里，从唐以来，以产茶著名。

[33] 机锋：我国古代禅宗和尚们彼此用语言互相启发，称机锋。

[34] 软壶子：阮胡子的谐音，即阮大铖。

[35] “晚妆楼上杏花残”二句：这是王实甫《西厢记》第三本第二折里的两句曲文。

[36] “樱桃红绽”二句：原文引自《西厢记》第一本第一折。

[37] 柳圈儿：江南一带风俗，清明时节用柳条编成圈儿，戴在小孩子的头上。

[38] 巫峰：传说楚襄王到高唐游玩，梦见一个女子愿和他合欢。临别时，她说："妾在巫山之阳，高丘之阻。朝为行云，暮为行雨，朝朝暮暮，阳台之下。"（见宋玉《高唐赋》）后人因用巫山、云雨、高唐、阳台等来形容男女性爱。

[39] 黄将军船泊水西门：黄将军即黄得功，辽宁开原卫人，以武功任总兵官，崇祯十七年，进封靖南伯。水西门，南京城门名。

[40] 丁继之、沈公宪、张燕筑：都是明末有名的戏曲演员。

第二出　眠香

【临江仙】〔小旦艳妆上〕

短短春衫双卷袖，

调筝花里迷楼[1]。

今朝全把绣帘钩，

不教金线柳，

遮断木兰舟[2]。

妾身李贞丽，只因孩儿香君，年及破瓜，梳栊无人，日夜放心不下。幸亏杨龙友，替俺招了一位世家公子，就是前日饮酒的侯朝宗，家道才名，皆称第一。今乃上头[3]吉日，大排筵席，广列笙歌，清客俱到，姊妹全来，好不费事。

〔唤介〕保儿那里？

〔杂扮保儿搧搧慢上〕席前搀趣话，

花里听情声。

Scene 2 Wedding Night

(Enter Mother Lee in rich attire.)

Mother (Singing to the tune of ***Riverside Daffodils***):

In short spring coat with uprolled sleeves,

I play on lute, bewildered amid flowers and leaves.

I draw up curtain new

Lest its golden threads keep orchid boat out of view.

I am Mother Lee. My daughter Fragrant has come of age and I am worried day and night to find for her a life companion. Fortunately our friend Yang Longyou has introduced to us Master Hou Chaozong (Fangyu) of a noble family, an ace of the young scholars, who came to the box party the other day. Today is an auspicious day for their wedding, a sumptuous feast is provided and happy music will be played by the band, honorable guests are invited and beautiful sisters have gathered here. How much labor for such a happy day!

(Calling) Where is the maid?

Maid (Coming fan in hand):

I make fun in the feast and in the bowers,

And overhear the lovers amid flowers.

妈妈唤保儿那处送衾枕[4]么?

〔小旦怒介〕啐！今日香姐上头，

贵人将到，

你还做梦哩。

快快卷帘扫地，

安排桌椅。

〔杂〕是了。

〔小旦指点排席介〕

【一枝花】〔末新服上〕

园桃红似绣，

艳覆文君酒[5]；

屏开金孔雀，

围春昼。

涤了金瓯，

点着喷香兽[6]。

这当垆红袖，

谁最温柔，

拉与相如消受[7]。

下官杨文骢，

受圆海嘱托，

采送梳栊之物。

〔唤介〕贞娘那里?

〔小旦见介〕多谢作伐，

喜筵俱已齐备。

〔问介〕怎么官人还不见到?

〔末〕想必就来。

Dear Mother Lee, are you calling me for the coverlet and pillows?

Mother (Angry): Today is Fragrant's wedding day, and the bridegroom will soon be here. How can you be still dreaming away your time? Why not draw up the curtain and sweep the floor clean and put chairs and tables in order?

Maid: Oh, yes, it will soon be done.

(Mother Lee gives orders for the arrangement.)

(Enter Yang Wencong [Longyou] in new dress.)

Yang (Singing to the tune of ***A Sprig of Flowers***):

Peach blossoms red as brocade fine
Intoxicate as beauty's wine.
The phoenix spreads its golden wing
To beautify the noonday spring.
From golden cup comes wit,
The incense burner lit.
Who will enjoy the pure delight
Of the rosy-sleeved beauty fair and bright?

I am Yang Wencong coming with the dowry for Fragrant Lee.

(Calling) Where is Mother Lee?

Mother: Welcome! Many thanks for your arrangement of Fragrant's marriage. Now the wedding feast is ready. Why has the bridegroom not yet come?

Yang: I think he will soon be here. (Smiling) I have brought with

〔笑介〕下官备有箱笼数件，

为香君助妆，教人搬来。

〔杂抬箱笼、首饰、衣物上〕

〔末吩咐介〕抬入洞房，铺陈齐整着！〔杂应下〕

〔小旦喜谢介〕如何这般破费，多谢老爷！

〔末袖出银介〕还有备席银三十两，交与厨房；

一应酒肴，俱要丰盛。

〔小旦〕益发当不起了。

〔唤介〕香君快来！

〔旦盛妆上〕

〔小旦〕杨老爷赏了许多东西，上前拜谢。

〔旦拜谢介〕

〔末〕些须薄意，何敢当谢，请回，请回。

〔旦即入介〕

〔杂急上报介〕新官人到门了。

〔生盛服，从人上〕

虽非科第天边客，

也是嫦娥月里人。

〔末、小旦迎见介〕

〔末〕恭喜世兄，得了平康佳丽，

小弟无以为敬，草办妆奁，

粗陈筵席，聊助一宵之乐。

me the dowry for Fragrant. Will you please let me show you? (Boxes large and small of the dowry are brought in.) Carry them to the nuptial chamber and put them in order!

Mother (Happy)**:** A thousand thanks cannot express my hearty gratitude.

Yang (Taking out silver coins)**:** Here are thirty pieces of silver for the expenditure of the feast.

Mother: I do not know how to express my gratitude.

(Calling) Fragrant, come out at once!

(Enter Fragrant in splendid attire.)

Show our gratitude for Master Yang, whose generosity is beyond our thanks.

(Fragrant bows to show her gratitude.)

Yang: Your beauty is worth much more than these humble gifts. Please do not mention it. I dare not delay you here long. Will you please not be disturbed? (Exit Fragrant.)

(Enter a servant.)

Servant (Announcing)**:** Here comes the bridegroom.

(Enter Master Hou in splendid attire, followed by attendants)

Hou: *Though not a winner of laurel crown,*

From the moon palace I am coming down.

(Yang and Mother Lee salute Hou.)

Yang: *Congratulations, my dear Master Hou!*

What more felicity can fall on you

Than to win a beauty incomparable in view!

I offer a humble dowry to show my delight

〔生揖介〕过承周旋，何以克当。

〔小旦〕请坐，献茶。
〔俱坐〕〔杂捧茶上，饮介〕
〔末〕一应喜筵，安排齐备了么？
〔小旦〕托赖老爷，件件完全。
〔末向生拱介〕今日吉席，
　　小弟不敢搀越，
　　竟此告别，
　　明日早来道喜罢。
〔生〕同坐何妨。
〔末〕不便，不便。〔别下〕
〔杂〕请新官人更衣。
〔生更衣介〕
〔小旦〕妾身不得奉陪，替官人打扮新妇，撺掇[8]喜酒罢。
〔别下〕
〔副净、外、净扮三清客上〕
　　一生花月张三影[9]，
　　五字宫商李二红[10]。
〔副净〕在下丁继之。
〔外〕在下沈公宪。
〔净〕在下张燕筑。
〔副净〕今日吃侯公子喜酒，只得早到。

〔净〕不知请那几位贤歌[11]来陪俺哩。

In your felicitous wedding night.

Hou (Saluting with clasped hands)**:** I have owed you so much that I do not know how to repay you.

Mother: Will you please sit down and drink tea?

(Tea is served. They sit down and drink.)

Yang: Is the wedding feast well arranged?

Mother: It is arranged in compliance with your order.

Yang (Saluting Hou with clasped hands)**:** Today is your happy wedding day, I should not divert your attention by my presence. So I beg to take leave and tomorrow I will come again for congratulations.

Hou: The longer you stay, the happier we shall be.

Yang: I would not divert your happy attention. (Exit.)

Announcer: Will it please the bridegroom to change his dress?

(Hou changes for the wedding attire.)

Mother: I beg to leave you for Fragrant's attire and preparations for the wedding feast. (Exit.)

(Enter three guests: Ding Jizhi, Shen Gongxian and Zhang Yanzhu.)

Guests: *We spend our life with flowers under the moon,*

Play music light and sing to joyful tune.

Ding: I am Ding Jizhi.

Shen: I am Shen Gongxian.

Zhang: I am Zhang Yanzhu.

Ding: Today is Master Hou's wedding day, so I am obliged to come early.

Zhang: Do you know which songstresses are invited in our company?

〔外〕说是旧院几个老在行[12]。

〔净〕这等都是我梳栊的了。

〔副净〕你有多大家私，梳栊许多。

〔净〕各人有帮手，你看今日侯公子，何曾费了分文。

〔外〕不要多话，侯公子堂上更衣，大家前去作揖。

〔众与生揖介〕

〔众〕恭喜，恭喜！

〔生〕今日借光。

〔小旦、老旦、丑扮三妓女上〕

情如芳草连天醉，
身似杨花尽日忙。

〔见介〕

〔净〕唤的那一部歌妓，都报名来。

〔丑〕你是教坊司[13]么，叫俺报名。

〔生笑介〕正要请教大号。

〔老旦〕贱妾卞玉京[14]。

〔生〕果然玉京仙子。

〔小旦〕贱妾寇白门。

〔生〕果然白门[15]柳色。

〔丑〕奴家郑妥娘。

〔生沉吟介〕果然妥当不过。

〔净〕不妥，不妥！

〔外〕怎么不妥？

Shen: Can it be other than the famed sisters of the delightful resort?

Zhang: Should I pay for the expenditure?

Ding: Could you afford to pay so much?

Zhang: Heaven helps those who help themselves. Master Hou need not pay the expenditure.

Shen: Do not talk too much! Master Hou is now in his wedding dress. Let us go to the hall for congratulations.

All (Saluting Hou with clasped hands)**:** Congratulations, congratulations!

Hou: Let us share the delight together!

(Enter three courtesans: Jade Bian, White Kou and Safe Zheng.)

Courtesans: *Drunken in love, we spread as grass all the way;*

Like willow-down we're busy all the day.

(They salute Hou and other guests.)

Zhang: Are you all famed songstresses? Would you please tell us your name?

Zheng: Are you master in charge of musicians? Why should we tell our names to you?

Hou (Smiling)**:** Excuse us for our ignorance of your high fame.

Bian: I am Jade Bian.

Hou: You are indeed a fairy from the Jade Capital.

Kou: I am White Kou.

Hou: You are really as tender as the willow of White Gate.

Zheng: I am Safe Zheng.

Hou (Hesitating)**:** It is indeed safe...

Zhang: It is not safe, not safe at all.

Zheng: Why not safe? Why not?

〔净〕好偷汉子。

〔丑〕呸！我不偷汉，你如何吃得恁胖。

〔众诨笑[16]介〕

〔老旦〕官人在此，快请香君出来罢。

〔小旦、丑扶香君上〕

〔外〕我们做乐迎接。

〔副净、净、外吹打十番[17]介〕

〔生、旦见介〕

〔丑〕俺院中规矩，不兴[18]拜堂，就吃喜酒罢。

〔生、旦上坐〕

〔副净、外、净坐左边介〕

〔小旦、老旦、丑坐右边介〕

〔杂执壶上〕

〔左边奉酒，右边吹弹介〕

【梁州序】〔生〕

齐梁词赋，
陈隋花柳[19]，
日日芳情迤逗[20]。
青衫偎倚，
今番小杜扬州[21]。
寻思描黛[22]，
指点吹箫，
从此春入手。
秀才渴病急须救，
偏是斜阳迟下楼，
刚饮得一杯酒。

Zhang: How can I feel safe when you flirt with a new gallant?

Zheng: If I did not satisfy a new gallant, could I be satisfied with you? (All burst in laughter.)

Bian: The bridegroom is already here. Why is the bride late?

(Enter Fragrant Lee, accompanied by White Kou and Safe Zheng.)

Shen: Music should be played for the congratulatory ceremony.

(Ding, Zhang, Shen and musicians play the wedding music.)

(Hou and Fragrant salute each other.)

Zheng: In accordance with the custom of the green mansions, there should be no wedding ceremony but a wedding feast. (Hou and Fragrant take the honorable seats, Ding, Shen, Zhang on their left and White Kou, Jade Bian and Safe Zheng on their right. Wine is served. Guests on the left hold up their cups and those on the right play music.)

Hou (Singing to the tune of ***Liangzhou Prelude***):

We read verse and prose as we please
Among flowers and willow trees.
What felicity is on the way
For us today?
My blue gown clings to you,
As happy as the poet in Yangzhou.
I ponder how
To pencil your green brow,
And how to play on flute and sing
Of happiness in spring.

〔右边奉酒，左边吹弹介〕

【前腔】〔旦〕
楼台花颤，
帘栊风抖，
倚着雄姿英秀。
春情无限，
金钗肯与梳头[23]。
闲花添艳，
野草生香，
消得夫人做。
今宵灯影纱红透，
见惯司空[24]也应羞，
破题儿真难就。
〔副净〕你看红日衔山，
乌鸦选树，
快送新人回房罢。
〔外〕且不要忙，
侯官人当今才子，
梳栊了绝代佳人，
合欢有酒，岂可定情无诗乎？
〔净〕说的有理，待我磨墨拂笺，伺候挥毫。

You bring fresh shower
For my long thirsting flower.
The setting sun on the decline,
I have just drunk a cup of wine.

(Guests on the right hold up their cups and those on the left play music.)

Fragrant (Singing to ***the previous tune***):

The flower shivers, if you please;
The screen is wrinkled with the breeze.
In face of such a hero as you,
Boundless is spring in view.
My golden hairpin can't adorn my head,
It's not so charming as a flower red,
Nor so fragrant as wild grass green.
It cannot beautify the bride behind the screen.
Tonight the candle flame will redden the curtained bed.
Even a veteran would feel shy at the sight.
What can I say for my first night?

Ding: Behold! The sun is sinking behind yonder hills and crows are hovering over their nest. It is time to see the newly-weds to their nuptial bed.

Shen: No hurry. Master Hou is the talent of the day, while Fragrant is the incomparable beauty of the age. Their wedding is celebrated with wine. How could there be no verse to celebrate their love?

Zhang: You are right. Let me get ink and paper ready for Master

〔生〕不消诗笺，
小生带有宫扇一柄，
就题赠香君，永为订盟之物罢。
〔丑〕妙，妙！我来捧砚。
〔小旦〕看你这嘴脸，只好脱靴罢了。

〔老旦〕这个砚儿，倒该借重香君。
〔众〕是呀！
〔旦捧砚，生书扇介〕
〔众念介〕夹道朱楼一径斜，
王孙初御富平车。
青溪尽是辛夷树，
不及东风桃李花。
〔众〕好诗，好诗！香君收了。
〔旦收扇袖中介〕
〔丑〕俺们不及桃李花罢了，
怎的便是辛夷树？
〔净〕辛夷树者，枯木逢春也。
〔丑〕如今枯木逢春，
也曾鲜花着雨来。
〔杂持诗笺上〕
杨老爷送诗来了。
〔生接读介〕生小倾城是李香，
怀中婀娜袖中藏；
缘何十二巫峰女，

Hou to write.

Hou: You need not prepare any paper, for I have brought a palace fan as my gift for Fragrant and I may write my verse on it to eternalize this memorable night.

Zheng: Good! I will hold the inkstand in my hand.

Kou: You are not a hand to hold the inkstand but to take off the boots of the drunken.

Bian: Only Fragrant's hand is qualified to hold the fragrant inkstand.

All: That is right.

(Fragrant holds the inkstand for Hou to write on the fan.)

All (Reading): A slanting way leads to a crimson bower;

The prince drives his carriage in search of the flower.

Along the stream stand only withered trees;

They lead to the peach blooming in the eastern breeze.

All: Who could be sought after but Fragrant?

(Fragrant puts the fan into her sleeve.)

Zheng: We are not as good as the peach blooming in the eastern breeze. But are we already withered trees?

Zhang: Even withered trees may bloom again when comes spring.

Zheng: *Then let the withered trees*

Bloom in rain and in breeze!

(Enter a servant with a billet.)

Servant: Here comes a poem from Master Yang.

Hou (Taking the poem and singing):

Fragrant while young is fairer than we can believe;

She is too tender to be hidden in the sleeve.

梦里偏来见楚王。

〔生笑介〕此老多情，

送来一首催妆诗，

妙绝，妙绝！

〔净〕“怀中婀娜袖中藏”，说的香君一搦身材，

竟是个香扇坠儿。

〔众笑介〕

〔副净〕大家吹弹起来，

劝新人多饮几杯。

〔丑〕正是带些酒兴，好入洞房。

〔左右吹弹，生、旦交让酒介〕

【节节高】〔生、旦〕

金樽佐酒筹，

劝不休，

沉沉玉倒[25]黄昏后。

私携手，

眉黛愁，香肌瘦。

春宵一刻天长久，

人前怎解芙蓉扣。

盼到灯昏玳筵收，

宫壶滴尽莲花漏[26]。

〔副净〕你听谯楼二鼓[27]，天气太晚，撤了席罢。

〔净〕这样好席，不曾吃净就撤去了，岂不可惜。

〔丑〕我没吃够哩，众位略等一等儿。

Why should the fairy come down from Witch Mountain proud
To bring fresh shower for the dreaming prince like a cloud?
(Smiling) Master Yang is still as young as his name. Though old, he has not forgotten the nuptial bed.

Zhang: When he says Fragrant can be hidden in the sleeve, is he not comparing her to the fan pendant?

(All burst in laughter.)

Ding: Let us play music and drink to the newly-weds and offer our best wishes!

Zheng: Only when tipsy can they enjoy the nuptial night all the better.

(All play music and the newly-weds drink their nuptial cups.)

Hou and Fragrant (Singing together to the tune of ***Higher and Higher***):

Golden cup full of wine,
We drink till the sun is on the decline.
Hand in hand, with eyebrows so slender,
And skin so tender,
We wish the nuptial night to be endless.
But how could we before all unbutton our dress?
We'd wait till over is the feast,
Dim is lamplight and mute the water clock at least.

Ding: Listen! The drumbeats announce the second watch. It is late now. We must withdraw from the feast.

Zhang: How can we leave such good wine undrunk?

Zheng: I have not eaten enough. Would you please wait a little longer?

〔老旦〕休得胡缠，大家奏乐，送新人入房罢。

〔众起吹打十番，送生、旦介〕

【前腔】〔合〕

笙箫下画楼，
度清讴[28]，
迷离灯火如春昼。
天台岫，
逢阮刘[29]，
真佳偶。
重重锦帐香熏透，
旁人妒得眉头皱。
酒态扶人太风流，
贪花福分生来有。

〔杂执灯，生、旦携手下〕

〔净〕我们都配成对儿，也去睡罢。

〔丑〕老张休得妄想，我老妥是要现钱的。

〔净数与十文钱，拉介〕

〔丑接钱再数，换低钱[30]，诨下〕

【尾声】〔合〕

秦淮烟月无新旧，
脂香粉腻满东流，
夜夜春情散不收。

〔副净〕江南花发水悠悠，

〔小旦〕人到秦淮解尽愁；

Bian: Do not disturb the happy night of the newly-weds! Let us play wedding music and see the bride and the bride-groom to their nuptial chamber!

(Wedding music is played for their departure.)

All (Singing to ***the previous tune***):

The lute and flute are played in painted bower
To celebrate the happy hour.
Dim lamplight turns the night into spring day.
The lovers on their way
With hand in hand
To the fairy dreamland.
Incense permeates the curtained bed,
Envy is aroused in green eyes and frowning forehead.
Seeing the drunken lovers would intoxicate.
Who would not be the beloved mate?

(Exeunt the lovers hand in hand in lantern light.)

Zhang: Let us go to bed in pairs!

Zheng: Do you dream to sleep with me without paying in cash!

(Zhang gives her ten coins, and Zheng counts before they withdraw.)

All (Singing ***the Epilogue***):

The moons old and new shine alike on River Qinhuai;
The water stained with rouge and powder eastward goes by.
From night to night the joy of love spreads far and nigh.

Ding: *Flowers bloom and water flows by the southern shore.*

Kou: *Arriving at Qinhuai, lovers feel sorrow no more.*

〔外〕不管烽烟家万里，

〔老旦〕五更怀里啭歌喉。

〔众下〕

【注释】

[1] 迷楼：隋炀帝兴建的一座宫殿。这里借指媚香楼。

[2] “不教金线柳”二句：表示对新郎君的盼望。木兰舟，指用木兰树做成的舟。

[3] 上头：梳栊。

[4] 送衾枕：妓女被客人叫去宿夜，要送衾枕去。

[5] 文君酒：相传卓文君与司马相如私奔以后，曾在临邛市上当垆卖酒。

[6] 喷香兽：指制成兽形、香气从兽口中喷出的香炉。

[7] “这当垆红袖”三句：当垆红袖，即指卓文君。相如，即司马相如，汉代著名的辞赋家。

[8] 撺掇（cuān duo）：本是怂恿的意思，这里作催促、准备解。

[9] 张三影：北宋著名词人张先。

[10] 五字宫商李二红：疑是指元代的曲家红字李二，他曾与马致远合编《黄粱梦》杂剧。五字宫商，即宫、商、角、徵（读作 zhǐ）、羽五音。

[11] 贤歌：歌即歌妓，贤是宋元以来对下辈人称呼时一种表示尊敬的语词。

[12] 在行（háng）：内行。

[13] 教坊司：是隋唐以来管理乐舞和乐户承应事宜的机关。

[14] 卞玉京、寇白门、郑妥娘：都是明末清初南京著名的妓女。

[15] 白门：本是六朝时建康城的西门，后人往往以白门指建康。建康从明代永乐以后，改称南京。

Shen: *They do not care if war flames rise far, far away.*

Bian: *The midnight drinking song in their heart will long stay.*

(Exeunt.)

[16] 诨笑：诨即打诨，是中国戏剧里属于开玩笑性质的情节。

[17] 十番：是一种音乐合奏，所用乐器随时间、地点而变更，也不限于十种。常用的是唢呐、笙、海笛、星堂、小锣、齐钹、胡琴、怀鼓，等等。

[18] 不兴：不许，是不时兴、不习惯的意思。

[19] “齐梁词赋”二句：暗指封建没落王朝的文章风气与荒淫生活。

[20] 迤（tuó）逗：勾引、撩拨的意思。

[21] 小杜扬州：小杜即唐末诗人杜牧，与李商隐齐名，因别于杜甫，故称小杜。

[22] 描黛：画眉。

[23] “春情无限”二句：疑是说侯方域对她无限爱恋，哪肯把她当作一般侍妾看待的意思。

[24] 见惯司空：司空见惯。

[25] 玉倒：玉即玉山，用来比喻人的身材。玉倒即醉倒。

[26] 宫壶滴尽莲花漏：莲花漏是铜壶滴漏的一种，古人没有钟表，宫禁里用铜壶滴漏来计时。

[27] 谯楼二鼓：谯楼即城上鼓楼，二鼓是二更时候。

[28] 度清讴：唱清歌。

[29] 天台岫，逢阮刘：阮肇、刘晨到天台山上采药遇到仙女的故事。

[30] 换低钱：把成色差一些的钱换过。

第三出　却奁

【夜行船】〔末〕

人宿平康深柳巷，
惊好梦门外花郎[1]。
绣户未开，
帘钩才响，
春阻十层纱帐。

下官杨文骢，早来与侯兄道喜。你看院门深闭，侍婢无声，想是高眠未起。

〔唤介〕保儿，你到新人窗外，说我早来道喜。

〔杂〕昨夜睡迟了，今日未必起来哩。老爷请回，明日再来罢。

〔末笑介〕胡说！快快去问。

Scene 3 Dowry Rejected

(Enter Yang Wencong [Longyou])

Yang (Singing to the tune of ***Night Sailing Boat***):

Sleeping in the willow bower,

The lover wakes to hear "Buy my flower!"

Closed is the door,

Hooks ring no more.

Spring can't be seen

Within curtain and screen.

I am Yang Wencong, coming early in the morning for congratulations of Master Hou's happy wedding. But I find the door closed and the house quiet. Perhaps they are still lingering in their dreamland.

(Calling the maid): Maid, Will you go to tell the newly-weds inside the window screen that I am coming for congratulations?

Maid: Our master and mistress went to bed late last night, so they have not yet got up. Will you please go back and come tomorrow?

Yang (Smiling): Do not talk nonsense! Go and inform your master and mistress!

〔小旦内问介〕保儿！来的是那一个？
〔杂〕是杨老爷道喜来了。
〔小旦忙上〕

倚枕春宵短，
敲门好事多。

〔见介〕多谢老爷，成了孩儿一世姻缘。
〔末〕好说。
〔问介〕新人起来不曾？
〔小旦〕昨晚睡迟，都还未起哩。

〔让坐介〕老爷请坐，待我去催他。
〔末〕不必，不必。〔小旦下〕
【步步娇】〔末〕

儿女浓情如花酿，
美满无他想，
黑甜共一乡[2]。
可也亏了俺帮衬，
珠翠辉煌，
罗绮飘荡，
件件助新妆，
悬出风流榜。

〔小旦上〕好笑，好笑！两个在那里交扣丁香[3]，并照菱花[4]，梳洗才完，穿戴未毕。请老爷同到洞房，唤他出来，好饮扶头卯酒。

Mother Lee (Asking from within): Who is coming?

Maid: It is Master Yang coming for congratulations.

(Enter Mother Lee in haste.)

Mother (Singing): *The nuptial night is short in spring;*

A knock at the door would announce some happy thing.

(Saluting Yang) Many thanks for your dowry. Without you there could not have been such a happy wedding.

Yang: Well said. Are the newly-weds not yet up?

Mother: They went to bed late last night, so they cannot rise early. Will you please take a seat? I shall announce your arrival.

Yang: Please do not wake them from their sweet dream.

(Exit Mother Lee.)

(Singing to the tune of ***Charming Step by Step***):

Their love is sweet as honey in the flower,

Sweeter from hour to hour.

They linger still in their dreamland.

But can it be without my helping hand?

Could they have pearls and jades so bright?

Could their silk dress sway left and right?

Pearls and jades adorn their dress new,

And make their love happy in view.

(Re-enter Mother Lee.)

Mother: It is funny to see them button up each other's dress and gaze at each other in the mirror. They have not yet finished their make-up. Would you please go to their nuptial chamber and

〔末〕惊却好梦，得罪不浅。

〔同下〕

〔生、旦艳妆上〕

【沉醉东风】〔生、旦〕

这云情接着雨况[5]，
刚搔了心窝奇痒，
谁搅起睡鸳鸯。
被翻红浪，
喜匆匆满怀欢畅。
枕上余香，
帕上余香，
消魂滋味，
才从梦里尝。

〔末、小旦上〕

〔末〕果然起来了，恭喜，恭喜！

〔一揖，坐介〕

〔末〕昨晚催妆拙句，可还说的入情么。

〔生揖介〕多谢！

〔笑介〕妙是妙极了，只有一件。

〔末〕那一件？

〔生〕香君虽小，还该藏之金屋[6]。

〔看袖介〕小生衫袖，如何着得下？

〔俱笑介〕

drink their wedding cup together with them?

Yang: How dare I disturb their sweet hour without bearing the blame?

(Exeunt.)

(Enter Hou and Fragrant Lee in splendid dress.)

Hou & Fragrant (Singing to the tune of ***Intoxicated in the Eastern Breeze***):

The cloud has brought fresh shower
For the itching flower.
Who should awake the love-birds' dream
When love flows like a rosy stream?
We have drunk happy wine to the fill,
When fragrance lingers on the pillow still.
When fragrance on the handkerchief is felt,
Our heart and soul are melt
In a dream we can't belt.

(Re-enter Yang and Mother Lee.)

Yang: You are up now. Congratulations, congratulations!

(Saluting with clasped hands and then sitting down)

What do you think of my congratulatory poem of yesterday?

Hou (With clasped hands): Many thanks.

(Smiling) Your poem is very nice, but ...

Yang: But what?

Hou: Fragrant is so tender. How could she be put into the sleeve slender? Would it not be better a golden bower to lend her?

(Both laugh.)

〔末〕夜来定情，
必有佳作。
〔生〕草草塞责，不敢请教。
〔末〕诗在那里？
〔旦〕诗在扇头。
〔旦向袖中取出扇介〕
〔末接看介〕是一柄白纱宫扇。
〔嗅介〕香的有趣。
〔吟诗介〕妙，妙！只有香君不愧此诗。
〔付旦介〕还收好了。

〔旦收扇介〕
【园林好】〔末〕
正芬芳桃香李香，
都题在宫纱扇上；
怕遇着狂风吹荡，
须紧紧袖中藏，
须紧紧袖中藏。
〔末看旦介〕你看香君上头之后，更觉艳丽了。

〔向生介〕世兄有福，消此尤物[7]。

〔生〕香君天姿国色，今日插了几朵珠翠，
穿了一套绮罗，十分花貌，
又添二分，果然可爱。

Yang: Out of love of last night, there must be some verse bright.

Hou: It is only an unfinished draft. How can I show it to you?

Yang: Where is it written?

Fragrant: It is written on a fan.

(Taking the fan from her sleeve.)

Yang: It is a fan of pure silk.

(Smelling at it) Fragrant and tasteful.

(Reading the poem) Very nice. Only Fragrant is worthy of the verse. You must keep it along.

(Giving it back)

(Fragrant puts the fan into her sleeve.)

Yang: (Singing to the tune of ***A Nice Garden***):

See blooming peach and plum flowers
Leave shadows on the fan of palace bowers.
When the furious wind roars and grieves,
It should be hidden in the sleeves.
It should be hidden in the sleeves.

(Gazing at Fragrant) Fragrant looks all the more charming after she has dressed her hair.

(To Hou) What a felicity falls on you to have enjoyed the first night of such a beauty!

Hou: Fragrant was born a beauty. Now adorned with pearls and emerald and in a silk dress, her loveliness has increased. How can she not be adored!

〔小旦〕这都亏了杨老爷帮衬哩。

【江儿水】

送到缠头锦，
百宝箱，
珠围翠绕流苏帐[8]，
银烛笼纱通宵亮，
金杯劝酒合席唱。
今日又早早来看，
恰似亲生自养，
赔了妆奁，
又早敲门来望。

〔旦〕俺看杨老爷，虽是马督抚[9]至亲，却也拮据作客，为何轻掷金钱，来填烟花之窟？在奴家受之有愧，在老爷施之无名；今日问个明白，以便图报。

〔生〕香君问得有理，小弟与杨兄萍水相交[10]，昨日承情太厚，也觉不安。

〔末〕既蒙问及，小弟只得实告了。这些妆奁酒席，约费二百余金，皆出怀宁[11]之手。

〔生〕那个怀宁？

〔末〕曾做过光禄的阮圆海。

Mother: We are grateful for Master Yang's generous gift.

(Singing to the tune of ***A Running Stream***):

The jewel box and the headdress,
Pearls and emeralds on the tress.
The candles bright
Illumine window screens all night.
The golden cups of wine
With sumptuous feast combine.
You come for congratulations at dawn,
As if she were the daughter of your own.
And the dowry you bring
Announces a happy spring.

Fragrant: So far as I know, Master Yang is only a relative of Minister Ma Dacheng. You are not a very rich official. How can you spend so much to prepare a dowry for unworthy me? I feel regretful not to have inquired into the matter. So I venture to ask you today in order to repay you the debt we owe you.

Hou: It is right to make this inquiry. For on my part, I am afraid not to be on such intimate terms with you as to justify such a generous donation.

Yang: Since you want further information, I cannot but tell you the truth: the dowry and the feast cost two hundred gold coins in all, and they are all the donation of Huaining.

Hou: Who is Huaining?

Yang: It is none other than Secretary Ruan.

〔生〕是那皖人阮大铖么？

〔末〕正是。

〔生〕他为何这样周旋？

〔末〕不过欲纳交足下之意。

【五供养】〔末〕

羡你风流雅望，
东洛才名，西汉文章[12]。
逢迎随处有，
争看坐车郎[13]。
秦淮妙处，
暂寻个佳人相傍，
也要些鸳鸯被、
芙蓉妆；
你道是谁的，
是那南邻大阮，
嫁衣全忙。

〔生〕阮圆老原是敝年伯，小弟鄙其为人，绝之已久。他今日无故用情，令人不解。

〔末〕圆老有一段苦衷，欲见白于足下。

〔生〕请教。

〔末〕圆老当日曾游赵梦白[14]之门，原是吾辈。后来结交魏党，只为救护东林，不料魏党一败，东林反与之水火[15]。近日复社诸生，倡论攻击，大肆殴辱，岂非操同室之戈[16]

Hou: You mean Ruan Dacheng?

Yang: Yes, it is he.

Hou: Why should he give me such a generous donation?

Yang: He just wishes to build up a close relationship with you.

(Singing to the tune of ***Cultivations***):

He admires your literary renown
Wide spread east and west, up and down.
You are admired here and there,
In a carriage or in a chair.
Now in Qinhuai you abide,
You need a beauty by your side,
And a love-bird quilt to caress
Your beauty in lotus dress.
Who would spend so much gold for you,
But Secretary Ruan who thinks it his due.

Hou: Ruan Dacheng is a senior scholar whose behavior is not praiseworthy, so we are not on friendly terms. I do not know why he should be so generous to me.

Yang: There is some misunderstanding between Secretary Ruan and the Recovery Society, which he wishes to explain to you.

Hou: Please explain it.

Yang: Secretary Ruan was a disciple of Zhao Mengbai, who is on friendly terms with the Recovery Society. When Wei Zhongxian the eunuch persecuted the Society, Secretary Ruan tried

乎？圆老故交虽多，因其形迹可疑，亦无人代为分辩。每日向天大哭，说道："同类相残，伤心惨目，非河南侯君，不能救我。"所以今日谆谆纳交。

〔生〕原来如此，俺看圆海情辞迫切，亦觉可怜。就便真是魏党，悔过来归，亦不可绝之太甚，况罪有可原乎。定生、次尾，皆我至交，明日相见，即为分解。

〔末〕果然如此，吾党之幸也。

〔旦怒介〕官人是何说话，阮大铖趋附权奸，廉耻丧尽；妇人女子，无不唾骂。他人攻之，官人救之，官人自处于何等也？

【川拨棹】

不思想，
把话儿轻易讲。
要与他消释灾殃，
要与他消释灾殃，
也提防旁人短长[17]。

官人之意，不过因他助俺妆奁，便要徇私废公；那知

to dissuade the eunuch but failed. Now the eunuch is deprived of power, but the Society mistakes the secretary for their persecuter, so all rise to attack him. The secretary cannot defend himself and plead his innocence, so he wishes to rely on you to rehabilitate his reputation.

Hou: If such is the case, I think Secretary Ruan is pitiable and might win over our sympathy. Even if he belongs to the eunuch's party, he should not be rejected if he really regrets and repents. So you need not worry too much. Since Dingsheng and Ciwei of the Society are my good friends, I shall try to explain for him when I see them.

Yang: If you could succeed to rescue Secretary Ruan, I do not know how to express the gratitude of our party.

Fragrant (Angry): How could you do anything to the rescue of the eunuch's party, my dear? Do you not know that Ruan Dacheng is a shameless traitor blamed even by common people and housewives? How can you make any effort to rescue one who bears the blame of so many?

(Singing to the tune of ***Boat on the Stream***):

How can you say anything nice

Without pondering twice!

How could you rid him of shame!

How could you rid him of blame!

Do you not know it will undo your fame?

If I am not mistaken, you mean to rescue Ruan Dacheng so as

道这几件钗钏衣裙，原放不到我香君眼里。

〔拔簪脱衣介〕脱裙衫，

穷不妨；

布荆[18]人，

名自香。

〔末〕阿呀！香君气性，忒也刚烈[19]。

〔小旦〕把好好东西，都丢一地，可惜，可惜！

〔拾介〕

〔生〕好，好，好！这等见识，我倒不如，真乃侯生畏友也。

〔向末介〕老兄休怪，

弟非不领教，但恐为女子所笑耳。

【前腔】

〔生〕平康巷，

他能将名节讲；

偏是咱学校朝堂，

偏是咱学校朝堂，

混贤奸不问青黄[20]。

那些社友平日重俺侯生者，也只为这点义气；我若依附奸邪，那时群起来攻，自救不暇，焉能救人乎。

节和名，

非泛常；

to repay him the dowry he has provided for us. But do you not know that I care for our fame much more than for the dowry?

(Removing the headdress and the new dress.)

I take off my dress new.
To be poor is our due.
Though in plain simple dress,
We are famed nonetheless.

Yang: Why should Fragrant be so angry?

Mother: Why should you scatter the new dress and the head-dress on the ground? Is it not a pity!

(Trying to pick them up.)

Hou: Bravo! My dear Fragrant, you have a deeper insight than we men. I think you are incomparable for me.

(To Yang) Excuse us for not accepting the gift. For I would not be held to ridicule by my dear Fragrant.

(Singing to ***the previous tune***)

People without a name
Care for honor and fame.
How can we officials and scholars bright,
How can we officials and scholars bright
Not tell good from vice, black from white!

If the Recovery Society values me highly, it is for my lofty morality. If I adhere to those of doubtful morality, I can hardly defend myself against the reproach of my friends.

How can I defend and rescue others?

重和轻，
须审详。

〔末〕圆老一段好意，也还不可激烈。

〔生〕我虽至愚，亦不肯从井救人[21]。

〔末〕既然如此，小弟告辞了。

〔生〕这些箱笼，原是阮家之物，香君不用，留之无益，还求取去罢。

〔末〕正是
“多情反被无情恼，
乘兴而来兴尽还。”
〔下〕

〔旦恼介〕

〔生看旦介〕俺看香君天姿国色，摘了几朵珠翠，脱去一套绮罗，十分容貌，又添十分，更觉可爱。

〔小旦〕虽如此说，舍了许多东西，到底可惜。

【尾声】

金珠到手轻轻放，
惯成了娇痴模样，
辜负俺辛勤做老娘。

〔生〕些须东西，何足挂念，
小生照样赔来。

〔小旦〕这等才好。

〔小旦〕花钱粉钞[22]费商量，

Honor and fame

Should be free from blame.

Know right from wrong,

And short from long.

Yang: You should not belie Secretary Ruan's good intention.

Hou: I am not so foolish as to plunge into a well to rescue the drowned.

Yang: If such is the case, I have nothing more to say but goodbye.

Hou: These boxes are the dowry given by Secretary Ruan. Since Fragrant has no need of them, would you please take them back?

Yang: *The lover comes in spirits high.*

Rejected, what can he say but goodbye?

(Exit.)

(Fragrant looks vexed.)

Hou (Gazing at her) **:** You are a born beauty. Without the rich attire, you look all the more beautiful and lovely.

Mother: It is regrettable to forsake such a rich dowry.

(Singing ***the Epilogue***):

Why should you give up pearls and gold?

Spoiled, you don't care for your mother old.

Hou: *You need not regret for the trifling thing.*

On my order it will come on the wing.

Mother: *All is well that ends well.*

Do not lose what you gain!

〔旦〕裙布钗荆也不妨；
〔生〕只有湘君能解佩，
〔旦〕风标不学世时妆。

【注释】

[1] 花郎：指卖花人。
[2] 黑甜共一乡：一齐睡熟。
[3] 丁香：丁香结，本是丁香的花蕾，这里指衣服的纽扣。
[4] 菱花：镜子。古代的镜子是铜的，一面磨光，另一面铸成各种图案。最普通的图案是菱花，因此往往以菱花作为镜子的别称。
[5] 云情、雨况：指男女交欢时的情况。
[6] 金屋：意指极华贵的房子。
[7] 尤物：本指特殊的人物，一般用以称有特殊姿色的美人。
[8] 流苏帐：流苏是和丝绦类似的一种装饰品。流苏帐是用流苏装饰四周的帐子。
[9] 马督抚：马士英，当时任凤阳督抚。
[10] 萍水相交：以浮萍在水面漂流，比喻偶然相遇、交情短浅的朋友。
[11] 怀宁：阮大铖。大铖，怀宁人。
[12] “东洛才名”二句：这是比喻侯方域的才名大，文章写得好。东洛才名暗用晋代左思写《三都赋》的故事。西汉文章是指西汉时代一些伟大作家，如司马迁、司马相如等人的作品。
[13] 争看坐车郎：相传潘岳貌美，每坐车出游，妇女争看他。
[14] 赵梦白：赵南星。
[15] 水火：表示彼此不相容之意。
[16] 操同室之戈：同室操戈本指兄弟间自相残杀，这里意指同类人自相攻击。

Fragrant: *In plain dress, fair I still remain.*

Hou: *Unadorned, you're fair still.*

Fragrant: *Be yourself if you will!*

[17] 旁人短长：意指旁人评论。

[18] 布荆：布衣、荆钗。

[19] 忒也刚烈：过于刚烈。忒，意同太。

[20] 不问青黄：不管是非黑白的意思。

[21] 从井救人：意说不能救起别人，却害了自己。

[22] 花钱粉钞：指花费在花粉装饰等上面的钱钞。

第二本　一封书信阻刀兵

· · ·

ACT II　Word and Sword

第一出　抚兵

【点绛唇】〔副净、末扮二将官，杂扮四小卒上〕

旗卷军牙[1]，

射潮弩发鲸鲵怕[2]。

操弓试马，

鼓角斜阳下。

俺们镇守武昌兵马大元帅宁南侯麾下[3]将士是也。

今日点卯[4]日期，元帅升帐，

只得在此伺候。

〔吹打开门介〕

【粉蝶儿】〔小生戎装，扮左良玉[5]上〕

七尺昂藏，

虎头燕颔[6]如画，

莽男儿走遍天涯。

活骑人，

飞食肉，

风云叱咤[7]。

报国恩，

一腔热血挥洒。

Scene 1 The Army

(Enter two officers followed by four soldiers.)

Officers (Singing to the tune of ***Rouged Lips***):

Our flags and banners waft in flight;

Our arrows would put whale and fish in fright.

When our cavaliers bend the bow,

The sun would sink to hear our bugles blow.

We are officers and soldiers under General Zuo Liangyu.

By his order we are going to hold a manoeuvre today.

(The bugles blow and the camp gate opens.)

(Enter General Zuo Liangyu in military array.)

Zuo (Singing to the tune of ***Pink Butterfly***):

Hero of seven feet,

As tiger and swallow as fleet,

I've conquered as far as the border.

Riding on horse,

I've beaten hostile force,

With wind and cloud at my order.

Serving the State with might and main,

I would shed blood over the plain.

建牙吹角不闻喧，
三十登坛众所尊；
家散万金酬士死，
身留一剑答君恩[8]。

咱家左良玉，表字昆山，家住辽阳[9]，世为都司[10]，只因得罪罢职，补粮昌平。幸遇军门侯恂，拔于走卒，命为战将，不到一年，又拜总兵之官。北讨南征，功加侯伯；强兵劲马，列镇荆襄[11]。

〔作势介〕看俺左良玉，自幼习学武艺，能挽五石之弓，善为左右之射；那李自成、张献忠几个毛贼，何难剿灭。只可恨督师无人，机宜错过，熊文灿、杨嗣昌既以偏私而败绩，丁启睿、吕大器[12]又因怠玩而无功。只有俺恩帅侯公，智勇兼全，尽能经理中原；不意奸人忌功[13]，才用即休，叫俺一腔热血，报主无期，好不恨也！

〔顿足介〕罢，罢，罢！这湖南、湖北，也还可战可守，且观成败，再定行藏[14]。

〔坐介〕

〔内作众兵喊叫，小生惊问介〕辕门之外，何人喧哗？

〔副净、末禀介〕禀上元帅，辕门肃静，谁敢喧哗。

〔小生怒介〕现在喧哗，怎报没有！

〔副净、末〕那是饥兵讨饷，并非喧哗。

〔小生〕哇！前自湖南借粮三十船，不到一月，难道支完了？

〔副净、末〕禀元帅，本镇人马已足三十万了，些须粮草，那够支销。

Blowing my bugle, under flags in flight,
At thirty, I arrive at generalship's height.
Sparing no gold for gallant soldiers slain,
To serve the crown my sword will ever remain.

I am General Zuo Liangyu of a military family. Once degraded for offense against my superior, I was then promoted to the rank of general by Marshal Hou Xun (father of Hou Chaozong). After northern and southern expeditions I have won victory on victory and I am now ennobled governor of Jingzhou and Xiangyang. Having learned military arts since my youthful days, I can bend a strong bow without much effort and shoot with my left or right arm. Now Li Zicheng and Zhang Xianzhong rose in revolt, all our commanders-in-chief suffered defeat on defeat. Our victorious Marshal Hou is no longer in service. What can I do with my courage and strategy which seem useless under wrong leadership? (Stamping his feet) If necessary, I could advance or retreat from Hunan and Hubei. It would depend on the situation. (Sitting down)

(Soldiers' shout from within)

Zuo (Startled): How can such a tumult rise within the camp gate?

Officers: There is no tumult within the camp gate, general.

Zuo (Angry): Can you not hear the uproar of the soldiers?

Officers: It is the hungry soldiers who shout for food.

Zuo: I have just asked Hunan to transport thirty shipfuls of food supplies. Could they be eaten up within a month?

Officers: Now you have three hundred thousand soldiers under your command, general. The thirty shipfuls of food are not enough

〔小生拍案介〕呵呀！这等却也难处哩。

〔立起，唱介〕

【北石榴花】

你看中原豺虎乱如麻，

都窥伺龙楼凤阙帝王家；

有何人勤王[15]报主，

肯把义旗拿？那督师无老将，

选士皆娇娃[16]；

却教俺自撑达[17]，却教俺自撑达。

正腾腾杀气，

这军粮又早缺乏。

一阵阵拍手喧哗，

一阵阵拍手喧哗，

百忙中教我如何答话，

好一似薨薨白昼闹蜂衙。

〔坐介〕

〔内又喊介〕

〔小生〕你听外边将士，益发鼓噪，好像要反的光景，左右听俺吩咐。

〔立起，唱介〕

【上小楼】

您不要错怨咱家，

您不要错怨咱家。

谁不是天朝犬马[18]，

他三百年养士不差，

for one month.

Zuo (Striking at the table): Alas! What can I do?

(Standing up)

(Singing to the tune of ***Pomegranate***):

Behold! Tigers and pards run wild in Central Plain,
Invading royal domain with might and main.
Who would come to the rescue of the crown,
Erecting royal banners in the town?
No veteran general in command,
No soldier but a new hand.
O with such troops against the foe how can I stand?
The foe will come in speed;
Of food we stand in need.
They come with hue and cry.
What can I do in reply?
I seem to see a swarm of humming bees far and nigh.

(Sitting down)

(Soldiers' shout heard from within)

Listen to the shouts! Would the soldiers rise in revolt? Officers and men, listen to my orders.

(Standing up)

(Singing to the tune of ***Mounting the Attic***):

Do not complain of me!
Do not complain of me!
Who from service to the State can be free?
It has provided for us three hundred years.

三百年养士不差。

都要把良心拍打，

为甚么击鼓敲门闹转加?

敢则要劫库抢官衙。

俺这里望眼巴巴，

俺这里望眼巴巴，

候江州军粮飞下。

〔坐介〕

〔抽令箭掷地介〕

〔副净、末拾箭，向内吩咐介〕元帅有令，三军听者：目下军饷缺乏，乃人马归附之多，非粮草屯积之少。朝廷深恩，不可不报；将军严令，不可不遵。况江西助饷，指日到辕[19]，各宜静听，勿得喧哗。

〔副净、末回话介〕奉元帅军令，俱已晓谕三军了。

〔内又喊叫介〕

〔小生〕怎么鼓噪之声，渐入辕门，你再去吩咐。

〔立起，唱介〕

【黄龙犯】

您且忍枵腹[20]这一宵，盼江西那几艖[21]。

俺待要飞檄金陵，俺待要飞檄金陵，

告兵曹转达车驾[22]，许咱们迁镇移家，

许咱们迁镇移家。就粮东去，安营歇马，

驾楼船到燕子矶边耍。

〔副净、末持令箭向内吩咐介〕元帅有令，三军听者：粮船一到，即便支发。仍恐转运维艰，枵腹难待；不日撤兵汉口，就食[23]南京；永无缺乏之虞，同享饱腾[24]之乐。

It has provided for us three hundred years.
Can we not defend its frontiers?
Why should the rebels beat the drum in mutiny?
Would they plunder the royal treasury?
Don't soldiers know I'm waiting with longing eyes,
Do they not know I'm waiting with longing eyes
For ships from Jiangzhou loaded with food supplies?

(Sitting down again.)

(Giving order by throwing an arrow on the ground.)

Officers (Picking up the arrow and reading the order) :

By order of General Zuo, officers and soldiers should wait for the food supply which would come from Jiangxi in a few days.

(Soldiers' shouts again heard from within.)

Zuo (Singing to the tune of ***Golden Dragon***):

You can't but suffer hunger one more day;
Food supply would come from Jiangxi without delay.
I'll send a message to the minister of war
To station our army around the east food store,
To station our army around the east food store.

Officers (Reading the order of General Zuo)**:** By order of General Zuo, our army should have ample supply of food from Jiangxi. For fear

各宜静听，勿再喧哗！

〔内欢呼介〕好，好，好！大家收拾行装，豫备东去呀。

〔副净、末回生介〕禀上元帅，三军闻令，俱各欢呼散去了。

〔小生〕事已如此，无可奈何，只得择期移镇，暂慰军心。

〔想介〕且住，未奉明旨，辄自前行，虽圣恩宽大，未必加诛；只恐形迹之间，难免天下之议。事非小可[25]，再作商量。

【尾声】

慰三军没别法，
许就粮喧声才罢，
谁知俺一片葵倾向日花[26]。

〔下〕

〔内作吹打掩门，四卒下〕

〔副净向末〕老哥，咱弟兄们商量，天下强兵勇将，让俺武昌。明日顺流东下，料知没人抵当。大家拥着元帅爷，一直抢了南京，就扯起黄旗，往北京进取，有何不可。

〔末摇手介〕我们左爷爷忠义之人，这样风话[27]，且不要题。依着我说，还是移家就粮，且吃饱饭为妙。

of delay, our army may be stationed around the food stores in the Southern Capital so that we may suffer no more hunger.

Soldiers (Shouting from within)**:** Bravo, bravo, bravo! Let us get ready to go eastward around the food stores in the Southern Capital.

Officers (To General Zuo)**:** Would you please listen to our report: on hearing your order, the soldiers give three cheers and go back to their barracks.

Zuo: What can I do but send a message to the Minister of war! (Meditating) Wait a minute! If my army should march eastward on the Southern Capital without imperial authorization, it might incur blame though not punishment from the imperial court. So I must reconsider the matter.

(Singing ***the Epilogue***):

My army can't be pacified

Without my promise that food would be supplied.

Who knows I have used all my power

But only like a sunflower! (Exit.)

(The camp gate closed with trumpets and drumbeats.)

(Exit four soldiers.)

First Officer: Our army garrisoned in Wuchang is the strongest in the empire. If we sail our warships eastward to the Southern Capital, no force would dare to resist us on our way. If we occupy the Southern Capital under the orders of our General, who could prevent us from erecting a dragon flag and marching on the Northern Capital?

Second Officer (Waving the hand)**:** But our general is loyal to the empire, so we should not talk about insurrection. I think it

〔副净〕你还不知，一移南京，人心惊慌，就不取北京，这个恶名也免不得了。

〔　末　〕纷纷将士愿移家，

〔副净〕细柳营中起暮笳；

〔　末　〕千古英雄须打算，

〔副净〕楼船东下一生差。

〔众下〕

【注释】

[1] 旗卷军牙：牙即牙旗，是军前大旗。旗卷军牙，形容军前大旗在风中卷动。

[2] 射潮弩发鲸鲵怕：传说五代时吴越王钱镠曾经率领五千弓弩手，射退海潮。这里借来形容左良玉军队的威武。

[3] 麾下：部下。

[4] 点卯：古时官府办公从卯时开始，吏役都要在这时按名册点验，称作点卯。这里指军队里的点名报到。

[5] 左良玉：明末临清人，字昆山。早年在辽东与清军作战，以骁勇得侯恂所识拔。

[6] 虎头燕颔：旧时相家以为贵相。《后汉书·班超传》："相者（班超）曰：生燕颔虎颈，飞而食肉，此万里侯相也。"

[7] 风云叱咤：叱咤，怒声。

[8] "建牙吹角不闻喧"四句：借用唐刘长卿《献淮宁军节度使李相公》诗句。建牙，武将出镇，登坛，拜帅。

[9] 辽阳：今辽宁省辽阳县。

[10] 都司：官名，在明初职权很大，掌握一省的军政大权。

[11] 荆襄：今湖北省一带。

would be better for us to be stationed in the Southern Capital around the food stores so that we might suffer no more hunger.

First Officer: The occupation of the Southern Capital would excite alarm. Even if our army did not march on the Northern Capital, could it be free from blame?

Second Officer: *Officers and soldiers would eastward go.*

First Officer: *At twilight in the camp the bugles blow.*

Second Officer: *A hero should think it over at least.*

First Officer: *Before he sails his warships to the east.*

(Exeunt.)

[12] 熊文灿、杨嗣昌、丁启睿、吕大器：都是明末人，曾担任较高军职，并都统率过左良玉。

[13] “奸人忌功”二句：根据侯方域《宁南侯传》，崇祯时，朝廷曾命侯恂督师，后因有人从中挑拨，不久被免官。

[14] 行藏：出处。

[15] 勤王：以兵救援王室。

[16] 选士皆娇娃：意说挑选的兵士都像娇弱的女子，不能作战。

[17] 撑达：元明方言，本是漂亮、老练的意思，这里意为支持。

[18] 犬马：封建时代臣对君的卑称。

[19] 辕：辕门，是军营的大门。

[20] 枵（xiāo）腹：空腹。

[21] 艖：小船。

[22] 告兵曹转达车驾：兵曹即兵部；车驾代指皇帝。

[23] 就食：移兵到屯粮的地方去吃粮。

[24] 饱腾：士饱马腾，形容军队供应充足，士气高扬的气象。

[25] 小可：轻易。

[26] 葵倾向日花：葵花向日，用来比喻臣子对君主的忠心。

[27] 风话：疯话。

第二出　修札

〔丑扮柳敬亭上〕老子江湖漫自夸，

收今贩古是生涯[1]。

年来怕作朱门客，

闲坐街坊吃冷茶。

〔笑介〕在下柳敬亭，自幼无藉[2]，流落江湖，虽则为谈词之辈，却不是饮食之人[3]。

〔拱介〕列位看我像个甚的，好像一位阎罗王，掌着这本大账簿，点了没数的鬼魂名姓[4]；又像一尊弥勒佛，腆着这副大肚皮，装了无限的世态炎凉。鼓板轻敲，便有风雷雨露；舌唇才动，也成月旦春秋。这些含冤的孝子忠臣，少不得还他个扬眉吐气；那班得意的奸雄邪党，免不了加他些人祸天诛；此乃补救[5]之微权，亦是褒讥[6]之妙用。

〔笑介〕俺柳麻子信口胡谈，却也燥脾[7]。昨日河南侯公子，送到茶资，约定今日午后来听平话[8]，且把鼓板取出，打个招客的利市。

Scene 2 The Message

(Enter Liu Jingting.)

Liu (Singing)**:** *I am a braggart roving by waterside,*

Talking about ancient and modern far and wide.

A visitor to rich mansions I would not be,

At leisure I would drink a cup of cold tea.

(Laughing) I am Liu Jingting, homeless since my youthful days and roaming here and there by the waterside. Fond of talking about verse and prose, I am an eater or drinker in rich families.

(Saluting the audience with clasped hands) Dear spectators, what do you think I look like? A Satan or a Buddha? A Satan for I talk about spirits and demons as if they were under me; a Buddha for I have seen so many ups and downs. Hearing my clappers, you may see wind and rain; seeing my lips and tongue, you may feel spring pass as autumn. I will right the wrong done to filial sons and loyal officers, and punish evildoers and unfair partisans.That is my way to remedy the injustice of the world and render justice by praise and blame.

(Laughing) I, pockmarked Liu, talk at random to please my dear spectators. Master Hou told me yesterday that he would

〔取出鼓板敲唱介〕

无事消闲扯淡，
就中滋味酸甜；
古来十万八千年，
一霎飞鸿去远。
几阵狂风暴雨，
各家虎帐龙船，
争名夺利片时喧，
让他陈抟睡扁。

〔生上〕

芳草烟中寻粉黛[9]，
斜阳影里说英雄。
今日来听老柳平话，里面鼓板铿锵，早已有人领教。

〔相见大笑介〕看官俱未到，独自在此，说与谁听。

〔丑〕这说书是老汉的本业，譬如相公闲坐书斋，弹琴吟诗，都要人听么？

〔生笑介〕讲的有理。

〔丑〕请问今日要听那一朝故事？

come to hear me tell tales this afternoon. So I must take out my clappers and get ready for my random talk.

(Taking out the clappers)

(Singing to the tune of ***the Moon on the West River***):

I try to pass my leisure

By seeking bitter sweet pleasure.

Thousands of years have passed

Just as wild geese at last.

Furious wind and rain running riot

Disturb generals' camps and boats quiet.

You strive for fame or wealth as you will.

But immortals will sleep their fill.

(Enter Master Hou.)

Hou (Singing) **:** *I tread on sweet green grass for the beautiful one;*

You talk about heroes under the sinking sun.

I come today to hear Master Liu tell his tales accompanied by his clappers. Has he already begun?

(Saluting Liu in laughter) Your audience has not yet come. Why are you using your clappers alone?

Liu: My job is to tell tales just as yours is to read and write, to croon your verse and play on your lute. You do not care if there is any listener, nor do I.

Hou (Smiling) **:** You are right.

Liu: You want to hear tales, but of which dynasty?

Hou: I do not care which dynasty. Just tell what is interesting and

〔生〕不拘何朝，你只拣着热闹爽快的说一回罢。

〔丑〕相公不知，那热闹局就是冷淡的根芽，爽快事就是牵缠的枝叶；倒不如把些剩水残山，孤臣孽子[10]，讲他几句，大家滴些眼泪罢。

〔生叹介〕咳！不料敬老你也看到这个田地，真可虑也！

〔末扮杨文骢急上〕

休教铁锁沈江底，
怕有降旗出石头。

下官杨文骢，有紧急大事，要寻侯兄计议；一路问来，知在此处，不免竟入。〔见介〕

〔生〕来得正好，大家听敬老平话。

〔末急介〕目下何等时候，还听平话。

〔生〕龙老为何这样惊慌。

〔末〕兄还不知么，左良玉领兵东下，要抢南京，且有窥伺北京之意。本兵熊明遇[11]束手无策，故此托弟前来，恳求妙计。

〔生〕小弟有何计策？

〔末〕久闻尊翁老先生乃宁南之恩帅，若肯发一手谕，必能退却。

不知足下主意若何？

moving.

Liu: No tale is interesting unless you are interested, nor is it moving if you are not moved. So I shall try to make you burst into laughter or move you to tears.

Hou (Sighing): Ah! I do not expect you to see things in this way. You make me worry all the more.

(Enter Yang Wencong in haste.)

Yang (Singing): *The iron chains could not stop warships coming down.*

How can we not surrender the capital town?

I am Yang Wencong coming on an urgent mission for consultation with Master Hou. On inquiry I am told he is here, So I must intrude on him. (Saluting Hou)

Hou: You have just come in time to listen to Master Liu tell tales.

Yang (Anxious): How can you be interested in tales in such an urgent time?

Hou: Why are you coming in such an alarm?

Yang: Don't you know that General Zuo's army would come to occupy the Southern Capital and then march on the North? Governor Xiong of Nanjing is at his wit's end, so he sends me to consult with you about how to deal with this urgent matter.

Hou: How can I know what to do?

Yang: I am told that your respectable father was teacher of General Zuo. If he would write a letter to dissuade the general from marching eastward, then the safety of Nanjing might not be endangered.

〔生〕这样好事，怎肯不做；但家父罢政林居[12]，纵肯发书，未必有济。且往返三千里，何以解目前之危？

〔末〕吾兄素称豪侠，当此国家大事，岂忍坐视。何不代写一书，且救目前；另日禀明尊翁，料不见责也。

〔生〕应急权变，倒也可行；待我回寓起稿，大家商量。

〔末〕事不宜迟，即刻发书，还恐无及，那里等的商量。

〔生〕既是如此，就此修书便了。

〔写书介〕

【一封书】

老夫愚不揣，
劝将军自忖裁，
旌旗且慢来，
兵出无名道路猜。
高帝留都陵树在，
谁敢轻将马足踹[13]；
乏粮柴，
善安排，
一片忠心穷莫改。

Hou: It is a good idea. But my old father is a retired marshal living in the countryside a thousand miles away. How could he write a message to preserve the safety of Nanjing?

Yang: You are a renowned patriot. Now the state is at stake. Could you stand idly by without extending a helping hand? Why could you not write a letter in your father's name to preserve the town's safety and then report to your father later on? I do not think he will lay blame on you anyhow.

Hou: It is a workable idea on this urgent situation. So let me go back to write a draft for discussion.

Yang: This message can bear no delay. How can we wait for you to go back and then write the draft? It would be far better to write this message at once without further discussion.

Hou: Since such is the case, I must write this message right now.

(Writing the letter)

(Singing to the tune of ***A Message***):

Although unwise,

I would advise

Your generalship to think over again

Before you make your eastward campaign.

Your army cannot march down

Without the authorization of the crown.

The way for you is hard,

For here extends the imperial graveyard.

How dare you let your forces

〔写完，末看介〕妙，妙！写的激切婉转，有情有理，叫他不好不依，又不敢不依，足见世兄经济[14]。

〔生〕虽如此说，还该送与熊大司马，细加改正，方为万妥。

〔末〕不必烦扰，待小弟说与他便了。

〔愁介〕只是一件，书虽有了，须差一妥当家人早寄为妙。

〔生〕小弟轻装薄游，只带两个童子，那能下的书来。
〔末〕这样密书，岂是生人可以去得。
〔生〕这却没法了。
〔丑〕不必着忙，让我老柳走一遭，何如？

〔末〕敬老肯去，妙得狠了；只是一路盘诘，也不是当耍的。

〔丑〕不瞒老爷说，我柳麻子本姓曹，虽则身长九尺，却不肯食粟而已。那些随机应变的口头，左冲右挡的膂力，都还有些儿。
〔生〕闻得左良玉军门严肃，山人[15]游客，一概不容擅入。你这般老态，如何去的？

Tramp on the royal tombs their horses?

If you lack food supply,

You should solve your difficulty nearby.

Do not forget to hold your royal banner high!

Yang (Reading the message) : Well written, well written! It appeals to General Zuo's heart and mind. How could he do otherwise than in compliance with the advice? How dare he defy the imperial sovereignty! From this message we can see your remarkable talent to handle state affairs.

Hou: It would be better to submit the message to Governor Xiong for approval.

Yang: You need not worry about that, for it is my job. The question is who will send this message to General Zuo.

Hou (Worried): I am only a visitor here, followed by two attendants. I am afraid I cannot send the message by myself.

Yang: Who then can take such an urgent charge?

Hou: I wonder ...

Liu: Do not worry! I will take the charge.

Yang: Oh, yes, no one can take this charge better than you. But could you pass so many sentinels along the way?

Liu: To tell you the truth, though my face is pockmarked, I am tall of stature and strong enough to defend myself. Besides, I have ready wit to reply to any interrogation.

Hou: It is said General Zuo's camp gate is of difficult access, and visitors cannot have free entrance. Old as you are, how can you

〔丑〕相公又来激俺了，这是俺说书的熟套子。我老汉要去就行，不去就止，那在乎一激之力。

〔起唱介〕

【北斗鹌鹑】

你那里笔下诌文[16]，
我这里胸中画策[17]。
舌战群雄，
让俺不才；
柳毅传书，
何妨下海。
丢却俺的痴骏，
用着俺的诙谐，
悄去明来，
万人喝采。

〔末〕果然好个本领，只是书中意思，还要你明白解说，才能有济。

【紫花儿序】〔丑〕

书中意不须细解，
何用明白，费俺唇腮。
一双空手，也去当差，
也会拙乖[18]。
凭着俺舌尖儿把他的人马骂开，
仍倒回八百里外。

get access to the general?

Liu: My dear Master Hou, you need not stimulate a tale-teller who is used to stimulations. Heaven will help one who helps himself. I will go of my own will.

(Standing up)

(Singing to the tune of ***Fight of Quails***):

You may well write
With your pen bright,
While I will fight
With my tongue quick to bite.
To send a letter, I am free
To go uphill or down the sea.
I will not play my clownish part
But use my wit to win the heart.
I may come in light or at dark,
And win applause of those who hark.

Yang: You are indeed eloquent. But do you think it necessary to make clear the hidden meaning of the message?

Liu (Singing to the tune of ***Violet Flower***):

The meaning of the message is plain:
There is no need for me to explain.
I may go with bare hand,
My lips will make people understand.
My sharp tongue will persuade the army to stay
Eight hundred Li away.

〔生〕你怎的骂他？

〔丑〕则问他防贼自作贼，该也不该。

〔生〕好，好，好！比俺的书字还说得明白。

〔末〕你快进去收拾行李，俺替你送盘缠来，今夜务必出城才好。

〔丑〕晓得，晓得！

〔拱手介〕不得奉陪了。

〔竟下〕

〔末〕竟不知柳敬亭是个有用之才。

〔生〕我常夸他是我辈中人，说书乃其余技耳。

【尾声】

一封书信权宜代，
仗柳生舌尖口快，
阻回那莽元帅万马晨霜，
保住这好江城三山暮霭[19]。

〔末〕一纸贤于汗马才[20]，
〔生〕荆州无复战船开；
〔末〕从来名士夸江左[21]，
〔生〕挥尘今登拜将台。

〔众下〕

Hou: What would you say?

Liu: *I'll ask the general if it's his pleasure*

To rob himself of his own treasure.

Hou: A very sharp question! Better said than written.

Yang: Go and pack your baggage as soon as possible. I will get ready the money for your expenditure on the way. It would be better for you to leave the Southern Capital tonight.

Liu: You need not tell me that.

(With clasped hands) I will not delay any longer.

(Exit.)

Yang: I did not know that pockmarked Liu is so versatile.

Hou: He is one of our compeers, not merely a story-teller.

(Singing ***the Epilogue***):

To send the message to General Zuo, who is fit?

Pockmarked Liu has sharp tongue and quick wit

To stop the general's thousand steeds from marching down

And to preserve the mountain-girt riverside town.

Yang: *A message may dissuade war steeds from running down,*

Hou: *And warships from leaving Jingzhou the western town.*

Yang: *No talent can outshine those on the eastern shore.*

Hou: *A story-teller mounts the tower all adore.*

(Exeunt.)

【注释】

[1] 收今贩古是生涯：以演说古今故事过生活。

[2] 无藉：没有依靠。

[3] 饮食之人：只知吃喝，毫无用处的人。

[4] 没数的鬼魂名姓：指他话本里记载着的许多古今人姓名。

[5] 补救：指对世道人心的补救。

[6] 褒讥：褒，表扬；讥，讽刺。

[7] 燥脾：快意、开心之意。

[8] 平话：说书。

[9] 粉黛：本是妇女的化妆品，这里借指美女。

[10] 孽子：在封建社会，凡不是正妻生的儿子都称作孽子，他在家庭里一般是受到歧视的。

[11] 本兵熊明遇：熊明遇，字良孺，江西进贤人，是当时东林党里的重要人物。这时他正任兵部尚书，因此杨龙友称他本兵。

[12] 林居：退隐林下。

[13] 蹦：践踏。

[14] 经济：古时称有应付政治问题的实际才能的人为经济之才。这经济是经世济民的意思，跟现代所说的经济含义不同。

[15] 山人：是当时社会上的人物名色。他们大都是读书人，没有功名官职，靠着书画鉴赏或其他属于“雅道”的玩艺儿来流浪江湖混饭吃。

[16] 你那里笔下诌文：指上文侯方域代侯恂写的信。诌文，意即弄文。

[17] 画策：划策。

[18] 挝（zhuā）乖：乖字在俗语里一般有机灵之意。挝乖，抓住窍门。

[19] 好江城三山暮霭：指南京。

[20] 一纸贤于汗马才：意说这封信的力量胜过战场上立的功。汗马是指打仗时战马跑出了汗。

[21] 从来名士夸江左：历史上所称江左，指长江下游金陵一带。五胡之乱，北方许多名士纷纷渡江南来，集中金陵一带，建立东晋王朝。“从来名士夸江左”，即指东晋说的。

第三出　投　辕[1]

〔净、副净扮二卒上〕

〔净〕杀贼拾贼囊，
救民占民房，
当官领官仓，
一兵吃三粮。

〔副净〕如今不是这样唱了。

〔净〕你唱来！

〔副净〕贼凶少弃囊，
民逃剩空房，
官穷不开仓，
千兵无一粮。

〔净〕这等说，我们这穷兵当真要饿死了。

〔副净〕也差不多哩。

〔净〕前日鼓噪之时，元帅着忙，许俺们就粮南京，这几日不见动静，想又变卦了。

Scene 3 The Camp Gate

(Enter two soldiers.)

First Soldier (Singing):

Killing the foe, we take the things they leave;
We occupy their houses but none grieve.
Officers eat from the stores a great deal;
Soldiers have from dawn till dusk their meal.

Second Soldier: Now we do not sing like that.

First Soldier: How do you sing now?

Second Soldier (Singing):

We can take nothing the foe leave;
People's empty houses make us grieve.
Officers eat nothing from the store;
Soldiers can have their meals no more.

First Soldier: If what you sing is true, we poor soldiers would die of hunger.

Second Soldier: That is almost true.

First Soldier: Last time when we shouted for food supply, our general promised to station us around the food stores in the vicinity of the Southern Capital. But now days have passed without further

〔副净〕他变了卦，俺们依旧鼓噪，有何难哉。

〔净〕闲话少说，

且到辕门点卯，

再作商量。

正是“不怕饿杀，谁肯犯法”。

〔俱下〕

【北新水令】〔丑扮柳敬亭，背包裹上〕

走出了空林落叶响萧萧，

一丛丛芦花红蓼。

倒戴着接䍦帽[2]，

横跨着湛卢刀[3]，

白髯儿飘飘，

谁认的诙谐玩世东方老[4]。

俺柳敬亭冲风冒雨，沿江行来，并不见乱兵抢粮，想是讹传了。且喜已到武昌城外，不免在这草地下打开包裹，换了靴帽，好去投书。

〔坐地换靴帽介〕

【南步步娇】〔副净、净上〕

晓雨城边饥乌叫，

来往荒烟道，

军营半里遥。〔指介〕

information. Could our general have changed his mind?

Second Soldier: If he changes his mind, we may raise another tumult.

First Soldier: Do not talk about tumult. We had better go to the camp gate for the daily manoeuvre. Do not forget the punishment for violation of martial law is more terrible than hunger or even death. (Exeunt.)

(Enter Liu Jingting with his baggage on the back.)

Liu (Singing to the tune of ***New Water Song***):

Coming out of the forest where leaves fall in showers,
I see here and there green weeds and red flowers.
I wear my hat on the back side
And hang my sword on a belt wide.
My white beard hanging down,
Who knows I am the clown
Of undying renown?

I come along the river in wind and rain without seeing any soldier plundering the food store, so it must be a rumor. I am glad now I have arrived at the city wall of Wuchang. So I may take out of my baggage clean hat and shoes to put on in order that I may send the message to the general.

(Sitting down on the grass and changing his hat and shoes)

(Re-enter the two soldiers.)

First Soldier (Singing to the tune of ***Charming Step by Step***) :

On this rainy morning by town-walls cry hungry crows;
On the deserted path no people goes.
The camp is half a Li away. (Pointing)

风卷旌旗，
鼓角缥缈，
前面是辕门了，大家趱行几步。
饿腹好难熬，
还点三八卯[5]。

〔丑起拱介〕两位将爷，借问一声，那是将军辕门？

〔净向副净私语介〕这个老儿是江北语音，不是逃兵，就是流贼。

〔副净〕何不收拾起来，诈他几文，且买饭吃。

〔净〕妙！

〔副净问介〕你寻将军衙门么？

〔丑〕正是。

〔净〕待我送你去。

〔丢绳套住丑介〕

〔丑〕呵呀！怎么拿起我来了？

〔副净〕俺们是武昌营专管巡逻的弓兵，不拿你，拿谁呀。

〔丑推二净倒地，指笑介〕两个没眼色的花子，怪不得饿得东倒西歪的。

〔净〕你怎晓得我们捱饿。

〔丑〕不为你们捱饿，我为何到此？

〔副净〕这等说来，你敢是解粮来的么？

〔丑〕不是解粮的，是做甚的？

〔净〕啐！我们瞎眼了，快搬行李，送老哥辕门去。

Flags in the breeze stream and sway.
Hear the muffled drumbeats and bugles blow!
The camp gate stands ahead and there let us go!
Hunger is hard to bear.
For the manoeuvre, who would care?

Liu (Saluting the soldiers): Excuse me. May I ask where the camp gate of General Zuo is?

First Soldier (Whispering to Second Soldier): This old man speaks with a Northern accent. If he is not a deserted soldier, he must be one of the rebels.

Second Soldier: Why don't we cheat some money out of him to buy food?

First Soldier: Let us try.

Second Soldier (To Liu): You want to go to the general's camp gate?

Liu: Yes.

First Soldier: Let us lead you there. (Throwing a rope to bind Liu up)

Liu: Ah! Why should you bind me up?

Second Soldier: We are soldiers on patrol. Who should we arrest if not you?

Liu (Thrusting them down in laughter): You are two beggars without eyes. No wonder you are too hungry to stand up.

First Soldier: How can you know we are hungry?

Liu: Why should I come here if I do not know?

Second Soldier: Then are you coming with food supply?

Liu: For what am I coming if not for food?

First Soldier: Sorry, we have eyes but see not. Let us bear your baggage

〔副净、净同丑行介〕

【北折桂令】〔丑〕

你看城枕着江水滔滔，
鹦鹉洲阔，黄鹤楼[6]高。
鸡犬寂寥，
人烟惨淡，
市井萧条。
都只把豺狼喂饱，
好江城画破图抛。
满耳呼号，
鼙鼓声雄，
铁马嘶骄。

〔副净指介〕这是帅府辕门了。

〔唤介〕老哥在此等侯，待我传鼓。

〔击鼓介〕

〔末扮中军官[7]上〕封拜惟知元帅大，
征诛不让帝王尊。

〔问介〕门外击鼓，有何军情，速速报来。

〔净〕适在汛地[8]捉了一个面生可疑之人，口称解粮到此，未知真假，拿赴辕门，听候发落。

〔末问丑介〕你称解粮到此，有何公文？

〔丑〕没有公文，止有书函。

to the camp gate.

(They walk together.)

Liu (Singing to the tune of ***Laurel Branch***):

The city lies by undulating riverside
With Yellow Crane Tower high and Parrot Isle wide.
Few dogs bark and few cocks crow;
Few people on the street come and go.
But leopards have eaten their fill;
The riverside town lies deserted still.
We hear but hue and cry up to the cloud,
The drumbeats loud
And neighing battle horses proud.

Second Soldier (Pointing): Here is the camp gate of our general. Will you please wait here for me to beat the announcing drum?

(Beating the drum thrice)

(Enter an officer.)

Officer (Singing)**:** *We only obey our general's order,*
And make expedition within the empires border.

(Asking) What are you beating the announcing drum for? Is there anything important? Make your report to me.

First Soldier: We have caught a doubtful stranger, saying he comes for food supply. So we have brought him here for your disposal.

Officer (Asking Liu): You say you come for food supply. Have you any official message?

Liu: I have brought no official message but a personal letter.

〔末〕这就可疑了。

【南江儿水】

你的此来意费推敲，

一封书信无名号，

荒唐言语多虚冒，

凭空何处军粮到。

无端左支右调，看他神情，

大抵非逃即盗。

〔丑〕此话差矣，若是逃、盗，为何自寻辕门。

〔末〕说的也是。既有书函，待我替你传进。

〔丑〕这是一封密书，要当面交与元帅的。

〔末〕这话益发可疑了。你且外边伺候，待我禀过元帅，传你进见。

〔净、副净、丑俱下〕

〔内吹打开门，杂扮军卒六人各执械对立介〕

〔小生扮左良玉戎服上〕荆襄雄镇大江滨，

四海安危七尺身[9]。

日日军储[10]劳计画，

那能谈笑净烟尘[11]。

〔升坐，吩咐介〕昨因饥兵鼓噪，本帅许他就粮南京；后来细想：兵去就粮，何如粮来就兵。闻得九江助饷，不

Officer: If you have only a personal letter, then the matter is rather doubtful.

(Singing to the tune of ***Water in Southern River***):

I wonder why you come from Southern Capital
With nothing more than a letter personal.
How can I know you are not telling lies?
Where would come your food supplies?
Your talk now left now right, if I am not wrong,
To rebels you belong?

Liu: How can you not be wrong? If I were a rebel, why should I come to the camp gate?

Officer: Perhaps you are right. Since you have a letter to the general, give it to me and I will submit it for you.

Liu: This is a confidential message I must submit to the general in person.

Officer: So to speak, it is all the more doubtful. Anyhow, you may just wait here. I shall report to the general and see if he will grant you an audience. (Exeunt.)

(Trumpets within. The camp gate opens, and six soldiers come out, weapon in hand, and stand left and right, face to face. Then enter General Zuo in military array.)

Zuo (Singing): *My army stationed by the riverside,*
Its safety hinges on me far and wide.
I should make plans before and after.
How can I pacify the land in laughter!

(Taking his seat and giving orders) Last time I promised hungry soldiers to be stationed around the food stores in the Southern

日就到，今日暂免点卯，各回汛地，静候关粮。

〔末〕得令。
〔虚下[12]，即上〕奉元帅军令，挂牌免卯，三军各回汛地了。

〔小生〕有甚军情，早早报来。
〔末〕别无军情，只有差役一名，口称解粮到此，要见元帅。

〔小生喜介〕果然粮船到了，可喜，可喜！

〔问介〕所赍[13]文书，系何衙门？

〔末〕并无文书，止有私书，要当堂投递。
〔小生〕这话就奇了，或是流贼细作[14]，亦未可定。
〔吩咐介〕左右军牢[15]，小心防备，着他膝行而进。
〔众〕是！
〔末唤丑进介〕
〔左右交执器械，丑钻入见介〕
〔揖介〕元帅在上，晚生拜揖了。
〔小生〕咗！你是何等样人，敢到此处放肆？
〔丑〕晚生一介平民，怎敢放肆。
【北雁儿落带得胜令】
俺是个不出山老渔樵，

Capital. Upon second thought, to move the army is not so good as to provide food for them. It is said that food supply will soon come from Jiujiang. Officer on duty, there will be no roll-call for today. Tell soldiers to return to their barracks and wait for the arrival of food supplies.

Officer: Your order shall be obeyed. (Exit and re-enter.)

By the order of our general, there will be no roll-call for today, and soldiers may go back to their barracks.

Zuo: Have you any report to make?

Officer: There is a messenger coming with food supplies, who is waiting for an audience with your generalship.

Zuo: The food supply arrived at last! What good news! Where is the official message? By whose order is he coming?

Officer: There is no official message, but the messenger will submit a personal letter to your generalship in person.

Zuo: It is unusual. This messenger may be a spy from the rebels. (Giving orders) Officers and soldiers, beware of the spy! Order him to come in on his knees!

All: Yes, sir.

(Officer calling Liu to come in under the crossed arms of two rows of soldiers.)

Liu (Saluting General Zuo with clasped hands) I salute your generalship.

Zuo: Who are you? How dare you come here without an official message?

Liu: What dare a humble civilian do in the presence of your generalship? (Singing to the tunes of ***Northern Wild Geese and Triumphant Song***):

那晓得王侯大宾客小。
看这长枪大剑列门旗，
只当深林密树穿荒草。
尽著狐狸纵横虎咆哮，
这威风何须要。
偏吓俺孤身客无门跑，
便做个长揖儿不是骄。

〔拱介〕求饶，军中礼原不晓。
〔笑介〕气也么[16]消，有书函将军仔细瞧。
〔小生问介〕有谁的书函？
〔丑〕归德侯老先生寄来奉侯的。
〔小生〕侯司徒是俺的恩师，你如何认得？

〔丑〕晚生现在侯府。
〔小生拱介〕这等失敬了。
〔问介〕书在那里？
〔丑送上书介〕
〔小生〕吩咐掩门。
〔内吹打掩门，众下〕
〔小生〕尊客请坐。
〔丑傍坐介〕
〔小生看书介〕
【南侥侥令】
看他谆谆情意好，
不啻教儿曹。

How can a mountaineer like me know
Military officers high and low?
Your swords and spears under the flags frighten me;
I seem to pass in deep forest from tree to tree,
And see your forces run riot and tigers roar,
So terrifying that I try to flee by the door.
Since there is no escape, I clasp hands to ask grace;
I do not know how to salute you face to face.
(Laughing) *My anger vented, I am freed.*
Here is a letter for your generalship to read.

Zuo: Whose letter is it?

Liu: It is a letter from Marshal Hou.

Zuo: Marshal Hou was my respectable teacher. How could you know His Excellency?

Liu: I am now in His Excellency's service.

Zuo (With clasped hands)**:** Excuse me for my misbehavior. Where is the letter?

(Liu gives the message to General Zuo.)

Let the camp gate be closed!

(Trumpets blow and the camp gate is closed. Exeunt officers and soldiers.)

Will you please take your seat?

(Liu takes his seat. Zuo reads the letter.)

(Singing to the tune of ***A Charming Song***):
The letter is a sincere one,
As if a master were advising his son.

这书中文理，一时也看不透彻，无非劝俺镇守边方，不可移兵内地。

〔叹介〕恩师，恩师！那知俺左良玉，一片忠心天可告，怎肯背深恩，辱荐保[17]。

〔问丑介〕足下尊姓大号？

〔丑〕不敢，晚生姓柳，草号敬亭。

〔杂捧茶上〕

〔小生〕敬亭请茶。〔丑接茶介〕

〔小生〕你可知这座武昌城，自经张献忠一番焚掠，十室九空。俺虽镇守在此，缺草乏粮，日日鼓噪，连俺也做不得主了。

〔丑气介〕元帅说那里话，自古道“兵随将转”，再没个将逐兵移的。

【北收江南】

你坐在细柳营，
手握着虎龙韬[18]，
管千军山可动，令不摇。
饥兵鼓噪犯天朝，
将军无计，
从他去自逍遥。
这恶名怎逃？
这恶名怎逃？
说不起三军权柄帅难操。

〔摔茶钟于地下介〕

It is not easy to fully understand.

In short, I should not leave the garrisoned land.

(Sighing) Dear Marshal, dear Marshal!

I can avow to Heaven high,

Your advice I shall never belie.

(To Liu) Will you please tell me your name?

Liu: Your humble servant is named Liu Jingting.

(Tea is served.)

Zuo: Please take tea. (Liu takes tea.) You know the city of Wuchang has turned into a deserted town after the plunder of Zhang Xianzhong's rebels. My army is stationed here without enough food supply, so the soldiers shout for hunger from day to day, and would not listen to my orders.

Liu: I beg to differ with your generalship. Since the olden days soldiers are obediant to generals and no general is obedient to his soldiers.

(Singing to the tune of ***Recapture of the South***):

In the camp you are in charge of the cavalcade;

Your order moving mountains can't be disobeyed.

The hungry soldiers run riot against the crown,

Your generalship should calm them down.

If you allow their claim,

Can you be free from blame?

Can you be free from blame?

How dare your soldiers tarnish their general's name!

(Sweeping the tea cup down and breaking it on the ground)

Zuo (Angered)**:** Ah! How can you be so impolite as to sweep down

〔小生怒介〕呵呀！这等无礼，竟把茶杯掷地。

〔丑笑介〕晚生怎敢无礼，一时说的高兴，顺手摔去了。

〔小生〕顺手摔去，难道你的心做不得主么？
〔丑〕心若做得主呵，也不叫手下乱动了。

〔小生笑介〕敬亭讲得有理。只因兵丁饿得急了，许他就粮内里。亦是无可奈何之一着。

〔丑〕晚生远来，也饿急了，元帅竟不问一声儿。

〔小生〕我倒忘了，叫左右快摆饭来。
〔丑摩腹介〕好饿，好饿！
〔小生催介〕可恶奴才，还不快摆！
〔丑起介〕等不得了，竟往内里吃去罢。

〔向内行介〕
〔小生怒介〕如何进我内里？
〔丑回顾介〕饿得急了。
〔小生〕饿得急了，就许你进内里么？
〔丑笑介〕饿得急了，也不许进内里，元帅竟也晓得哩。

〔小生大笑介〕句句讥诮俺的错处，好个舌辩之士。俺这帐下倒少不得你这个人哩。

【南园林好】

the tea cup and break it on the ground!

Liu (Laughing) : How dare I am impolite before your generalship! It is only because I am so agitated that my hand sweeps the tea cup away with my sleeve.

Zuo: How could you allow your hand to do so?

Liu: If I could not allow my hand to sweep the cup away, how could your generalship allow your soldiers to run riot?

Zuo (Laughing): You are right. But when soldiers are hungry to death, what could I do but promise them to be stationed around the food stores in the Southern Capital?

Liu: Now coming from afar, I am hungry to death. Why don't your generalship condescend to offer me some food?

Zuo: Excuse me for my negligence.

Liu (Stroking his belly) : I am so hungry, so hungry!

Zuo: Soldier, make haste.

Liu: I am so hungry that I can no longer wait. Let me go in to take my meal!

(Going towards the inner part of the camp)

Zuo (Angered): How can you go into my camp!

Liu: (Turning back): I am hungry to death.

Zuo: Are you allowed to go into the camp even if you are hungry to death?

Liu (Laughing)**:** If the hungry are not allowed to go into the camp, could hungry soldiers be allowed to go into the Southern Capital?

Zuo (Laughing) **:** How eloquent you are! Each shot makes a hit. You are indeed the talent we need in our camp.

(Singing to the tune of t***he Southern Garden***):

俺虽是江湖泛交，
认得出滑稽曼老[19]；
这胸次包罗不少，
能直谏，
会旁嘲。

〔丑〕那里，那里！只不过游戏江湖，图铺啜耳。

〔小生问介〕俺看敬亭，既与缙绅[20]往来，必有绝技，正要请教。

〔丑〕晚生自幼失学，有何技艺。偶读几句野史，信口演说，曾蒙吴桥范大司马、桐城何老相国，谬加赏赞，因而得交缙绅，实堪惭愧。

【北沽美酒带太平令】

俺读些稗官词[21]，
寄牢骚，
稗官词，
寄牢骚，
对江山吃一斗苦松醪[22]。
小鼓儿颤杖[23]轻敲，
寸板儿软手频摇；
一字字臣忠子孝，
一声声龙吟虎啸；
快舌尖钢刀出鞘，

Though we have just made our acquaintance now,
I know you are the clown to whom all men bow.
There is nothing your fun cannot embrace;
You can blame face to face
Or admonish with grace.

Liu: You flatter me. I am only earning a living from hand to mouth, from mouth to hand.

Zuo: Since you have made friends with so many intelligentlemen, you must have your own long suit. Will you please tell me some?

Liu: How could I have any long suit since I did not attend any school while young? I have only read a few books of history and learned to speak at random. By luck I have won the appreciation of Minister Fan and Premier He, so some intelligentlemen condescend to make friends with me. In reality, I am not worthy of their friendship.

(Singing to the tune of ***Buy Good Wine and Peaceful Song***):

I have read unauthentic history to vent
My discontent, my discontent,
As if I had drunk the bitter wine
Made in the land of bitter pine.
Beating my little drum, I stand
And wave the clappers in my hand.
Word by word I talk about loyal and pious throng,
And imitate the tiger's and dragon's song.
My tongue is sharp as sword unsheathed under the sun,
My throat is loud as thundering gun.

响喉咙轰雷烈炮。
呀！似这般冷嘲热挑，
用不着笔抄、墨描[24]。
劝英豪，
一盘错帐速勾了。

〔小生〕说得爽快，竟不知敬亭有此绝技，就留下榻衙斋，早晚领教罢。

【清江引】
从此谈今论古日倾倒，
风雨开怀抱。
你那苏张[25]舌辩高，
我的巧射惊羿奡[26]，
只愁那匝地烟尘[27]何日扫。

〔丑〕闲话多时，到底不知元帅向内移兵，有何主见？

〔小生〕耿耿臣心，惟天可表，不须口劝，何用书责。

〔小生〕臣心如水照清霄，
〔丑〕咫尺天颜路不遥；
〔小生〕要与西南撑半壁，
〔丑〕不须东看海门潮[28]。
〔众下〕

I may jeer at one
Or sneer at none.
I need not write
In black and white.
I advise heroes, right or wrong,
To cancel the account however long.

Zuo: You may say what you will. I do not know you have such a long suit. Will you please stay in my camp so that I may consult you from time to time?

(Singing to the tune of ***the Clear River***):

From now on we may talk present or past;
In wind or rain we may talk heart to heart at last.
Your eloquence outshines from east to west;
I can shoot better than the archer best.
What fills our mind with woe
Is when to sweep away the foe.

Liu: You have talked so long without telling me if your army will march eastward.

Zuo: I have made my vow to Heaven, so I need neither man nor letter to dissuade me.

Zuo: *As sky and water my mind is as clear.*
Liu: *The way to the celestial court is near.*
Zuo: *I will uphold the state on southwest side.*
Liu: *You need not go east to see the high tide.*

(Exeunt.)

【注释】

[1] 投辕：辕即辕门。投辕是指柳敬亭到辕门去见左良玉。

[2] 接䍦（lí）帽：白接䍦，头巾的一种，因为用白鹭的羽毛来装饰，故称白接䍦。

[3] 湛（zhàn）卢刀：古代著名的剑，传说是春秋战国时的著名铸剑师欧冶子制造的。

[4] 东方老：东方朔，是汉代著名的滑稽人物。

[5] 三八卯：卯即点卯，点名的意思。三八卯是逢三、八（如三日、八日、十三日、十八日）日的例期点名。

[6] 鹦鹉洲、黄鹤楼：鹦鹉洲在今武昌西南江中；黄鹤楼在武昌西南江边，都是武昌的名胜。

[7] 中军官：明清时代，凡在统军将领本营里管理营务的首领官称作中军官。

[8] 汛地：军队防守的地方。

[9] 四海安危七尺身：意说他的七尺之身关系着四海安危。

[10] 军储：军需。

[11] 谈笑净烟尘：在谈笑之中平息了战乱。

[12] 虚下：戏曲演出时的术语，指演员到了舞台左边入口又上来，表示他已经离开了刚才演出的现场，到另一个场合来了。

[13] 赍（jī）：携带。
[14] 细作：军事上的暗探、间谍。
[15] 军牢：指卫兵。
[16] 也么：只是帮助腔调的两个音，没有什么意义。
[17] 辱荐保：荐保即推荐保举，辱是玷辱，亏负之意。
[18] 手握着虎龙韬：意指手握兵权。
[19] 滑稽曼老：东方朔，字曼倩。
[20] 缙绅：指一般官僚绅士。
[21] 稗官词：稗官野史。
[22] 松醪：酒名。
[23] 颤杖：抖动着小鼓槌。杖，指小鼓槌。
[24] “似这般冷嘲热挑”二句：说这些冷嘲热挑的话，比笔抄墨描的文章更有效。
[25] 苏张：苏秦、张仪，都是春秋战国时的著名说客。
[26] 羿奡（yì ào）：羿是夏时有穷的君主，也是我国神话传说里的有名射手。奡是夏时寒浞的儿子，相传他能陆地行舟。
[27] 匝地烟尘：遍地烟尘，指兵乱。
[28] 不须东看海门潮：不须引兵东下。

第三本　三罪阻立继位人

ACT III　Crime and Succession

第一出　辞院

【西地锦】〔末扮杨文骢冠带上〕

锦绣东南列郡，
英雄割据纷纷；
而今还起周郎恨，
江水向东奔[1]。

下官杨文骢，昨奉熊司马[2]之命，托侯兄发书宁南，阻其北上，已遣柳敬亭连夜寄去。还怕投书未稳，一面奏闻朝廷，加他官爵，荫他子侄；又一面知会各处督抚，及在城大小文武，齐集清议堂[3]，公同计议，助他粮饷，这也是不得已调停之法。下官与阮圆海虽罢闲流寓，都有传单，只得早到。

〔副净扮阮大铖冠带上〕黑白看成棋里事，须眉扮作戏中人。

Scene 1 Parting

(Enter Yang Wencong in official dress.)

Yang (Singing to the tune of ***Western Brocade***):

In the southeastern land

Heroes rose in command,

But General Zhou of bygone day

Has passed with waves on eastward way.

By order of Governor Xiong, I asked Master Hou to write a message for General Zuo in order to prevent his army from marching on the Southern Capital. This message was sent by Liu Jingting last night. Unsure if it could succeed, we requested the imperial court on the one hand to promote General Zuo's rank, and on the other, all civil and military officers are summoned to the assembly hall to discuss how to provide food supply to his army. That is the only precautionary measure we can take. Retired as we are from civil service, Ruan Dacheng and I are summoned for the discussion, so we come early to attend the meeting.

(Enter Ruan Dacheng in official dress.)

Ruan (Singing) : *Filling an office is like playing chess,*

〔见介〕龙友请了，今日会议军情，既传我们到此，也不可默默无言。

〔末〕事体重大，我们废员闲宦，立不得主意，身到就是了。

〔副净〕说那里话。

【啄木儿】

朝廷事，
须认真，
太祖神京今未稳，
莫漫愁铁锁船开[4]，
只怕有萧墙人引[5]。
角声鼓音城楼震，
帆扬帜飞江风顺，
明取金陵，
有人私启门。

〔末〕这话未确，且莫轻言。

〔副净〕小弟实有所闻，岂可不说。

〔丑扮长班[6]上〕处处军情紧，
朝朝会议多。

禀老爷，淮安漕抚史可法[7]老爷，凤阳督抚马士英老

An actor should play his role nonetheless.

(Saluting Yang) Dear Master Yang, summoned to discuss the military situation, we should not remain taciturn on this important matter.

Yang: Important as the matter is, but retired officials as we are, I am afraid we cannot have much to say, while our attendance has expressed our concern on the situation.

Ruan: I beg to differ from you.

(Singing to the tune of ***Wood Peckers***):

The state affair
Demands great care.
We are not sure
If the capital is secure.
Do not let warships break iron chains and come near.
A hidden traitor is what to fear.
Hearing the bugle and drumbeats, the town would shiver,
When warships sail down in the wind along the river.
I am afraid they try to change the city's fate;
A traitor may open the city gate.

Yang: Do not say what you are not sure!

Ruan: Why can I not say what I have heard?

(Enter an announcer.)

Announcer (Singing) **:** *When you see armies in array,*
Meetings are held from day to day.
Here comes His Excellence Shi Kefa.

爷俱到了。

〔末、副净出候介〕

〔外白须扮史可法，净秃须扮马士英，各冠带上〕

〔外〕天下军储一线漕[8]，

无能空佩吕虔刀[9]。

〔净〕长陵抔土关龙脉，

愁绝烽烟搔二毛。

〔末、副净见各揖介〕

〔外问介〕本兵熊老先生为何不到？

〔丑禀介〕今日有旨，往江上点兵去了。

〔净〕这等又会议不成，如何是好？

【前腔】〔外〕

黄尘起，王气昏[10]，

羽扇难挥建业军[11]；

幕府山蜡檄星驰，

五马渡[12]楼船飞滚。

江东应须夷吾镇，

清谈怎消南朝恨[13]，

少不得努力同捐衰病身。

〔末〕老先生不必深忧，左良玉系侯司徒旧卒，昨已发书劝止，料无不从者。

Here comes His Excellence Ma Shiying.

(Yang and Ruan come out in attendance.)

(Enter Shi Kefa and Ma Shiying in official dress.)

Shi (Singing): *Though in charge of military supply,*

In vain is my sword brandished high.

Ma (Singing): *On royal tombs the fate of empire lies.*

What can we do to see beacon fires rise!

(Yang and Ruan salute Shi and Ma.)

Shi: Why has Governor Xiong not yet come?

Announcer: By imperial order, Governor Xiong has gone to a manoeuvre on the river.

Ma: How can we discuss the matter at his absence?

Shi (Singing to ***the previous tune***):

Yellow dust rain

Dims royal reign.

A feathered fan cannot command soldiers to fight;

A message should be sent in starry night.

The warships sail on rolling waves like steeds in flight.

The eastern shore should listen to royal command.

How can lip service take revenge for southern land?

We do our best in vain

Although with might and main.

Yang: Your Excellecy need not worry too much. General Zuo was a subordinate officer under Marshal Hou, who has just sent a message to him, which must lead to good result.

〔外〕学生亦闻此举虽出熊司马之意，实皆年兄之功也。

〔副净〕这倒不知，只闻左兵之来，实有暗里勾之者。

〔外〕是那个？

〔副净〕就是敝同年侯恂之子侯方域。

〔外〕他也是敝世兄，在复社中铮铮有声，岂肯为此？

〔副净〕老公祖[14]不知，他与左良玉相交最密，常有私书往来，若不早除此人，将来必为内应。

〔净〕说得有理，何惜一人，致陷满城之命乎？

〔外〕这也是莫须有之事[15]，况阮老先生罢闲之人，国家大事也不可乱讲。

〔别介〕请了，正是

“邪人无正论，

公议总私情。”〔下〕

〔副净指恨介〕

〔向净介〕怎么史道邻就拂衣而去，小弟之言凿凿有据；闻得前日还托柳麻子去下私书的。

〔末〕这太屈他了，敬亭之去，小弟所使，写书之时，小弟

Shi: I have heard that it is you who, under the command of Governor Xiong, asked the Marshal to write this message.

Ruan: I have heard something to the contrary. It is the intrigue of some traitor who enticed Zuo Liangyu to march on the Southern Capital.

Shi: Who can this traitor be?

Ruan: It is Hou Fangyu, son of Marshal Hou.

Shi: He is a renowned member of the Recovery Society. How could it be possible for him to do such a base action?

Ruan: Your Excellency did not know that he is on intimate terms with Zuo Liangyu, so it would be necessary to get rid of this traitor.

Ma: You are right. For the security of the Southern Capital, I think it is safe to sacrifice this man.

Shi (To Ruan): Do not spread baseless rumor! A retired official like you should not damage the reputation of a renowed personage of the state.

(Leaving) I beg to leave the assembly.

(Singing): *We can tell right from wrong*

As we know short from long. (Exit.)

Ruan (Pointing to Shi and speaking to Ma): Why is His Excellency Shi displeased and leaves us? Will he not believe what I say is not baseless rumor? I am sure Pockmarked Liu sent a message for Hou Fangyu.

Yang: Witness to the message sent by Liu, I know it tries to dissuade

在傍；倒亏他写的恳切，怎反疑起他来？

〔副净〕龙友不知，那书中都有字眼暗号，人那里晓得？

〔净点头介〕是呀，这样人该杀的，小弟回去，即着人访拿。

〔向末介〕老妹丈，就此同行罢。
〔末〕请舅翁先行一步，小弟随后就来。
〔副净向净介〕小弟与令妹丈不啻同胞，常道及老公祖垂念，难得今日会着。小弟有许多心事，要为竟夕之谈。不知可否？
〔净〕久荷高雅，正要请教。〔同下〕
〔末〕这是那里说起！侯兄之素行虽未深知，只论写书一事呵。

【三段子】
这冤怎伸，硬叠成曾参杀人；
这恨怎吞，强书为陈恒弑君。
不免报他一信，
叫他趁早躲避。
〔行介〕眠香占花风流阵，今宵正倚薰笼[16]困，
那知打散鸳鸯金弹狠。
来此是李家别院，不免叫门。
〔敲门介〕
〔内吹唱介〕

General Zuo from marching eastward. How could he be suspected as traitor?

Ruan: You do not know that the message may say one thing and mean another.

Ma (Nodding): Such an insidious traitor must be executed. Back to my office, I will have him arrested. (To Yang) My dear nephew, I am going back now, will you go with me?

Yang: My dear uncle, please go ahead! I will go later.

Ruan (To Ma): On intimate terms with your nephew, I have many things to talk with you. I do not know if you have the time to listen.

Ma: You are welcome. Let us go together. (Exeunt.)

Yang: This is far beyond my knowledge. Though not on intimate terms with Master Hou, I know the whole process of the message.

(Singing to the tune of ***Three Stanzas***):

How could such a baseless rumor spread?

I must try to prevent such an unjust bloodshed

I think it would be better

To write a preventive letter. (Walking)

He sleeps with fragrant flower to sweeten his heart,

But golden balls would drive love-birds apart.

Here is Lee's Bower. I shall knock at the door.

(Knocking)

(Music and songs are heard within. Enter Su Kunsheng.)

〔净扮苏昆生上〕是那个？

〔末〕快快开门！

〔净开门见介〕原来是杨老爷，天色已晚，还来闲游。

〔末认介〕你是苏昆老。

〔问介〕侯兄在那里？

〔净〕今日香君学完一套新曲，都在楼上听他演腔。

〔末〕快请下楼！

〔净入唤介〕

〔小旦、生、旦出介〕

〔生〕浓情人带酒，
　　寒夜帐笼花。
　　杨兄高兴，也来消夜。

〔末〕兄还不知，有天大祸事来寻你了。

〔生〕有何祸事，如此相吓？

〔末〕今日清议堂议事，阮圆海对着大众，说你与宁南有旧，常通私书，将为内应。那些当事诸公，俱有拿你之意。

〔生惊介〕我与阮圆海素无深仇，为何下这毒手。

〔末〕想因却奁一事，太激烈了，故此老羞变怒耳。

Su: Who is knocking?

Yang: Open the door, please.

Su (Opening and saluting) : It is you, dear Master Yang. For what are you coming so late?

Yang: Oh, dear Master Su, will you please tell me where Master Hou is?

Su: Fragrant has just learned a new song and Master Hou is listening to her sing it upstairs.

Yang: Would you please ask him to come down?

Su (Calling) : Master Hou!

(Enter Hou with Fragrant and Mother Lee.)

Hou (Singing) : *Drunken with wine and love and sweet delight,*

Flowers in curtained bed fear no cold night.

Ah, dear Master Yang, are you coming to enjoy a sweet night?

Yang: Ah, Master Hou, you do not know disaster would come like a bolt out of the blue?

Hou: What disaster has frightened you so much?

Yang: Ruan Dacheng said in the assembly hall that you are on intimate terms with General Zuo and would open the city gate for him when his army march eastward. Some officials in charge who believe what they have heard would try to arrest you.

Hou (Startled) : I am not in enmity with him. Why should he spread such rumor against me?

Yang: Perhaps your rejection of the dowry he provided for you has angered him, so he would take revenge on you.

〔小旦〕事不宜迟，趁早高飞远遁，不要连累别人。

〔生〕说得有理。
〔愁介〕只是燕尔[17]新婚，如何舍得。
〔旦正色介〕官人素以豪杰自命，为何学儿女子态？
〔生〕是，是，但不知那里去好？
【滴溜子】

双亲在，
双亲在，
信音未准；
烽烟起，
烽烟起，
梓桑半损。
欲归，
归途难问。
天涯到处迷，
将身怎隐。
歧路穷途，
天暗地昏。

〔末〕不必着慌，小弟倒有个算计。
〔生〕请教！
〔末〕会议之时，漕抚史可法、凤抚马舍舅俱在坐。舍舅语言甚不相为[18]，全亏史公一力分豁[19]，且说与尊府原

Mother: If so, you had better leave here at once so as not to compromise others.

Hou: You are right. But how can I leave my darling bride!

Fragrant: How can a renowned intelligentleman like you hesitate like an undecisive woman!

Hou: Then where shall I go?

(Singing to the tune of ***Dripping Drop by Drop***)

I have not heard a word
From my family dear,
From my family dear.
When beacon fire
Runs higher and higher,
The state is devastated far and near,
Far and near.
Homeward I'd go,
But which way? I don't know.
I'm puzzled on my way.
Where can I stay?
Can I not stray?
Dark is the sky,
The earth is dim far and nigh.

Yang: Do not worry. I think there is a way for you.

Hou: Will you please tell me which?

Yang: His Excellency Shi Kefa came with my uncle Ma Shiying to the assembly hall. Ma did not say anything helpful for you. But Shi

有世谊的。

〔生想介〕是，是，史道邻是家父门生。

〔末〕这等何不随他到淮，再候家信。

〔生〕妙，妙！多谢指引了。

〔旦〕待奴家收拾行装。

〔旦束装介〕

【前腔】

欢娱事，
欢娱事，
两心自忖；
生离苦，
生离苦，
且将恨忍，
结成眉峰一寸。
香沾翠被池，
重重束紧。
药裹巾箱[20]，
都带泪痕。

〔丑上，挑行李介〕

〔生别旦介〕暂此分别，后会不远。

〔旦弹泪介〕满地烟尘，重来亦未可必也。

【哭相思】

离合悲欢分一瞬，

did not believe the rumor at all. On the contrary, he said your respectable father Marshal Hou has been very kind to him.

Hou: Oh, yes, my father was in charge when he passed the civil service examinations.

Yang: If so, why do you not go to his office and wait for the message from your father?

Hou: Good. Thank you for your timely advice.

Fragrant: Then I will go to pack your baggage.

(Singing to ***the previous tune***):

Thinking of the delight we share,
Deep in the heart,
Deep in the heart,
How can we bear,
How can we bear,
Each from the other to part!
What can I do but knit my brow
And pack up your things now?
Although your fragrant quilt and box in places
Are stained with tear traces?

(Enter a servant carrying the baggage.)

Hou (Bidding adieu): We part now but soon we shall meet again.

Fragrant (Shedding tears): The land is torn by war, can we not be torn apart?

(Singing to the tune of ***Longing in Tears***):

Soon we shall part in sorrow.

后会期无凭准。

〔小旦〕怕有巡兵踪迹，快行一步罢。

〔生〕吹散俺西风太紧，

停一刻无人肯。

〔生〕但不知史漕抚寓在那厢。

〔净〕闻他来京公干，常寓市隐园，待我送官人去。

〔生〕这等多谢。

〔生、净、丑急下〕

〔小旦〕这桩祸事，都从杨老爷起的，也还求杨老爷归结。

明日果来拿人，作何计较？

〔末〕贞娘放心，侯郎既去，都与你无干了。

〔末〕人生聚散事难论，

〔旦〕酒尽歌终被尚温；

〔小旦〕独照花枝眠不稳，

〔末〕来朝风雨掩重门。

〔众下〕

When shall we meet again? Never tomorrow.

Mother: You had better go at once for fear of the patrols.

Hou (Singing): *The west wind hastens me to depart,*

But who cares for my broken heart?

(To Yang) Do you know where His Excellency Shi dwells?

Yang: It is said when he comes to the Southern Capital on mission, usually he dwells in the Secluded Garden. I may ask someone to accompany you to go there.

Hou: Thanks a lot.

(Exeunt.)

Mother: Dear Master Yang, it is you who have caused this disaster. So I can only ask you to avert it. What if men should come here to arrest Master Hou?

Yang: Do not worry, dear Mother Lee. Since Master Hou is gone, no one shall be arrested.

Epilogue of the Scene

Yang: In our life we cannot drink together for long.

Fragrant: When wine is drunk, in warm quilt we hear no more song.

Mother: How can a lonely blooming branch fall into sleep,

Yang: When over double door wind and rain swiftly sweep!

(Exeunt.)

【注释】

[1]“而今还起周郎恨”二句：周郎即周瑜，周瑜为吴将时，曹操自荆州顺流东下，引起赤壁之战。江水向东奔，暗指左兵的东下。

[2]熊司马：兵部尚书熊明遇。

[3]清议堂：当时朝廷大臣商议军政大事的地方。

[4]铁索船开：这里引用了王濬的故事。《晋书·王濬传》：西晋太康元年，龙骧将军王濬带兵攻打吴国。吴人在长江中要害之处横拦铁锁链，并在江中放置大铁锥，以阻挡王濬船舰。王濬造了几十只大木筏，上面绑着草人，让会水的军士驾着行驶在船队前头，木筏遇到铁锥，就将锥带走。又造了长十几丈的大火把，灌上麻油，放在船前，点燃烧断锁链，使船队顺利通过。后吴王孙皓投降。

[5]只怕有萧墙人引：祸起于内部的往往叫作祸起萧墙。

[6]长班：官僚的仆从。

[7]史可法：字宪之，号道邻，河南祥符人，崇祯进士，曾任南京兵部尚书。

[8]天下军储一线漕：天下的军需靠一线漕河来运输。

[9]吕虔刀：吕虔，三国时期魏国人，他有一把宝刀，铸工说：“要位

登三公的人才可佩带它。”史可法在上场诗里用这典故，表示他才德不称官位。

[10]“黄尘起”二句：我国古时传说，认为金陵有王者之气。

[11] 羽扇难挥建业军：《晋书·顾荣传》中说陈敏在江南作乱时，顾荣以羽扇指挥三军，与他交战，陈敏的兵纷纷溃散。这里借用这故事。建业，南京。

[12] 五马渡：南京地名，在旧上元县西北二十三里。

[13] 清谈怎消南朝恨：南朝士大夫往往排弃世务，从事清谈；南朝各代国力不振，和这种风尚有关。

[14] 老公祖：明清时绅士称地方官作公祖。

[15] 莫须有之事：指凭空诬陷的冤狱。

[16] 薰笼：有笼子罩着的薰炉。

[17] 燕尔：安乐。

[18] 不相为：不相助。

[19] 分豁（huò）：开脱。

[20] 巾箱：指放头巾的箱子。

第二出　哭主

〔副净扮旗牌官[1]上〕汉阳烟树隔江滨，
影里青山画里人，
可惜城西佳绝处，
朝朝遮断马头尘。
在下宁南帅府一个旗牌官的便是，俺元帅收复武昌，功封侯爵。昨日又奉新恩，加了太傅[2]之衔；小爷左梦庚[3]，亦挂总兵之印，特差巡按御史黄澍[4]老爷到府宣旨。今日九江督抚袁继咸[5]老爷，又解粮三十船，亲来给发。元帅大喜，命俺设宴黄鹤楼，请两位老爷饮酒看江。

〔望介〕遥见晴川树底，芳草洲边[6]，万姓欢歌，三军嬉笑，好一段太平景象也。远远喝道[7]之声，元帅将到，不免设起席来。

〔台上挂黄鹤楼匾〕

Scene 2 The Emperor's Death

(Enter an Officer on Duty.)

Officer (Singing): *By riverside loom mist-veiled trees,*

In picturesque blue hills men stay.

Though scenic spots in west town please,

War steeds raise dust from day to day.

I am an officer on duty in Marshal Zuo's camp. Since the recovery of the lost land, our general is promoted to the rank of marshal and ennobled as marquees. His son is also appointed officer in charge of a town. The imperial edict will be announced by Advisor Huang Shu, who will come to our marshal's camp today. Besides, Governor Yuan Jixian has come from Jiujiang with thirty ships loaded with food supply. Our marshal, highly delighted, orders me to prepare a banquet at Yellow Crane Tower so that he may invite the governor and the advisor to feast on wine and on the scenic beauty by the riverside.

(Gazing) I see from afar by the riverside, in the shade of trees, on the carpet of grass, people and soldiers are making merry. What a peaceful sight! The trumpets announce the arrival of our marshal. I must get the banquet ready. (Arranging the seats

〔副净设席安座介〕

〔杂扮军校旗仗鼓吹引导〕

〔小生扮左良玉戎装上〕

【声声慢】

逐人春色，

入眼晴光，

连江芳草青青。

百尺楼高，

吹笛落梅风景。

领着花间小乘[8]，

载行厨，

带缓衣轻；

便笑咱将军好武，

也爱儒生。

咱家左良玉，今日设宴黄鹤楼，请袁、黄两公饮酒看江，只得早候。

〔吩咐介〕大小军卒楼下伺候。

〔众应下〕

〔作登楼介兰〕三春云物归胸次[9]，

万里风烟到眼中。

〔望介〕你看浩浩洞庭，苍苍云梦[10]，控西南之险，当江汉之冲[11]；俺左良玉镇此名邦，好不壮哉！

in the tower)

(Enter soldiers, flag in hands, playing music with bugles and drums.)

(Enter Marshal Zuo in military array.)

Zuo (Singing to ***the Slow, Slow Tune***):

The charming spring
Makes my eyes sing
By riverside overgrown with grass sweet.
In tower high
The flute is played and flowers fly.
Coming along the path in cabs with cooks,
In light dress and loose belt we meet.
People may laugh and say
A general should love military array.
But I am also fond of books.

I invite Governor Yuan and Advisor Huang to a banquet in Yellow Crane Tower in order to entertain them with wine and scenic beauty. I must come early to attend to them.

(Giving orders) Sergeants and soldiers, wait on us downstaris.

(Exeunt soldiers.)

Zuo (Going upstairs and singing):

Before my breast late spring clouds rise,
The breeze brings smoke into my eyes.

(Looking out) Behold! How vast is the Dongting Lake! So green is the Dreaming Cloud. Commanding the southwest

〔坐呼介〕旗牌官何在？

〔副净跪介〕有。

〔小生〕酒席齐备不曾？

〔副净〕齐备多时了。

〔小生〕怎么两位老爷还不见到？

〔副净〕连请数次，袁老爷正在江岸盘粮，黄老爷又往龙华寺[12]拜客，大约傍晚才来。

〔小生〕在此久候，岂不困倦。叫左右速接柳相公上楼，闲谈拨闷。

〔杂跪禀介〕柳相公现在楼下。

〔小生〕快请。

〔杂请介〕

〔丑扮柳敬亭上〕气吞云梦泽，声撼岳阳楼。

〔见介〕

〔小生〕敬亭为何早来了。

〔丑〕晚生知道元帅闷坐，特来奉陪的。

〔小生〕这也奇了，你如何晓得。

〔丑〕常言"秀才会课，点灯告坐[13]"。天生文官，再不能爽快的。

〔小生笑介〕说得有理。

〔指介〕你看天才午转，几时等到点灯也。

region and controlling the two rivers, what an important post do I hold! It should be occupied by none other than a hero. (Calling) Officer on Duty!

Officer (Kneeling): Here, sir.

Zuo: Is the banquet ready?

Officer: It is ready for a long time.

Zuo: Why have Governor Yuan and Advisor Huang not yet come?

Officer: On inquiry, Governor Yuan is busy with food supply by the riverside, and Advisor Huang is visiting the Dragon Temple. They cannot be here till dusk.

Zuo: I am tired of waiting here so long. Ask Master Liu to come upstairs so that we may while away the time.

Servant (Kneeling): Master Liu is downstairs.

Zuo: Invite him to come upstairs.

(Enter Liu Jingting.)

Liu (Singing): *Clouds rise from Dreaming Lake;*

My voice makes towers shake.

(Saluting Zuo)

Zuo: Why are you here so early?

Liu: I come early to beguile your leisure with my tales.

Zuo: How could you know I am at leisure?

Liu: It is said a story-teller is as good as a fortune-teller. What is there that a story-teller does not know?

Zuo: You are right. (Pointing skywards) It is past noon. How long shall we wait for dusk to come?

〔丑〕若不嫌聒噪呵，把昨晚说的“秦叔宝见姑娘”，再接上一回罢。

〔小生〕极妙了。

〔问介〕带有鼓板么？

〔丑〕自古“官不离印，货不离身”，老汉管着做甚的。

〔取出鼓板介〕

〔小生〕叫左右泡开岕片[14]，安下胡床。咱要纱帽隐囊[15]，清谈消遣哩。

〔杂设床、泡茶，小生更衣坐，杂捶背搔痒介〕

〔丑旁坐敲鼓板说书介〕

大江滚滚浪东流，
淘尽兴亡古渡头；
屈指英雄无半个，
从来遗恨是荆州。

按下新诗，还提旧话。且说人生最难得的是乱离之后，骨肉重逢。总是地北天南，时移物换，经几番凶荒战斗，怎免得梗泛萍漂[16]。可喜秦叔宝解到罗公帅府，枷锁连身，正在候审；遇着嫡亲姑娘，卷帘下阶，抱头大哭。当时换了新衣，设席款待，一个候死的囚徒，登时上了青天。这叫作“运去黄金减价，时来顽铁生光”。

Liu: My story may make a long day short. If you are not displeased with it, I shall tell you the story of *Qin Qiong meeting his aunt*.

Zuo: It would be interesting. Have you brought your clappers with you?

Liu: I cannot go out without my clappers just as an official cannot leave his seal.

(Taking out the clappers)

Zuo: Let tea be served and seats be provided. I will while away this afternoon in civilian dress.

(Seats are arranged and tea served. Zuo changes his dress and takes his seat, an attendant is doing massage.)

Liu (Taking his seat at a table and telling his tale to the rhythm of his clappers and singing):

The great river rolls its endless waves to the east,
The old ferry has witnessed rise and fall at least.
Have any heroes outlived the river flowing down?
All their regret is to have lost the southwest town.

What more felicity can fall to a creature than to meet one near and dear to you in time of trouble? I shall continue to tell you the story of Qin Qiong, a hero defeated after furious battles, captured and sent in fetters to Marshal Luo's camp. What was not his joy when, as a prisoner waiting for trial, he was discovered to be a nephew-in-law of the marshal. When his aunt rolled up the curtain, came down from the hall, held him in warm embrace and shed copious tears, he seemed to have flown up

〔拍醒木介〕

〔小生掩泪介〕咱家也都经过了。

〔丑〕再说那罗公问及叔宝的武艺，满心欢喜，特地要夸其本领，即日放炮传操。下了教场，雄兵十万，雁翅排开。罗公独坐当中，一呼百诺，掌着生杀之权。秦叔宝站在旁边，点头赞叹，口里不言，心中暗道：大丈夫定当如此！

〔拍醒木介〕

〔小生作骄态，笑介〕俺左良玉也不枉为人一世矣。

〔丑〕那罗公眼看叔宝，高声问道："秦琼，看你身材高大，可曾学些武艺么？"叔宝慌忙跪下，应答如流："小人会使双锏[17]。"罗公即命家人，将自己用的两条银锏，抬将下来。那两条银锏，共重六十八斤，比叔宝所用铁锏，轻了一半。叔宝是用过重锏的人，接在手中，如同无物。跳下阶来，使尽身法，左轮右舞，恰似玉蟒缠身，银龙护体。玉蟒缠身，万道毫光台下落；银龙护体，一轮月影面前悬。罗公在中军帐里，大声喝采道："好呀！"那十万雄兵，一齐答应。

from the hell to the paradise. Having changed his dress, he was entertained with a high feast. Like the iron with rust rubbed off, he appeared even brighter than gold.

(Striking the table with a slab)

Zuo (Shedding tears): That is my personal experience.

Liu: When Marshal Luo asked Qin about his skills in using weapons, he was delighted to learn Qin's craft and he would give him a chance to show his skills. So by his order, the booming of the cannon announced the manoeuvre on the parade ground and the army spread out two wings in display. The marshal took his seat in the centre while Qin stood by his side in admiration. That is what a hero should do, said Qin to himself. (Striking the table with a slab)

Zuo (In proud laughter): What I have done is not unworthy of a heroic generalship.

Liu: Marshal Luo, looking at Qin in the face, asked him: "Bright and brave as you looked, have you learned how to use weapons?" At once Qin answered on his knee, "I have learned to wield two iron clubs." The marshal ordered the attendant to bring the two silver clubs of sixty-eight *jin* which he used himself, but which were not so weighty as Qin's iron clubs. So Qin brandished the weapons up and down, left and right, as two jade serpents or silver dragons which shed brilliance here and there like moonbeams which dazzled the eyes. The marshal applauded in the central seat and the army burst in thunderous echoes heard

〔作喊介〕如同山崩雷响，十里皆闻。

〔拍醒木介〕

〔小生照镜镊鬓介〕俺左良玉立功边塞，万夫不当，也是天下一个好健儿。如今白发渐生，杀贼未尽，好不恨也。

〔副净上〕禀元帅爷，两位老爷俱到楼了。

〔丑暗下〕

〔小生换冠带、杂撤床排席介〕

〔外扮袁继咸，末扮黄澍，冠带喝道上〕

〔外〕长湖落日气苍茫，
黄鹤楼高望故乡。

〔末〕吹笛仙人称地主，
临风把酒喜洋洋。

〔小生迎揖介〕二位老先生俯临敝镇，曷胜光荣；聊设杯酒，同看春江。

〔外、末〕久钦威望，喜近节麾，高楼盛设，大快生平。

〔安席坐，斟酒欲饮介〕

〔净扮塘报[18]人急上〕忙将覆地翻天事，
报与勤王救主人。

far and near. (Striking the table with a slab)

Zuo (Looking at his white hair in the mirror): Irresistible on the frontier, I am also a hero who has won victory on victory. But now age begins to snow white hair on my forehead, while the foe is not yet vanquished. What a deep regret!

(Enter an Officer in Charge.)

Officer: Governor Yuan and Advisor Huang have arrived at the tower.

(Exit Liu unobserved.)

(General Zuo puts on his official dress, while the table and the seat for the story-teller are removed and the banquet seats are arranged.)

(Enter Governor Yuan and Advisor Huang in official dress.)

Yuan (Singing): *The boundless lake at sunset takes a crimson dye.*

I can't see my home on Yellow Crane Tower high.

Huang (Singing): *The immortal flutist invites us to his land.*

How happy we're to drink in the breeze, cup in hand!

Zuo (Saluting them): What a great honor for me to invite Your Excellencies to dinner by the riverside, where scenic splendor is as enjoyable as wine!

Yuan & Huang: What a great pleasure for us to be invited by Your Generalship to such a sumptuous feast on this lofty tower! (Taking their seats and ready to drink)

(Enter a messenger.)

Messenger (Singing): *The empire is turned upside down.*

I shall report to the commander of the town.

禀元帅爷，不好了，不好了！

〔众惊起介〕有甚么紧急军情，这等喊叫？

〔净急白介〕禀元帅爷：

大伙流贼[19]北犯，层层围住神京[20]；

三天不见救援兵，暗把城门开禁。

放火焚烧宫阙，持刀杀害生灵。

〔拍地介〕可怜圣主好崇祯，

〔哭说介〕缢死煤山树顶。

〔众惊问介〕有这等事，是那一日来？

〔净喘介〕就是这、这、这三月十九日。

〔众望北叩头，大哭介〕

〔小生起，搓手跳哭介〕我的圣上呀！我的崇祯主子呀！我的大行皇帝[21]呀！孤臣左良玉，远在边方，不能一旅勤王，罪该万死了。

【胜如花】

高皇帝在九京[22]，

不管亡家破鼎[23]，

那知他圣子神孙，

反不如飘蓬断梗。

Alas! Dire news! Dire news! Your Generalship.

Zuo (Startled) : What urgency makes you shout with such alarm!

Messenger (In tears): I come to report to Your Generalship.

(Singing): *The rebels surrounded the helpless capital,*

And in three days they broke into the city wall.

They set fire to imperial palace hall,

And killed defenceless people and plundered all.

(Stamping on the ground)

Alas! The emperor could not be free.

(Weeping) *He hanged himself upon a tree.*

All (Astonished): How could it be so! Do you know when did it take place?

Messenger (Out of breath): It was on the nineteenth day of the third month.

(All kowtowing to the north and bursting into tears)

Zuo (Rising, stamping on the ground and crying): Alas! Your Majesty! My dear emperor!

Your humble servant is so far away from the capital that we could not come to your rescue. How could I be exempted from condemnation!

(Singing to the tune of ***Better than Flower***):

The emperor in the celestial town

Could not foretell the empire would be overthrown.

How could he know his sons and grandsons

Would become shelterless wandering ones!

十七年忧国如病，
呼不应天灵祖灵，
调不来亲兵救兵；
白练无情，
送君王一命。
伤心煞煤山私幸[24]，
独殉了社稷苍生，
独殉了社稷苍生！

〔众又大哭介〕

〔外摇手喊介〕且莫举哀，还有大事相商。

〔小生〕有何大事？

〔外〕既失北京，江山无主，将军若不早建义旗，顷刻乱生，如何安抚。

〔末〕正是。〔指介〕这江汉荆襄，亦是西南半壁，万一失守，恢复无及矣。

〔小生〕小弟滥握兵权，实难辞责，也须两公努力，共保边疆。

〔外、末〕敢不从事。

〔小生〕既然如此，大家换了白衣，对着大行皇帝在天之灵，恸哭拜盟一番。

〔唤介〕左右可曾备下缞衣[25]么？

Worried for the empire for seventeen years,
Without the help of holy spirits on high
Nor rescue armies coming far and nigh,
He hanged himself with white silk stained with tears.
With broken heart the hill feels sad and drear
To see the empire lose its emperor dear,
To see the empire lose its emperor dear!

(All weeping in hot tears)

Yuan (Waving the hand): There is something more important than going into mourning.

Zuo: What is it?

Yuan: Since the Northern Capital is lost, the empire has no sovereign. If your generalship does not raise the royal flag, who could pacify the empire if disorder should break out?

Huang: You are right. (Pointing outwards) This riverside town is the most important land in the southwest. If it were lost to the rebels, the empire's recovery would be more difficult.

Zuo: As commander-in-chief of the Southwestern armies, I cannot shirk my responsibility. But I still need the support of Your Excellencies.

Yuan & Huang: Glad to be at your service.

Zuo: Let us then put on mourning and declare alliance to console the emperor's holy spirit in Heaven.

(To Attendant) Is the mourning dress ready?

〔副净〕一时不能备及，暂借附近民家素衣三领，白布三条。

〔小生〕也罢，且穿戴起来。

〔吩咐介〕大小三军，亦各随拜。
〔小生、外、末穿衣裹布介〕
〔领众齐拜，举哀介〕我那先帝呀，
【前腔】〔合〕
　　宫车出[26]，庙社倾，
　　破碎中原费整。
　　养文臣帷幄无谋[27]，
　　豢武夫疆场不猛；
　　到今日山残水剩，
　　对大江月明浪明，
　　满楼头呼声哭声。

〔又哭介〕这恨怎平，
　　有皇天作证：
　　从今后戮力奔命[28]，
　　报国仇早复神京，
　　报国仇早复神京。

〔小生〕我等拜盟之后，义同兄弟；临侯督师，仲霖监军，我左昆山操兵练马，死守边方。倘有太子诸王，中

Attendant: We have no time to get it ready. But here are some white suits of civilian dress.

Zuo: All right, we shall wear them in mourning.

(Giving orders) Let all officers and soldiers attend the mourning service.

(Zuo, Yuan and Huang put on mourning dress and kneel down with officers and soldiers.)

All: Repose in Heaven, Your Majesty!

(Singing to ***the previous tune***):

Imperial carriages overturned
And ancestral temples burned,
Destroyed is the Central Plain.
Ministers have no plan in hand,
Soldiers cannot guard the land,
But barren mountains and shallow rivers remain.
We only see the waves and the moon shine,
And hear in Yellow Crane Tower but cry and whine.
(Weeping) *How can we calm our revengeful mind down!*
We make a vow
To Heaven now:
We will do our best to revenge for the crown
And to recapture Northern Capital town!
And to recapture Northern Capital town!

Zuo: Since our alliance is formed, we should cooperate like brothers.

I shall drill the army to guard the frontier and wait for the heir

兴定鼎，那时勤王北上，恢复中原，也不负今日一番义举。

〔外、末〕领教了。

〔副净禀介〕禀元帅，满城喧哗，似有变动之意，快请下楼，安抚民心。

〔俱下楼介〕

〔小生〕二位要向那里去？

〔外〕小弟还回九江。

〔末〕小弟要到襄阳。

〔小生〕这等且各分手，请了。〔别介〕

〔小生呼介〕转来，若有国家要事，还望到此公议。

〔外、末〕但寄片纸，无不奔赴。请了。

〔外、末下〕

〔小生〕呵呀呀！不料今日天翻地覆，吓死俺也！

飞花送酒不曾擎，
片语传来满座惊，
黄鹤楼中人哭罢，
江昏月暗夜三更。

〔下〕

to the throne to lead our northern expedition. Then we shall recapture the Central Plain to console the emperor's holy spirit in Heaven.

Yuan & Huang: We are ever at your service.

Officer: The whole city is in uproar for the emperor's death. Will Your Generalship go down to pacify the people?

(All go downstairs.)

Zuo (To Yuan & Huang): Where are Your Excellencies going?

Yuan: I am going back to Jiujiang.

Huang: I am leaving for Xiangyang in the west.

Zuo: Then let us part here. Adieu! (They bid adieux.) But wait a minute. Will you please come here again if something important should happen?

Yuan & Huang: We are ever at your order.

(Exeunt.)

Zuo: Alas! What disaster! How could the empire be turned thus!

(Singing)

Before we drink, all flowers fly down;
Words come about the death of the crown.
In Yellow Crane Tower tears turn into blood red;
On midnight River sad moonbeams are shed.

(Exit.)

【注释】

[1] 旗牌官：替主将掌管令旗、令牌的官，地位跟中军官相近。

[2] 太傅：明代称太师、太傅、太保作三公。

[3] 左梦庚：左良玉的儿子。

[4] 巡按御史黄澍：黄澍，字仲霖，曾被派到湖广任巡按御史，监左良玉的军队。

[5] 督抚袁继咸：督抚即总督。袁继咸，字临侯，明末人，崇祯十二年任兵部侍郎，总督江、楚、赣、皖等地，曾代吕大器督左良玉军队。左梦庚降清时，他不屈而死。

[6] “晴川树底”二句：唐人崔颢《黄鹤楼》诗：“晴川历历汉阳树，芳草萋萋鹦鹉洲。”芳草洲指在汉阳西南长江中的鹦鹉洲。

[7] 喝道：过去官僚出行时，前列仪仗及卫士高声呵喝，禁止行人，称“喝道”。

[8] 小乘：小车。

[9] 胸次：胸中。

[10] 云梦：泽名，在今湖北安陆县内。

[11] 冲：指险要的地方。

[12] 龙华寺：在武昌宾阳门内。

[13] “秀才会课”二句：意说秀才们约会做功课，往往要到点灯时才到齐。

[14] 岕（jiè）片：岕茶，产于浙江长兴县境罗岕山，故此得名。

[15] 隐囊：即靠褥。

[16] 梗泛萍漂：意指像断梗、浮萍似的在水面上东漂西泛。

[17] 锏：通“简”，是一种鞭类的兵器。

[18] 塘报：提塘邸报，是由都城发出的一种情报。

[19] 流贼：当时对李自成等起义军的蔑称。

[20] 神京：京师，这里指北京。

[21] 大行皇帝：古时称刚死而未有谥号的天子作大行皇帝。

[22] 九京：这里指九泉，即地下。

[23] 破鼎：亡国。

[24] 煤山私幸：古时天子出行叫巡幸。煤山私幸，就是说崇祯皇帝私下跑到煤山去。

[25] 缞（cuī）衣：丧服。

[26] 宫车出：古时为了忌讳，一般称皇帝死为“宫车晏出”，即宫车迟出的意思。

[27] 帷幄无谋：帷幄，军中的帐幕。帷幄无谋是指谋士无用。

[28] 奔命：哪里有使命就赶到哪里。

第三出　阻奸

【绕地游】〔生上〕

飘飖家舍，
怎把平安[1]写，
哭苍天满喉新血。
国仇未雪，
乡心难说，
把闲情丢开后些。

小生侯方域，自去冬仓皇避祸，夜投史公，随到淮安漕署[2]，不觉半载。昨因南大司马熊公内召[3]，史公即补其缺，小生又随渡江。亏他重俺才学，待同骨肉。正思移家金陵，不料南北隔绝。目今议立纷纷，尚无定局，好生愁闷。且候史公回衙，一问消息。〔暂下〕

Scene 3 Succession to the Throne

(Enter Master Hou Fangyu.)

Hou (Singing to the tune of ***Going around the Earth***):

I roam and roam
Far, far from home.
How could I tell her that I'm safe? I cry
With bleeding throat to Heaven high.
The death not avenged of the crown,
How could I care for my hometown?
I must put apart
What else in my heart.

In order to avert the disaster fallen on me last winter, I came to seek patronage of His Excellency Shi in Huai'an. Half a year has passed since then. His Excellency was appointed last month as minister of defence to replace Governor Xiong in the Southern Capital, and I was ordered to follow him to cross the River. He values talents and treats me as his kin. Now obsessed with the heated argument over the succession to the throne, I am eager to know the result and would like to inquire for further information, so I must wait for His Excellency's return. (Exit.)

【三台令】〔外扮史可法忧容，丑扮长班随上〕

山河今日崩竭，
白面谈兵掉舌；
弈局事堪嗟，
望长安谁家传舍[4]。

下官史可法，表字道邻，本贯河南，寄籍燕京。自崇祯辛未，叨[5]中进士，便值中原多故，内为曹郎[6]，外作监司[7]，敭历[8]十年，不曾一日安枕。今由淮安漕抚升补南京兵部尚书。那知到任一月，遭此大变；万死无裨，一筹莫展。幸亏长江天险，护此留都。但一月无君，人心皇皇，每日议立议迎，全无成说。今早操兵江上，探得北信，不免请出侯兄，大家快谈。

〔丑〕侯爷，有请。

〔生上见介〕请问老先生，北信若何？

〔外〕今日得一喜信，说北京虽失，圣上无恙，早已航海而南；太子亦间道[9]东奔，未知果否？

〔生〕果然如此，苍生之福也。

〔小生扮差役上〕朝廷无诏旨，将相有传闻。

(Enter Shi Kefa followed by attendants.)

Shi (Looking worried and singing to the tune of ***Three Terraces***):

The ruined land in great alarms,
How could scholars talk about arms?
For State affairs I sigh;
To recapture the north, on whom can we rely?

In imperial service for ten years long, I was appointed minister of defence of the Southern Capital last month. Having not foreseen such imperial disaster, I do not know what to do but guard the River lest the security of the south should be endangered. But how could there be no sovereign on the throne? The question of succession is vehemently argued. When the morning manoeuvre was held, an intelligence report came from the North, so I must consult Master Hou about the matter.

Attendant: Here comes Master Hou.

(Re-enter Hou Fangyu.)

Hou (Saluting Shi): Is there any news from the north, Your Excellency?

Shi: We have received a good news today, saying that His Majesty survived the disaster and escaped by the sea. He is now sailing south with the heir apparent. But this report is not yet verified.

Hou: It would be the supreme bliss for the empire if the news proved true.

(Enter a Messenger.)

Messenger (Singing):

From the palace there comes no imperial decree,

〔到门介〕门上有人么？

〔丑问介〕那里来的？

〔小生〕是凤抚衙门来的，有马老爷候札[10]，即讨回书。

〔丑〕待我传上去。

〔入见介〕禀老爷，凤抚马老爷差人投书。

〔外拆看，皱眉介〕这个马瑶草，又讲甚么迎立之事了。

【高阳台】

清议堂中，
三番公会，
攒眉仰屋蹴靴；
相对长吁，
低头不语如呆。
堪嗟！军国大事非轻举，
俺纵有庙谟[11]难说。
这来书谋迎议立，
邀功情切。

〔向生介〕看他书中意思，属意福王。又说圣上确确缢死煤山，太子奔逃无踪。若果如此，俺纵不依，他也竟自举行了。况且昭穆伦次[12]，立福王亦无大差。罢，罢，罢！答他回书，明日会稿，一同列名便了。

But between generals and ministers rumors run free.

(Arriving at the door) Is there anyone within?

Concierge: Where do you come from?

Messenger: I come from Governor Ma's office at Fengyang. Here is a letter from him for His Excellency Shi. I am ordered to wait for the reply.

Concierge: I shall transmit the letter for you. (Entering and Saluting Shi) Your Excellency, here is a letter from Governor Ma at Fengyang.

Shi (Reading the letter with a frown): Again he will talk about the succession.

(Singing to the tune of ***High Sunny Terrace***):

Thrice have we met in the Assembly Hall,

Looking up with a frown and stamping, we sighed all,

Or bowing mutely as if stupefied,

We did nothing but look aside.

We'd not make light of State affairs.

What could I say though I had my cares?

This letter talks about the royal heir.

I seem to see an intrigue there.

(To Hou) In his letter Ma seems to propose that the Blissful Prince should succeed to the throne, for the late emperor had hanged himself on the coal hill in the imperial garden, and the imperial Prince had fled nobody knows where. If this were true, it would be the Blissful Prince's turn to succeed with or

〔生〕老先生所言差矣。福王分藩敝乡[13]，晚生知之最详，断断立不得。

〔外〕如何立不得?

〔生〕他有三大罪，人人俱知。

〔外〕那三大罪?

〔生〕待晚生数来:

【前腔】

福邸藩王，神宗骄子，
母妃郑氏淫邪。
当日谋害太子，欲行自立，
若无调护良臣，几将神器夺窃。

〔外〕此一罪却也不小。〔问介〕还有那一罪？

〔生〕骄奢，盈装满载分封去，
把内府金钱偷竭。
昨日寇逼河南，
竟不舍一文助饷，
以致国破身亡，
满宫财宝，徒饱贼囊。

〔外〕这也算的一大罪。〔问介〕那第三大罪呢?

without our support. According to age, it would not be wrong for him to become heir to the throne. Why then should I raise any objection to his succession? So I think I may tell Ma I agree to his proposal and will sign and put my seal on the document. What do you think of it?

Hou: I beg to differ from Your Excellency's approval. My homeland is a fief of the Blissful Prince and I know in detail what he has done there. I do not think he is a worthy successor to the throne.

Shi: Will you please tell me why?

Hou: He has committed three grave crimes well-known in his fief.

Shi: What are they?

Hou: Let me tell you one by one.

(Singing to ***the previous tune***):

The Blissful Prince is insidiou since
He plotted to murder the imperial prince
With his lascivious mother. This plot laid bare,
How could he succeed to the throne as heir?

Shi: This is indeed a grave crime. What next?

Hou: *His avarice and greed*
Made him steal from the treasury to meet his need.
When the rebels invaded his fief in the south,
He would not pay to feed his soldiers' mouth.
As a result, he lost his land,
His treasure fell into the rebels' hand.

Shi: This is the second crime. What is the third?

〔生〕这一大罪，就是现今世子德昌王[14]，
父死贼手，暴尸未葬，竟忍心远避。
还乘离乱之时，纳民妻女。
这君德全亏尽丧，怎图皇业。
〔外〕说的一些不差，果然是三大罪。
〔生〕不特此也，还有五不可立。

〔外〕怎么又有五不可立？
【前腔】〔生〕
第一件，车驾存亡，传闻不一，天无二日同协。
第二件，圣上果殉社稷，尚有太子监国，
为何明弃储君，翻寻枝叶旁牒。
第三件，这中兴之主，原不必拘定伦次的分别，
中兴定霸如光武，要访取出群英杰[16]。
第四件，怕强藩乘机保立。
第五件，又恐小人呵，将拥戴功挟[17]。

〔外〕是，是，世兄高见，虑的深远。前日见副使雷缜祚、礼部周镳[18]，都有此论，但不及这番透彻耳。就烦世兄把这三大罪、五不可立之论，写书回他便了。
〔生〕遵命。
〔点烛写书介〕

〔副净扮阮大铖，杂扮家僮提灯上〕
须将奇货归吾手，

Hou: He did not bury his father dead,

But far away he fled.

Besides, he took another man's wife as his own.

How could such a vile prince succeed to the throne?

Shi: You are right. He has indeed committed three grave crimes.

Hou: What is more, there are five reasons why we oppose to his succession.

Shi: What are they?

Hou (Singing to ***the previous tune***):

First, we are not sure if the emperor did die.

How could we have two suns in the same sky?

Secondly, if the emperor is no more,

The successor should be the prince we all adore.

Thirdly, the heir need not be the oldest in age,

But an outstanding talent, hero or sage.

Fourthly, he should not be arrogant and strong.

Lastly, his supporters are not those who do wrong.

Shi: You have a deep insight, far deeper than other officials. So, would you please write down the three crimes and five reasons in reply to Ma's letter?

Hou: It shall be done at once.

(A candle is lit and Hou writes the letter in reply to Ma.)

(Enter Ruan Dacheng, followed by an attendant, lantern in hand.)

Ruan (Singing): *I will not lose what I gain*

莫把新功让别人。

下官阮大铖，潜往江浦，寻着福王，连夜回来，与马士英倡议迎立。只怕兵部史可法临时掣肘。今日修书相商，还恐不妥，故此昏夜叩门，与他细讲。

〔见小生介〕你早来下书，如何还不回去。

〔小生〕等候回书，不见发出。

〔喜介〕阮老爷来的正好，替小人催一催。

〔杂〕门上大叔那里？

〔丑〕是那个？

〔副净见，作足恭[19]介〕烦位下[20]通报一声，说裤子裆里阮，求见老爷。

〔丑诨介〕裤子裆里软，这可未必。常言“十个胡子九个骚”，待我摸一摸，果然软不软。

〔副净〕休得取笑，快些方便罢。

〔丑〕天色已晚，老爷安歇了，怎敢乱传。

〔副净〕有要话商议，定求一见的。

〔丑〕待我传上去。

〔进禀介〕禀老爷，有裤子裆里阮，到门求见。

But keep it with might and main.

I am Ruan Dacheng. Having found the Blissful Prince by riverside, I came back by night to consult with Ma Shiying about the Prince's succession to the throne. But afraid that our proposal may not win the support of Shi Kefa, Minister of Defence, I wrote him a letter by day. For fearing that letter might not secure his support, I come in person to persuade him by night. (Seeing the messenger) You came to send a message by day. Why are you still here by night, without bringing back the reply?

Messenger: I am still waiting for the reply. Since Your Excellency has come in person, will you please ask them to give me the reply at once?

Attendant: Where is the concierge?

Concierge: Who is coming so late?

Ruan (Saluting with respect): Would you please report to His Excellency Shi that Ruan Soft Root is coming to pay a visit?

Concierge (Making fun): How can I know if your root is soft or hard?

Ruan: Do not make fun, please. Would you report to His Excellency?

Concierge: It is late now and His Excellency has taken rest. How dare I disturb his repose?

Ruan: I come here for something important. Would you please report for me?

Concierge: In that case, I shall try to report for you.

(To Shi) Your Excellency, here comes Ruan Soft Root on night

〔外〕是那个姓阮的?

〔生〕在裤子裆里住，自然是阮胡子了。

〔外〕如此昏夜，他来何干?

〔生〕不消说，又是讲迎立之事了。

〔外〕去年在清议堂诬害世兄的便是他。这人原是魏党，真正小人，不必理他，叫长班回他罢了。

〔丑出，怒介〕我说夜晚了，不便相会，果然惹个没趣。请回罢!

〔副净拍丑肩介〕位下是极在行的，怎不晓得。夜晚来会，才说的是极有趣的话哩;那青天白日，都是些扫帐儿[21]。

〔丑〕你老说的有理，事成之后，随封[22]都要双分的。

〔副净〕不消说，还要加厚些。

〔丑〕既是这等，待我再传。

〔进禀介〕禀老爷，姓阮的定求一见，要说极有趣的话。

〔外〕哇,放屁!国破家亡之时,还有甚么趣话说!快快赶出，闭上宅门。

〔丑〕凤抚回书尚未打发哩。

〔生〕书已写就，求老先生过目。

〔外读介〕

【前腔】

二祖列宗[23]，

visit.

Shi: Who is this Ruan?

Hou: It must be Ruan Dacheng.

Shi: Why does he come so late in the night?

Hou: No doubt, he comes to talk about the prince's succession.

Shi: It was he who spread the rumor against you in the Assembly Hall last year. He belongs to Eunuch Wei's party. (To Concierge) Tell him I have nothing to do with him.

Concierge (Coming out and speaking with anger): I have told you it is too late for His Excellency to see a guest. You ask me to incur his displeasure. Now you can do nothing but go back.

Ruan (Tapping the concierge on the shoulder): You know a visitor by night would offer you more interest than a visitor by day.

Concierge: What interest? Would you give me half of it?

Ruan: I would offer you more.

Concierge: In this case, I will report once more for you.

(Entering and reporting to Shi) Your Excellency, the visitor says that he has something to say which would offer you great interest.

Shi: How could he have anything of great interest to say when the empire is in danger? Tell him to get away and close the door!

Concierge: Your Excellency has not yet given a reply to the messenger from Fengyang.

Hou (To Shi): Here is the reply. Would Your Excellency read it over?

Shi (Reading and singing to ***the previous tune***):

It's hard to build the empire and come to the throne;

经营垂创，

吾皇辛苦力竭。

一旦倾移，

谁能重续灭绝[24]。

详列：

福藩罪案三桩大，

五不可、

势局当歇。

再寻求贤宗雅望[25]，

去留先决。

〔外〕写得明白，料他也不敢妄动了。

〔吩咐介〕就交与凤抚家人，

早闭宅门，不许再来啰唣。

〔起介〕正是江上孤臣生白发，

〔生〕灯前旅客罢冰弦。

〔外、生下〕

〔丑出呼介〕马老爷差人呢？

〔小生〕有。

〔丑〕领了回书，快快出去，我要闭门哩。

〔小生接书介〕还有阮老爷要见，怎么就闭门？

〔副净向丑介〕正是，我方才央过求见老爷的，难道忘了。

Our crown should prevent it from being overthrown.
If it were overthrown,
Who should succeed to the throne?
We should discuss in great detail. Three times
The Blissful Prince has committed grave crimes.
Besides, there are five reasons why he can't succeed,
For we should elect a prince of good renown
To rule the empire up and down.

All is clearly written. I think they cannot make light of it. (To Attendant)

Give the reply to the messenger and close the door.
Let no visitor disturb us any more.

(Rising) *By riverside age snows on my forehead hair white.*

Hou: *I will no longer play on strings by candlelight.*

(Exeunt Shi and Hou.)

Concierge (Coming out): Where is the messenger from Fengyang?

Messenger: Here.

Concierge: Here is the reply. Take it and go back. I am ordered to close the door.

Messenger (Taking the letter): Why should you close the door? Have you forgotten His Excellency Ruan is still here?

Ruan (To Concierge): Have you forgotten the interest we have just talked about?

〔丑佯问介〕你是谁呀?

〔副净〕我便是裤子裆里阮哪。

〔丑〕啐！半夜三更，只管软里硬里，奈何的人不得睡。

〔推介〕好好的去罢。

〔竟闭门入介〕

〔小生〕得了回书，我先去了。〔下〕

〔副净恼介〕好可恶也，竟自闭门不纳了。

〔呆介〕罢了！俺老阮十年之前，这样气儿也不知受过多少，且自耐他。

〔搓手介〕只是当前机会，不可错过。这史可法现掌着本兵之印，如此执拗起来，目下迎立之事，便行不去了，这怎么处？

〔想介〕呸！我到呆气了，如今皇帝玉玺且无下落，你那一颗部印有何用处。

〔指介〕老史，老史，一盘好肉包掇上门来，你不会吃，反去让了别人，日后不要见怪。正是：

穷途才解阮生嗟，
无主江山信手拿；
奇货居[26]来随处赠，
不知福分在谁家。

Concierge (Playing the ignorant): Who are you?

Ruan: I am Ruan Soft Root.

Concierge: I do not care if your root is soft or hard. I shall go to sleep. (Thrusting him out)

Get away!

(Exit.)

Messenger: I shall go back with the letter in reply. (Exit.)

Ruan (Angered) How hateful! But this is not the first time for me to be maltreated. I must bear it as ten years ago.

(Rubbing his hands anxiously) But how could I let go such a chance? What to do with Shi who is Minister of Defense in charge of military affairs, but who is so obstinate against the Blissful Prince!

(Pondering): What a fool I am! Now even the imperial edict will not work. Why should we care for a Minister of Defence!

(Pointing where Shi exits): Old Shi! Old Shi! You do not eat the meal I offer to you. Is there no one else who would eat it? I shall consult other ministers and generals. (Singing):

When poor, you understand why the hungry sigh;
The land without owner is free to occupy.
When fortune falls on me, I may give what I please,
Though I don't know who can be fortunate with ease.

(Exeunt.)

【注释】

[1] 平安：家信。

[2] 淮安漕署：明代于江苏淮安设漕抚，总督漕运。漕署即漕抚的官署。

[3] 南大司马熊公内召：熊公即熊明遇。

[4] 望长安谁家传舍：传舍是驿站供应过路客人住的房舍。长安是历代的帝都，这里借指北京。

[5] 叨：表示谦虚语气的副词。

[6] 曹郎：部曹，是部属各司的官。

[7] 监司：监察州郡的官，如按察使之类。

[8] 勷（yáng）历：指仕宦的经历。

[9] 间道：偏僻的路径。

[10] 候札：指立等回信的书札。

[11] 庙谟：指大臣为朝廷计议的谋划。

[12] 昭穆伦次：宗庙的次序。

[13] 分藩敝乡：福王分封河南，是侯方域的故乡。

[14] 德昌王：福王由崧，初封德昌王，进封福王世子。

[15] 枝叶旁牒：牒指封建时代宗族里的谱牒。枝叶旁牒，意说福王在

皇族里是旁枝侧叶，不是嫡派子孙。

[16]“中兴定霸如光武”二句：意说如要立中兴之主，就应访取像汉光武这样的英雄人物。光武即刘秀，是汉高祖的九世孙，王莽篡汉之后，光武起兵春陵，打败王莽的军队，自立为帝。

[17]将拥戴功挟：凭拥戴天子的功来要挟朝廷。

[18]雷缜（yǎn）祚、周镳：雷缜祚，字介之，太湖人。周镳，字仲驭，号鹿溪，金坛人，都是东林党的健将，后来被马士英、阮大铖害死。

[19]足恭：过分谦卑地谄媚人的样子。

[20]位下：对门下人的敬称。

[21]扫帐儿：犹言“零头数”。商业或债务上结算时的零数，往往可以免除。

[22]随封：封包、赏钱。

[23]二祖列宗：二祖指明太祖与明成祖，列宗指明仁宗以后的列朝皇帝。

[24]重续灭绝：把已经灭绝的国家重新继承下来。

[25]贤宗雅望：宗室里贤德而有名望的人。

[26]居：积贮，把货物积存起来，等价格高时出售。

第四本　三番两次逼香君

·

·

·

ACT IV　Persecution on Persecution

第一出　拒媒

【燕归梁】〔末扮杨文骢冠带上〕

南朝领略风流尽，
新立个妙龄君；
清江[1]隔断浊烟尘，
兰署[2]里买香薰。

下官杨文骢，因叙迎驾之功，补了礼部主事[3]。盟兄阮大铖，仍以光禄起用。又有同乡越其杰、田仰[4]等，亦皆补官，同日命下，可称一时之盛。目下漕抚缺人，该推升田仰。适才送到聘金三百，托俺寻一美妓，要带往任所。我想青楼色艺之精，无过香君，不免替他去问。

〔唤介〕长班走来。

〔杂扮长班上〕胸中一部缙绅，脚下千条衚衕。

〔见介〕老爷有何使唤？

Scene 1 Refusal

(Enter Yang Wencong in official dress.)

Yang (Singing to the tune of ***Swallow on the Beam***):

At the end of the Southern Dynasty's splendor
Is elected a sovereign of age tender.
War dust can't cross the river clear;
The orchid office needs a fragrant dear.

I, Yang Wencong, was appointed secretary in charge of ceremony as a result of my support for the Blissful Prince's succession to the throne. My friends Ruan Dacheng and Tian Yang were also appointed as high officials on the same day, Ruan in Ministry of Internal Affairs and Tian in charge of transportation. Recently Tian has sent me three hundred pieces of gold in order to find a beautiful courtesan and bring her to accompany him in his office. As for courtesans in the Green Mansions, no one is more beautiful than Fragrant Lee. I shall send someone to inquire after her. (Calling) Attendant! (Enter an attendant.)

Attendant (Singing): I know all the officials low and high
And all the roads and by-roads far and nigh.
(Saluting Yang) What is your order, sir?

〔末〕你快请清客丁继之，女客卞玉京，到我书房说话。

〔杂〕禀老爷，小人是长班，只认的各位官府，那些串客[5]、表子，没处寻觅。

〔末〕听我吩咐：

【渔灯儿】

闹端阳，
正纷纭，
水阁含春。
便有那乌衣子弟[6]伴红裙，
难道是织女牵牛天汉津[7]。

〔杂〕就在那秦淮河房么，小人晓得了。

〔末指介〕你望着枣花帘影杏纱纹，那壁厢款问殷勤。

〔副净扮丁继之，外扮沈公宪，净扮张燕筑上〕

院里常留老白相，
朝中新聘大陪堂。

〔副净〕来此是杨老爷私宅，待我叫门。

〔叫介〕位下那里？

〔杂出见介〕众位何来？

〔副净〕老汉是丁继之，同这沈、张两敝友，求见杨老爷；烦位下通报一声。

Yang: Go and tell Courtesan Jade Bian and Green Mansion visitor Ding Jizhi to come here.

Attendant: I am a humble servant of your office, who knows only officials high and low, but not the courtesans and their visitors far and near.

Yang: Listen to me.

(Singing to the tune of ***Fisherman's Lantern***):

On the Dragon Boat Day

We see all on display.

In poolside bowers

Will bloom spring flowers.

Then rosy faces and their visitors will come nigh,

Not so far away as Cowherd and Maid in the sky.

Attendant: You mean they're in riverside bower? I know the place.

Yang (Pointing): *Behind the rippled screen you'll find the rosy face.*

(Enter Ding Jizhi, Shen Gongxian and Zhang Yanzhu.)

Ding, Shen, Zhang (Singing): *Old visitors to the green mansions need not pay;*

Officials without portfolio have nowhere to stay.

Ding: Here is Secretary Yang's private residence. Let me knock at the door. (Knocking)

Is there anyone at the door?

Servant: Where are you coming from?

Ding: I am Ding Jizhi coming with two friends. Will you please announce to your master?

〔杂喜介〕正要去请，来的凑巧，待我通报。

〔欲入介〕

〔老旦扮卞玉京，小旦扮寇白门，丑扮郑妥娘上〕

紫燕来何早，

黄莺到已迟。

〔小旦叫介〕三位略等一等，同进去罢。

〔副净〕原来是你姊妹们。

〔净〕你们来此何干？

〔丑〕大家是一样病根，你们怕做师父，我们怕做徒弟的。

〔俱入介〕

〔末喜介〕如何来的恰好。

〔众〕无事不敢轻造，今日特来恳恩，尚容拜见。

〔俱叩介〕

〔末拉起介〕请坐，有何见教？

〔副净问介〕新补光禄阮老爷是杨老爷至交么？

〔末〕正是。

〔副净〕闻得新主登极，阮老爷献了四种传奇，圣心大悦，把《燕子笺》钞发总纲[8]，要选我们入内教演，有这话么？

〔末〕果然有此盛举。

〔净〕不瞒老爷说，我们两片唇，养着八张嘴。这一入内

Servant: You are coming in time, for we are told to invite you. Let me go in to announce your arrival.

(Enter Jade Bian, White Kou and Safe Zheng.)

Bian, Kou & Zheng (Singing): *The violet swallows early fly;*

Late golden orioles come nigh.

Kou (To Ding): Wait a minute! Let us go in together.

Ding: It is you, dear sisters?

Zhang: What are you coming for?

Zheng: We come for the same reason as you. You are afraid to teach in the palace theatre and we are to learn on the palatial stage.

(All come in.)

Yang (Happy): How can you come all in the same time?

All: We come here to ask a favor of you.

(Saluting on the knee)

Yang (Raising them): Take your seats please. What can I do for you?

Ding: Is Secretary Ruan Dacheng one of your good friends?

Yang: Yes, he is.

Ding: It is said that Secretary Ruan has written four dramas and presented them to the regent who has just succeeded to the throne. The regent was pleased and ordered *the Swallow's Letter* be copied, studied and put on the stage. So we may be summoned to teach actors or actresses. Is that true?

Yang: It is true.

Zhang: To speak the truth, we rely on our lips to feed our families. If we come to teach in the palatial theatre, who then will feed our

庭[9]，岂不“灭门绝户了一家儿”[10]？

〔丑〕我们也是八张嘴，靠着两片皮哩。

〔末笑介〕不必着忙，当差承应，自有一班教坊男女；你们都算名士数里的，谁好拿你。

〔众〕只求老爷护庇则个[11]。

〔末〕明日开列姓名，送与阮圆海，叫他一概免拿便了。

〔众〕多谢老爷。

【前腔】看一片秣陵春，
烟水消魂，
借着些笙歌裙屐[12]醉斜曛。
若把俺尽数选入呵，
从此后江潮暮雨掩柴门，
再休想白舫青帘载酒樽。
老爷果肯见怜，
这功德不小，
保秦淮水软山温。

〔末〕下官也有一事借重。

〔副净〕老爷有何见教？

〔末〕舍亲田仰，不日就升漕抚，适才送到聘金三百，托俺寻一小宠[13]。

families?

Zheng: The same is true with us.

Yang (Smiling): You need not worry about that. Dramas will be performed by actors and actresses of the palatial theatre. You are well-known scholars and courtesans. Who would force you to perform on the palatial stage?

All: We pray for your protection.

Yang: You may give me a list of names, and I will send it to Secretary Ruan and ask him to exempt you from the service.

All: Our hearty thanks, sir.

(Singing to ***the previous tune***)

We all enjoy the Southern spring
And drink wine, play music and sing.
If we come to the palace to sing,
Or to perform the play,
Who would come to help our families night and day?
We can no longer drink behind the screen,
So we come to pray you to protect our mansions green.

Yang: I also have something which needs your service.

Ding : What is it?

Yang: My kinsman Tian Yang is newly appointed secretary in charge of transportations and needs a beautiful courtesan to accompany him in his new office. Here are three hundred pieces of gold as engagement money.

〔丑〕让我去罢。

〔净〕你去不得，你去了，这院中便散了板儿了。

〔丑〕怎的便散了板儿?

〔净〕没人和我打钉了。

〔老旦〕是那个?

〔末〕便是李家的香君。

〔副净摇头介〕这使不得。

〔末〕如何使不得?

〔副净〕他是侯公子梳栊过的。

【锦渔灯】

现有个秦楼上吹箫旧人，
何处去觅封侯柳老三春。
留着他燕子楼[14]中昼闭门，
怎教学改嫁的卓文君。

〔末〕侯公子一时高兴，如今避祸远去，那里还想着香君哩。但去无妨。

〔老旦〕香君自侯郎去后，立志守节，不肯下楼，岂有嫁人之理，去也无益。

【锦上花】

似一只雁失群，
单宿水，
独叫云，
每夜里月明楼上度黄昏。

Zheng: May I go to accompany him?

Zhang: If you go, who then will play music in your bower?

Ding: Is there anyone you like for his company?

Yang: There is one for whom I need a go-between.

Bian: Who is it?

Yang: It is Fragrant Lee.

Ding (Waving his head): That will not do.

Yang: Why not?

Ding: She is already wedded to Master Hou.

(Singing to the tune of ***Fisherman's Lantern***):

She is a flutist in her bower,

Who has her lord, though far away.

She shuts herself up in the Swallow's Tower.

Why with another lover will she stay?

Yang: Master Hou is a whimsical lover who is now far, far away to avert the disaster. How could he still think of his old lover? So I think you may go and ask her.

Bian: Since the departure of Master Hou, Fragrant will not go downstairs to see any new visitor. How could she be willing to remarry? I think it useless to ask her.

(Singing to the tune of ***Flowers on Brocade***):

Like one of the wild geese astray,

Perching lonely by riverside,

Who into the cloud alone cried,

She passed the night

洗粉黛，
抛扇裙，
罢笛管，
歇喉唇，
竟是长斋绣佛女尼身，
怕落了风尘。

〔末〕虽如此说，但有强如侯郎的，他自然肯嫁。

〔副净〕香君之母，原是老爷厚人，倒是老爷面讲更好。

〔末〕你是知道的，侯郎梳栊香君，原是下官作伐。今日觌面，如何讲说，还烦二位走走，自有重谢。

〔净、外〕这等我们也去走走。
〔小旦、丑〕呸！皮肉行里经纪[15]，只许你们做么，俺也同去。
〔末〕不必争闹，待他二位说不来时，你们再去。

〔众〕是，是！辞过老爷罢。
〔末〕也不远送了。
狎客满堂消我闷，
嫁衣终日为人忙[16]。〔下〕
〔副净、老旦〕杨老爷免了咱们差事，莫大的恩典哩。

〔外、净〕正是。

In the moonlight
And in her bower passed the day
With powder from her face washed away.
She wore no fan-like dress of spring,
On flute she would no longer play,
Nor would she sing,
Like a Buddhist careless of everything.

Yang: What you say is not wrong. But I think she would not be unwilling to remarry a man better than Master Hou.

Ding: Her mother is your old acquaintance. Why do you not go and ask her in person?

Yang: You know it was I who proposed her wedding with Master Hou. How could I go and persuade her to change her mind? It would be better for you two to go in my place.

Zhang & Shen: We would like to go, too.

Kou & Zheng: How could you go there without us?

Yang: Would it not be better for you to go when they have failed in the business?

All: You are right. Now let us say goodbye.

Yang: You are welcome to come again. (Singing)

They try to please me with music and song;
I am busy for others all the day long. (Exit.)

Ding & Bian: We are grateful to him for exempting us from service in the palace, so we are obliged to render this service for him.

Zhang & Shen: We are grateful to him, too.

〔副净〕你四位先回，俺要到香君那边，替杨老爷说事去了。
〔丑〕赚了钱不可偏背，大家八刀[17]才好。
〔众诨下〕
〔副净、老旦同行介〕
〔副净〕记得侯公子梳栊香君，也是我们帮衬来。
【锦中拍】
　　想当初华筵盛陈，
　　配才子佳人，
　　排列着花林粉阵，
　　逐趁着筝声笛韵。
　　如今又去帮衬别家，
　　好不赧颜，
　　似邮亭马厮，
　　迎官送宾。
〔老旦〕我们不去何如？
〔副净〕俺若不去呵，又怕他
　　新铮铮春官匣印，硬选入秋官院门。
〔老旦〕这等如之奈何？
〔副净〕俺自有个两全之法，
　　到那边款语[18]商量，柔情索问，
　　做一个闲蜂蝶[19]花里混。
〔老旦〕妙，妙！
〔副净〕来此已是，不免竟进。

〔唤介〕贞娘出来。

Ding: Would you go back now that I am going to see Fragrant Lee?

Zheng: Do not forget to share your gain with us!

(Exeunt all but Ding and Bian, who walk together.)

Ding: If my memory does not fail me, I think it was we who went together to congratulate Master Hou's wedding with Fragrant.

(Singing to the tune of ***Beats on the Brocade***):

Do you remember when the sumptuous feast was spread,
The talent and the beauty were wed?
Flowers and powdered faces on display,
On flute and strings we hear them play.
How can we not feel shy,
If to persuade her to re-wed we try?
What can we do on hearing horses neigh
But welcome the new and say to the old "Good day"?

Bian: What if we do not go to see her?

Ding: *If we do not, can we avert the fate*
To be forced to perform within the palace gate?

Bian: What can we do then?

Ding: I think the only way is to imitate
The butterfly or the bee at leisure,
To talk and gratify his pleasure.

Bian: Good.

Ding: Here is Fragrant's bower. Let us go in!

(Calling): Is Mother Lee at home?

(Enter Fragrant.)

〔旦上〕空楼寂寂含愁坐，

长日恹恹带病眠。

〔问介〕楼下那个？

〔老旦〕丁相公来了。

〔旦望介〕原来是卞姨娘同丁大爷光降，请上楼来。

〔副净、老旦见介〕令堂怎的不见？

〔旦〕往盒子会里去了。

〔让介〕请坐，献茶。

〔同坐介〕

〔老旦〕香君闲坐楼窗，和那个顽耍！

〔旦〕姨娘不知：

【锦后拍】

俺独自守空楼，

望残春，

白头吟[20]罢泪沾巾。

〔老旦〕何不招一新婿？

〔旦〕奴家已嫁侯郎，岂肯改志？

〔副净〕我们晓你苦心。今日礼部杨老爷说，有一位大老田仰，肯输三百金，娶你作妾，托俺来问一声。

〔旦〕这题目错认，

这题目错认，

可知定情诗红丝拴紧，

抵过他万两雪花银。

Fragrant (Singing): *In the empty bower lonely I stay;*

Tired I lie in bed all the tiresome day.

(Asking) Who is dowstairs?

Bian: It is Master Ding.

Fragrant (Looking downstairs): It is Aunt Bian and Master Ding. Would you please come upstairs?

Ding & Bian (Saluting her): Where is your mother?

Fragrant: She has gone for a box party. Would you please sit down and take tea?

(They take their seats.)

Bian: What are you doing by the windowside?

Fragrant: You do not know, Aunt Bian.

(Singing to the tune of ***Beats on Brocade***):

Lonely in empty bower, I see late is spring;

Tears stream down when Song of White Hair I sing.

Bian: Why do you not find another lover?

Fragrant: How could I find another since I am wedded to Master Hou?

Ding: We know your heart. But today Secretary Yang told us that a rich official named Tian Yang would offer three hundred pieces of gold to ask your hand.

Fragrant: *To talk about remarriage is wrong,*

To talk about remarriage is wrong,

For my heart is tied up with Love's red silk for long.

It's worth more than a thousand pieces of gold.

〔老旦〕这事凭你裁酌，你既不肯，另问别家。

〔旦〕卖笑哂[21]，
有勾栏[22]艳品。
奴是薄福人，
不愿入朱门。
〔老旦〕既如此说，回他便了。
〔副净〕令堂回家，不要见钱眼开。
〔旦〕妈妈疼奴，亦不肯相强的。

〔副净〕如此甚好，可敬，可敬！
〔起介〕别过了。

〔外、净、小旦、丑急上〕两处红丝千里系[23]，一条黑路六人忙。
〔净〕快去，快去！他二人说成，便偏背我们了。
〔丑〕我就不依他，饶他吃到口里，还倒出脏来。
〔进介〕

〔净〕香君恭喜了。
〔旦〕喜从何来？
〔小旦〕双双媒人来你家，还不喜哩。

〔旦〕敢也说田仰的事么？

So I will not remarry even if I grow old.

Bian: It is up to you to remarry or not. If you refuse, we shall try to ask another.

Fragrant: *I could not sell my smiling face;*

Others may sell their smile with grace.

I was not born so fortunate

To enter the red mansion's gate.

Bian: Then we shall refuse him for you.

Ding: Will your mother not regret when she comes back?

Fragrant: My mother loves me more than gold. She will not force me to remarry.

Ding: You are indeed worthy of our respect.

(Rising) Then we shall say goodbye to you.

(Enter Shen, Zhang, Kou and Zheng.)

Shen etc.: *Could Love's silk two persons unite?*

We are six busy on dark night.

Zhang: Be quick! If they succeed, we shall have nothing to do.

Zheng: I will not allow them to succeed. Even if they have swallowed the profit, I would make them vomit. (They enter Fragrant's bower.)

Zhang: Congratulations, Fragrant.

Fragrant: What for?

Kou: Should we not congratulate you when so many go-betweens come to your bower?

Fragrant: Are you also coming on the part of Secretary Yang?

〔净〕便是。

〔旦〕方才奴已拒绝了。

〔外〕杨老爷的好意，如何拒得。

【北骂玉郎带上小楼】

他为你生小绿珠花月身，
寻一个金谷绮罗里石季伦。

〔旦〕奴家不图富贵，这话休和我讲。

〔副净、老旦〕我二人在此劝了半日，他决不肯嫁人的。

〔小旦〕他不嫁人，明日拿去学戏，要见个男子的面，也不能够哩。

歌残舞罢锁长门[24]，
卧氍毹夜夜伤神。

〔旦〕奴便终身守寡，有何难哉，只不嫁人。

〔丑〕难道三百两花银，买不去你这黄毛丫头么?

〔旦〕你要银子，你便嫁他，不要管人家闲事。

〔丑怒介〕好丫头，抢白起姨娘来了，我就死在你家。

〔撒泼介〕小私窠[25]贱根，小私窠贱根，掉巧舌讪谤尊亲。

〔净发威介〕好大胆奴才！杨老爷新做了礼部，连你们官儿都管的着[26]，明日拿去拶[27]掉你指头。

管烟花要津[28]，
管烟花要津；
触恼他风狂雨迅，

Zhang: Yes.

Fragrant: But I have already refused him.

Shen: How could you decline Secretary Yang's good will?

(Singing to the tunes of ***Jade Gallant & Mounting the Attic***):

You are beautiful as Green Pearl or moonlit flower.

We try to find for you a man of Golden Bower.

Fragrant: I need neither wealth nor title. Do not talk about that please.

Ding & Bian: We have long tried to persuade her but she is determined not to marry again.

Kou: She will not marry again. All right, let her go to be shut up in the palace without seeing the face of any man. (Singing)

She'd sing and dance within the locked gate,

And lie in bed by night early or late.

Fragrant: It is not hard to live a widow's life, but I will not marry again.

Zheng: Do you not need the three hundred pieces of gold or silver?

Fragrant: If you need them, why not marry him yourself? Please mind your own business.

Zheng: How dare you contradict your elders! Will you anger me to death? You clandestine prostitute! You base whore! How dare you speak against your elders!

Zhang (In anger): You base maid! Do you not know that Secretary Yang is in charge of the civil service and all the directors of green mansions are under his command? (Singing)

If he is angered, he will be

准备着桃伤柳损。

〔旦〕尽你吓唬，奴的主意已定了。

〔老旦〕看他小小年纪，倒有志气。

〔副净〕吓他不动，走罢，走罢。

〔丑〕我这里撒泼，没个人来拉拉，气死我也。他不嫁人，我扭也扭他下楼。

硬推来门外双轮，
硬推来门外双轮；
兜折[29]宝钏，扯断湘裙[30]。

〔副净〕自古有钱难买不卖货，撒了赖当不的，大家散罢。

〔外、小旦〕我两个原要不来，吃亏老燕、老妥强拉到此，惹了这场没趣。走，走，走！快出门，掩羞面，气忍声吞。

〔净、丑〕我们也走罢，干发虚[31]，没钞分，遗臊撒粪。

〔外、净、小旦、丑俱诨下〕

〔副净、老旦〕香君放心，我们回绝杨老爷，再不来缠你便了。

〔旦拜介〕这等多谢二位。

A violent storm destroying peach or willow tree.

Fragrant: I am determined in spite of threat and menace.

Bian: Though young, she has a lofty ideal.

Ding: She is not moved by threats. Why should we stay here any longer?

Zheng: Why is there no one to help me to threaten her into submission? She will not marry again. But I will pull her down for a second marriage. (Singing)

I will thrust her into a carriage of two wheels,

I will thrust her into a carriage of two wheels,

Break her hairpin, tear her skirt, care not how she feels.

Ding: How can we buy anything which the owner will not sell? What is the use of threats? I think it better to go back.

Shen & Kou: We will not come, but you force us to suffer this displeasure. Now let us go.

(Singing): *Let us go with ashamed face.*

Why should we suffer such disgrace!

Zhang & Zheng: We shall go, too. (Singing):

We have come in vain

Without any gain.

(Exeunt Shen, Zhang, Kou and Zheng.)

Ding & Bian: Fragrant, you need not care for what they say. We shall go to tell Secretary Yang about your refusal and will not come to trouble you any more.

Fragrant (Bowing): Thank you very much.

〔作别介〕

〔副净〕蜂媒蝶使闹纷纷，
〔旦〕　阑入红窗搅梦魂，
〔老旦〕一点芳心采不去，
〔旦〕　朝朝楼上望夫君。

【注释】

[1] 清江：地名，即江苏的清江浦。

[2] 兰署：兰台。兰台是汉代宫中藏书的地方。这里借指礼部衙门。

[3] 礼部主事：明代中央政府六部，于所属各司置主事官，职位次于员外郎。

[4] 越其杰、田仰：越其杰，贵阳人，擅长诗文，善于骑射，官至河南巡抚。田仰，是马士英的亲戚，弘光时奉命巡抚淮扬。

[5] 串客：清客。串，指串戏。

[6] 乌衣子弟：富贵人家的子弟。

[7] 难道是织女牵牛天汉津：天汉即天河。中国神话，天河的东边有织女，嫁给河西的牵牛郎，他们一年才相会一次。

[8] 总纲：戏曲术语，也称总讲，即脚本。

[9] 内庭：皇宫。

[10] 岂不“灭门绝户了一家儿”：引自《西厢记》第三本第一折。

[11] 则个：语助词，在这里表示祈求的语气。

[12] 笙歌裙屐：指擅长笙歌的清客与歌妓。

[13] 小宠：侍妾。

[14] 燕子楼：燕子楼在江苏铜山县西北。

(They bid goodbye.)

Epilogue of the Scene

Ding: *The go-betweens like buzzing bees come in a stream.*

Fragrant: *They fly into my window to disturb my dream.*

Bian: *But they cannot disturb your fragrant heart.*

Fragrant: *I'll wait for him upstairs though we are far apart.*

(Exeunt.)

[15] 皮肉行里经纪：指妓馆里的交易。

[16]嫁衣终日为人忙：替人辛苦，自己得不到享受。

[17] 八刀：拆"分"字。

[18] 款语：软语。

[19] 闲蜂蝶：指帮衬风月的人物做蜂媒蝶使。

[20] 白头吟：相传汉司马相如和卓文君结婚后不久，相如又爱上了另一个人。卓文君写了一首《白头吟》，表示她的怨恨。

[21] 卖笑哂（shěn）：意指妓女出卖色相。

[22] 勾栏：妓馆。

[23] 两处红丝千里系：意指相互间有婚姻的因缘。

[24] 长门：汉宫名，陈皇后失宠后曾在长门宫居住。

[25] 私窠：元明人称私娼为私窠。

[26] 连你们官儿都管的着：你们官儿即指教坊司，它属礼部管。

[27] 拶（zǎn）：夹手指的一种刑法。

[28] 要津：津本是渡口。要津，一般人用来比喻官居显要的地位。

[29] 兜折：拗折之意。

[30] 湘裙：缃裙。缃，浅黄色。

[31] 干发虚：疑是空费力气之意。

第二出　守楼

〔外、小生拿内阁灯笼、衣、银跟轿上〕

天上从无差月老，
人间竟有错花星[1]。

〔外〕我们奉老爷之命，硬娶香君，只得快走。

〔小生〕旧院李家母子两个，知他谁是香君。

〔末急上呼介〕转来同我去罢。

〔外见介〕杨姑老爷肯去，定娶不错了。

〔同行介〕

〔末〕月照青溪水，
霜沾长板桥。
来此已是，快快叫门。

〔叫门介〕

〔杂扮保儿上〕才关后户，又开前庭；迎官接客，卑职驿丞[2]。

Scene 2 Fragrant in Her Bower

(Enter a messenger of Prime Minister Ma and an attendant following a palankeen.)

Messenger: *The go-between will do no wrong under the sky;*

A beauty-seeker may have no discerning eye.

By order of Prime Minister Ma, we are going to take a bride, so we must make haste.

Attendant: In Lee's Bower the mother is said as fair as the daughter. How can we distinguish one from the other?

(Enter Yang Wencong in haste.)

Yang: Come back! I shall go with you.

Messenger (Saluting Yang): Since Secretary Yang condescends to go with us, we are sure to make no mistake.

(They walk together.)

Yang: *The clear stream is steeped in moonlight;*

The wooden bridge is covered with frost white.

Here is Lee's Bower. Let us knock at the door. (Knocking)

(Enter a Maid Servant)

Maid: I have just closed the door;

Again I come to the fore.

〔问介〕那个叫门？

〔外〕快开门来。

〔杂开门惊介〕呵呀！灯笼火把，轿马人夫，杨老爷来夸官[3]了。

〔末〕哇！快唤贞娘出来。

〔杂大叫介〕妈妈出来，杨老爷到门了。

〔小旦急上问介〕老爷从那里赴席回来么？

〔末〕适在马舅爷相府，特来报喜。

〔小旦〕有什么喜？

〔末〕有个大老官来娶你令爱哩。

〔指介〕

【渔家傲】

你看这彩轿青衣[4]门外催，

你看这三百花银，一套绣衣。

〔小旦惊介〕是那家来娶，怎不早说？

〔末〕你看灯笼大字成双对，是中堂[5]阁内。

〔小旦〕就是内阁老爷自己娶么？

〔末〕非也。漕抚田公，同乡至戚，赠个佳人捧玉杯。

〔小旦〕田家亲事，久已回断，如何又来歪缠？

〔小生拿银交介〕你就是香君么，请受财礼。

Who is knocking?

Messenger: Open the door!

Maid (Startled on opening the door): Ah! Lanterns and torches, palankeen and footmen! It is Secretary Yang coming.

Yang: Tell Mother Lee to come down.

Maid: Will you please come down, Mother Chaste? Here comes Secretary Yang. (Enter Mother Lee in haste.)

Lee (Saluting Yang): Are you coming back from a feast, Secretary Yang?

Yang: I am coming on behalf of Prime Minister Ma to congratulate you.

Lee: For what?

Yang: A high official would ask your daughter's hand.

(Pointing to three hundred pieces of gold and singing to the tune of ***Fishermen's Pride***):

Here are three hundred pieces of gold, what's more,

A sumptuous palankeen with footmen at your door.

Lee (Startled): Which high official? Why not inform us beforehand?

Yang: Have you not seen the characters on the lantern? We are coming from the mansion of the Prime Minister.

Lee: Is the high official the prime minister himself?

Yang: No, *the prime minister would send a beautiful maid*

To Secretary Tian for holding his cup of jade.

Lee: We have already refused Tian. Why is he coming again?

Messenger (Giving her the gold): Are you Fragrant? Please take the

〔小旦〕待我进去商量。

〔外〕相府要人，还等你商量；快快收了银子，出来上轿罢。

〔末〕他怎敢不去，你们在外伺候，待我拿银进去，催他梳洗。

〔末接银，杂接衣，同小旦作进介〕

〔小生、外〕我们且寻个老表子燥脾去。

〔俱暂下〕

〔小旦、末、杂作上楼介〕

〔末唤介〕香君睡下不曾？

〔旦上〕

有甚紧事，一片吵闹。

〔小旦〕你还不知么？

〔旦见末介〕想是杨老爷要来听歌。

〔小旦〕还说甚么歌不歌哩。

【剔银灯】

忙忙的来交聘礼，

凶凶的强夺歌妓；

对着面一时难回避，

执着名别人谁替。

〔旦惊介〕唬杀奴也！又是那个天杀的？

〔小旦〕还是田仰，又借着相府的势力，硬来娶你。

engagement money.

Lee: I shall go in to consult with her.

Messenger: The prime minister is waiting. How can you waste time in consultation? Take the money and mount the palankeen, please.

Yang: We shall not delay long. You may wait outside. I take the money and go in to hasten her. (Yang takes the gold, the maid takes the embroidered dress, and Mother Lee goes upstairs with them.)

Messenger & Attendant: Let us go to see another songstress.

(Exeunt.)

(Mother Lee and Yang go upstairs with the maid.)

Yang (Calling): Fragrant, have you gone to bed or not yet?

(Enter Fragrant.)

Fragrant: What noise! Is there anything unexpected?

Lee: You have not yet heard it?

Fragrant (Saluting Yang): Are you coming to hear songs, Secretary Yang?

Lee: How can we have time to hear songs?

(Singing to the tune of ***A Silver Lamp***):

They come in haste to send us gold

And force you to wed a man old.

What with their power could we do?

Who might go with them if not you?

Fragrant (Statled)**:** It is again that old villain. He has frightened me to death.

Lee: It's Tian relying on Prime Minister Ma's power

堪悲，青楼薄命，

一霎时杨花乱吹。

〔小旦向末介〕杨老爷从来疼俺母子，为何下这毒手？

〔末〕不干我事，那马瑶草知你拒绝田仰，动了大怒，差一班恶仆登门强娶。下官怕你受气，特为护你而来。

〔小旦〕这等多谢了，还求老爷始终救解。

〔末〕依我说三百财礼，也不算吃亏；香君嫁个漕抚，也不算失所；你有多大本事，能敌他两家势力？

〔小旦思介〕杨老爷说得有理，看这局面，拗不去了。孩儿趁早收拾下楼罢！

〔旦怒介〕妈妈说那里话来！当日杨老爷作媒，妈妈主婚，把奴嫁与侯郎，满堂宾客，谁没看见。现收着定盟之物。

〔急向内取出扇介〕这首定情诗，杨老爷都看过，难道忘了不成？

【摊破锦地花】

案齐眉[6]，

To force you to go to his bower.

What grief for flowerlike beauty to be blown

Away like willow down!

(To Yang) You are always kind to us. How can you allow Tian to do so?

Yang: This is beyond my power. Prime Minister Ma is angry at your refusal to Tian, so he orders his lackeys to take Fragrant by force. I come with them only to prevent them from using violence.

Lee: We should be grateful to you for that, but I hope you will help us to the end.

Yang: In my opinion three hundred pieces of gold is not a small sum of money, and Secretary Tian is not an unworthy match for Fragrant. Besides, do you think you are in a position to oppose the prime minister and his favorite secretary?

Lee (Meditating): What you say is right. We can by no means oppose the authorities. My dear daughter, I think you cannot but go with them.

Fragrant (Angry): How can you say that, dear mother? Have you forgotten that it was you who gave my hand to Master Hou, and Secretary Yang also attended the wedding? Here is the token of our love.

(Taking out the fan) Secretary Yang, you did read the poem on the fan. How could all this be forgotten?

(Singing to the tune of ***Embroidered Flowers***):

We are vowed man and wife;

他是我终身倚，
盟誓怎移。
宫纱扇现有诗题，
万种恩情，
一夜夫妻。

〔末〕那侯郎避祸逃走，不知去向；设若三年不归，你也只顾等他么？

〔旦〕便等他三年；便等他十年；便等他一百年；只不嫁田仰。

〔末〕呵呀！好性气，又像摘翠脱衣骂阮圆海的那番光景了。

〔旦〕可又来，阮、田同是魏党，阮家妆奁尚且不受，倒去跟着田仰么？

〔内喊介〕夜已深了，快些上轿，还要赶到船上去哩。

〔小旦劝介〕傻丫头！嫁到田府，少不了你的吃穿哩。

〔旦〕呸！我立志守节，岂在温饱。

忍寒饥，
决不下这翠楼梯。

I will rely on him throughout my life.

And I will keep my vow;

The verse is still on the fan now.

One night we were made man and wife,

We are married all through our life.

Yang: But Master Hou, to escape the disaster, has fled far away and no one knows where. Would you wait for him if he did not come back for three years?

Fragrant: I will wait for him not only three years, but ten years or even a hundred years. But I will never give my hand to Secretary Tian.

Yang: Ah! What a strong character! You play the same part as you rejected Ruan's dowry by taking off the embroidered dress and the jade hairpin.

Fragrant: You need not tell the old tale. Both Ruan and Tian belong to Eunuch Wei's party. How can I accept Tian's gold?

Voice within: It is late in the night. Will the bride come out and sit in the palankeen at once? It will be a long way for us to go back by boat.

Lee: My unwise daughter, why will you not go to Tian's mansion where you will have more than enough to eat and to dress?

Fragrant: I am determined to be true to Master Hou. How could I care for food and dress?

It is neither hunger nor cold for which I care.

I am determined not to go there.

〔小旦〕事到今日，也顾不得他了。

〔叫介〕杨老爷放下财礼，大家帮他梳头穿衣。
〔小旦替梳头，末替穿衣介〕
〔旦持扇前后乱打介〕

〔末〕好利害，一柄诗扇，倒像一把防身的利剑。

〔小旦〕草草妆完，抱他下楼罢。
〔末抱介〕
〔旦哭介〕奴家就死不下此楼。
〔倒地撞头晕卧介〕

〔小旦惊介〕呵呀！我儿苏醒，竟把花容，碰了个稀烂。

〔末指扇介〕你看血喷满地，连这诗扇都溅坏了。
〔拾扇付杂介〕
〔小旦唤介〕保儿，扶起香君，且到卧房安歇罢。
〔杂扶旦下〕
〔内喊介〕夜已三更了，诓去银子，不打发上轿；我们要上楼拿人哩。

〔末向楼下介〕管家略等一等，他母子难舍，其实可怜的。

〔小旦急介〕孩儿碰坏，外边声声要人，这怎么处？

Lee: We have no time to lose. I can no longer wait for you to change your mind. (To Yang)

Secretary Yang, would you please leave the gold here. Let us help her put on her wedding dress. (Lee tries to comb her hair and Yang to put the wedding dress on her.)

(Fragrant brandishes the fan to strike whoever comes near her.)

Yang: How angry she is! The word on the fan seems sharper than the sword.

Lee: Now she is hastily dressed. Let us hasten her downstairs.

(Yang tries to carry her down.)

Fragrant (Weeping): I would rather die than go there. (Falling on the floor with her head knocked on the corner stone and fainting away)

Lee (Startled): Alas! Wake up, my dear daughter! How can you destroy your flowerlike face in such a way!

Yang (Pointing to the fan): Even the poetic fan is stained with blood.

(Picking up the fan and giving it to the maid)

Lee: Maid, help to raise her and lay her on bed!

(The maid helps her to rise.)

Voice within: It is midnight now. You have taken the gold. Why not come down and ride in the palankeen? Should we go upstairs and help you to come down?

Yang (To the lackey): Wait a little bit longer. It is pitiable to see the daughter torn away from the mother.

Lee (Anxious): Fragrant is badly hurt and the lackey is pressing us.

〔末〕那宰相势力，你是知道的，这番羞了他去，你母子不要性命了。

〔小旦怕介〕求杨老爷救俺则个。

〔末〕没奈何，且寻个权宜之法罢！

〔小旦〕有何权宜之法？

〔末〕娼家从良，原是好事，况且嫁与田府，不少吃穿，香君既没造化，你倒替他享受去罢。

〔小旦急介〕这断不能。一时一霎，叫我如何舍得。

〔末怒介〕明日早来拿人，看你舍得舍不得。

〔小旦呆介〕也罢！叫香君守着楼，我去走一遭儿。

〔想介〕不好，不好，只怕有人认得。

〔末〕我说你是香君，谁能辨别。

〔小旦〕既是这等，少不得又妆新人了。

〔忙打扮完介〕

〔向内叫介〕香君我儿，好好将息，我替你去了。

What can I do?

Yang: You know the authority of the prime minister. What will he not do if he feels himself offended! Would he not take your life and your daughter's?

Lee: Would you please save us?

Yang: We must think of a way out.

Lee: What way?

Yang: It is not a bad thing for your daughter to be married again. You need not worry about your meals and dress if she were wedded with Secretary Tian. Since your daughter is not willing to share such fortune, would you go in her place?

Lee (Anxious): That will not do. How can I leave my daughter and my bower!

Yang: If they seize you by force, could you say you would not leave your bower?

Lee (Stupefied): What can I do but leave the bower to Fragrant? I cannot but go to Tian's mansion instead of my daughter. (Thinking over) What if they find I am not Fragrant?

Yang: If I say you are what we want, who could tell mother from daughter?

Lee: In that case, what can I do but disguise myself as an old new bride.

(Busy in making up and dressing up)

(To Fragrant) My dear daughter, I cannot but go in your stead, but you must repose yourself. As for the three hundred pieces of

〔又嘱介〕三百两银子，替我收好，不要花费了。

〔末扶小旦下楼介〕

【麻婆子】〔小旦〕

下楼下楼三更夜，
红灯满路辉；
出户出户寒风起，
看花未必归。

〔小生、外打灯抬轿上〕

好，好，新人出来了，快请上轿。

〔小旦别末介〕别过杨老爷罢。

〔末〕前途保重，后会有期。

〔小旦〕老爷今晚且宿院中，照管孩儿。

〔末〕自然。

〔小旦上轿介〕

萧郎从此路人窥，
侯门再出岂容易[7]。

〔行介〕舍了笙歌队，今夜伴阿谁。〔俱下〕

〔末笑介〕贞丽从良，香君守节，雪了阮兄之恨，全了马舅之威！将李代桃[8]，一举四得，倒也是个妙计。

gold, you must keep them in safety. Do not spend them without my permission.

(Yang helps her go downstairs.)

(Singing to the tune of ***A Pock marked Woman***):

I go downstairs late at midnight.

With red lanterns the road is bright.

The cold wind blows when I leave my bower.

Could I come back when there is no more flower?

(Enter the messenger and the attendant with the palankeen.)

Messenger: Well, at last comes the bride. Would you please mount the palankeen?

Lee (To Yang): Goodbye, Secretary Yang.

Yang: Heaven bless you. I will see you later.

Lee: Would you please stay in my bower for one night and take care of my daughter?

Yang: You need not tell me that.

(Lee mounts the palankeen.)

Lee: *The gallant is no longer a lord I adore.*

Could it be easy to come out of a mansion's door?

I have left my bower of music bright

To accompamny a new lord tonight. (Exit.)

Yang (Smiling): *The mother wed, the daughter in the bower.*

Ruan is revenged and Ma has shown his power.

One stone has killed four birds. What an ingenious intrigue!

(Sighing)

〔叹介〕只是母子分别，
未免伤心。
匆匆夜去替蛾眉，
一曲歌同易水悲[9]；
燕子楼中人卧病，
灯昏被冷有谁知。

【注释】

[1] 花星:《帝京景物略》中有“女怕花星照。”花星是古代江湖术士推算星命时的一种术语。本是表示婚姻的征兆，对妇女说有男女风情的纠葛。

[2] 驿丞: 掌管驿站的官，经常要迎官接客。

[3] 夸官：士子考中进士或官员升迁时，排列鼓乐仪仗游街，叫作夸官。

[4] 青衣: 指奴仆。古时奴婢一般是穿青衣的。

[5] 中堂: 唐代在中书省设政事堂，是宰相办事的地方，后人因此称宰相作中堂。

[6] 案齐眉: 形容夫妻相敬。东汉时梁鸿的妻子孟光每次吃饭都举案

But it would break my heart
To see mother and daughter part.
One takes the other's place on this night long.
The river would be grieved to hear their farewell song.
The daughter lies in bed ill in the Swallow's Bower.
Who knows by dim lamplight in cold quilt her sad hour!

齐眉，表示对梁鸿的尊敬。

[7]"萧郎从此路人窥"二句：这两句是李贞丽引崔郊的故事来说明自己这一入田府，恐怕再难出来。萧郎是唐代一般美好的男子的通称。

[8]将李代桃：乐府《鸡鸣》篇："桃生露井上，李树生桃傍。虫来齧桃根，李树代桃僵。"后人因此用李代桃僵，表示代人受罪或彼此顶替的意思。

[9]一曲歌同易水悲：借用战国荆轲与燕太子丹在易水分别的故事来形容李香君母子的分别。

第三出　寄扇

【醉桃源】〔旦包帕病容上〕

寒风料峭[1]透冰绡，
香炉懒去烧。
血痕一缕在眉梢，
胭脂红让娇[2]。
孤影怯，
弱魂飘，
春丝命一条。
满楼霜月夜迢迢，
天明恨不消。

〔坐介〕奴家香君，一时无奈，用了苦肉之计，得遂全身之节。只是孤身只影，卧病空楼，冷帐寒衾，无人作伴，好生凄凉。

【北新水令】

冻云残雪阻长桥，
闭红楼冶游人少。
栏杆低雁字[3]，
帘幙挂冰条；

Scene 3 The Fan

(Enter Fragrant ill.)

Fragrant (Singing to the tune of ***Drunk at Peach Blossom Fountain***):

The chilly wind pierces my bed curtain ice-white;
I am too tired the incense to light.
The trace of a wreath of blood left on my forehead
Outshines the rouge on my lips red.
My lonely shadow feels shy,
My soul is too weak to fly.
My life hangs on a vernal thread,
My bower steeped in frosty moonbeams in the long night.
My sorrow won't dissolve in daylight.

(Sitting) My chastity is preserved at my mother's sacrifice. But I am left lonely and ill in an empty bower with a cold curtain and a chilly quilt without a companion. How sad and dreary I am!

(Singing to the tune of ***New Water Song***):

The Long Bridge barred by frozen cloud and snow,
To a closed rosy mansion few visitors would go.
Beyond the balustrade wild geese fly low,
Icicles hang like a curtain show.

炭冷香消，
人瘦晚风峭。
奴家虽在青楼，
那些花月欢场，
从今罢却了。

【驻马听】
绣户萧萧，
鹦鹉呼茶声自巧；
香闺悄悄，
雪狸[4]偎枕睡偏牢。
榴裙裂破舞风腰，
鸾靴剪碎凌波靿[5]；
愁多病转饶[6]，
这妆楼再不许风情闹。
想起侯郎匆匆避祸，不知流落何所；怎知奴家独住空楼，替他守节也。

〔起唱介〕

【沉醉东风】
记得一霎时娇歌兴扫，
半夜里浓雨情抛；
从桃叶渡头寻，
向燕子矶边找，

To ashes coal is burned,
And cold is fragrance turned
How can I not grow lean
To hear the chilly evening wind blow
Over the mansions green?
What could I know
Of pleasures among the flowers
Or in the moonlit bowers?

(Singing to the tune of ***Stopping a Horse***):

In shady bower without glee
A clever parrot calls for tea.
My fragrant boudoir in silence deep,
Relying on my pillow, in fur coat I sleep.
My waist can't dance in rosy skirt torn apart,
Nor can my love-bird shoes tread on waves with art.
My sorrow aggravates my illness long;
My bower hears no more amorous song.

To escape from the disaster, dear Master Hou is roaming I know not where. Does he know how I live lonely and chaste in my deserted bower? (Rising)

(Singing to the tune of ***Intoxicated in the East Wind***):

I still remember songs no longer sung in my bower,
Your midnight love brings no more fresh shower
For my thirsting flower.
I try to find you at the ferry of Peach Leaf

乱云山风高雁杳。
那知道梅开有信，
人去越遥；
凭栏凝眺，
把盈盈秋水，
酸风冻了。
可恨恶仆盈门，硬来娶俺；俺怎肯负了侯郎。

【雁儿落】

欺负俺贱烟花薄命飘飖，
倚着那丞相府忒骄傲。
得保住这无瑕白玉身，
免不得揉碎如花貌。
最可怜妈妈替奴当灾，
飘然竟去。

〔指介〕你看床榻依然，归来何日。

【得胜令】

恰便似桃片逐雪涛，
柳絮儿随风飘；
袖掩春风面，
黄昏出汉朝。
萧条，
满被尘无人扫；
寂寥，
花开了独自瞧。
说到这里，

And on the rock of Swallow's Grief.

But the wind drives away message-bearing wild geese,

So none will bring your letter from on high.

Leaning on balustrade, I gaze with longing eye,

Frozen by the sour breeze.

How hateful are those lackeys who forced me to marry again!

How could I be ungrateful to my beloved lord?

(Singing to the tune of ***Falling Wild Geese***):

They bully us songstresses with a hand high;

On arrogant prime minister they rely.

In order to preserve my purity and grace

I can't but hurt my rosy face.

What pity for my mother to go in my place!

(Pointing to the bed) Her curtained bed is still there. But when can she come back?

(Singing to the tune of ***Triumphant Song***):

As peach petals buried in snow

Or willow down when wild winds blow,

Her rosy face is covered with her sleeves;

When night falls on the palace, the beauty leaves.

What gloomy day!

No one will sweep the dust away.

Lonely I stay.

Who would enjoy the flowers on display?

So sad and drear,

不觉一阵酸心。

〔掩泪坐介〕

【乔牌儿】

这肝肠似搅，

泪点儿滴多少。

也没个姊妹闲相邀，

听那挂帘栊的钩自敲。

独坐无聊，不免取出侯郎诗扇，展看一回。

〔取扇介〕嗳呀！都被血点儿污坏了，这怎么处。

【甜水令】

你看疏疏密密，

浓浓淡淡，

鲜血乱蘸[7]。

不是杜鹃抛[8]；

是脸上桃花做红雨儿飞落，

一点点溅上冰绡。

侯郎！侯郎！

这都是为你来。

【折桂令】

叫奴家揉开云髻，

折损宫腰；

睡昏昏似妃葬坡平，

血淋淋似妾堕楼高。

怕旁人呼号，

How can I not shed tear on tear!

(Shedding tears. Singing to the tune of ***Pseudo Song***):
With broken heart,
How many tears fall apart!
No sister comes to see me;
Only the curtain hooks are ringing without glee.

Sitting alone with nothing to do, why not take out the fan left by my dear lord and read the verse he wrote on it? (Taking out the fan) Alas! It is stained with blood. What can I do!

(Singing to the tune of ***Sweet Water Song***):
You see the blood in deep or bright red
Densely or sparsely spread.
It is not cuckoo's tears fallen in showers
But my own blood blent with peach flowers.
It pours out of my heart and from my face,
And leaves on icy silk its trace.
My dear lord, it is all for you.

(Singing to the tune of ***Laurel-Plucking Song***):
I have untied my chignon in haste,
And do not fear to hurt my waist.
I sleep my time away like buried Queen,
and let my head bleed like Pearl Green.
I won't listen to others' call and cry

舍着俺软丢答的魂灵没人招。

银镜里朱霞残照[9]，

鸳枕上红泪春潮。

恨在心苗，

愁在眉梢，

洗了胭脂，

涴了鲛绡[10]。

一时困倦起来，

且在妆台盹睡片时。

〔压扇睡介〕

〔末扮杨文骢便服上〕认得红楼水面斜，一行衰柳带残鸦。

〔净扮苏昆生上〕银筝象板佳人院，风雪今同处士家。

〔末回头见介〕呀！苏昆老也来了。

〔净〕贞丽从良，香君独住，放心不下，故此常来走走。

〔末〕下官自那日打发贞丽起身，守了香君一夜，这几日衙门有事，不能脱身；方才城东拜客，便道一瞧。

〔入介〕〔净〕香君不肯下楼，我们上去一谈罢。

〔末〕甚好。

〔登楼介〕

〔末指介〕你看香君抑郁病损，困睡妆台，且不必唤他。

For fear of hearing my soul's sigh.

My mirror shows a face in sunset dyed,

My pillow wet with tears like vernal tide.

Regret deep in my heart,

My eyebrows frown apart.

The rouge is washed away,

Stains on my face still stay.

I feel so tired that I shall take a short rest.

(Sleeping with one hand on the fan.)

(Enter Yang Wencong in civilian dress.)

Yang: This is the poolside rosy bower I know;

Crows hover over withered willow trees in row.

(Enter Su Kunsheng in music-composer's dress.)

Su: *In Beauty's Bower silver lute and clappers glow;*

I come to Talent's Residence in wind and snow.

Yang (Turning back and saluting Su): Ah, it is you, Master Su.

Su: I come to take care of Fragrant who lives alone after her mother's departure.

Yang: I watched over her on the night of separation. Since then busy in my office, I have no time to come to see her. Today on paying a visit to the eastern town, I come again.

Su (Entering with Yang): Fragrant will not come downstairs. Let us go up.

Yang: Very well. (Going upstairs with Yang and pointing to Fragrant asleep) Ill and tired, she is dozing at her dressing table. We had

〔净看介〕这柄扇儿展在面前，怎么有许多红点儿？

〔末〕此乃侯兄定情之物，一向珍藏不肯示人，想因面血溅污，晾在此间。

〔抽扇看介〕几点血痕，红艳非常，不免添些枝叶，替他点缀起来。

〔想介〕没有绿色怎好？

〔净〕待我采摘盆草，扭取鲜汁，权当颜色罢。

〔末〕妙极！

〔净取草汁上〕

〔末画介〕叶分芳草绿，花借美人红。

〔画完介〕

〔净看喜介〕妙，妙！竟是几笔折枝桃花。

〔末大笑指介〕真乃桃花扇也。

〔旦惊醒见介〕杨老爷、苏师父都来了，奴家得罪。

〔让坐介〕

〔末〕几日不曾来看，额角伤痕渐已平复了。

〔笑介〕下官有画扇一柄，奉赠妆台。

better not awaken her.

Su (Looking at the fan): Why are there so many blood stains on the fan?

Yang: This fan is the token of her love with her lord, which she would not show to others. It is spread out here perhaps because she will expose the blood stain in the air.

(Taking the fan from under her hand) The blood stains strike the eye. It would be better to add a few green leaves to the red flowers. (Pondering) But where can I find green colour?

Su: I may squeeze green juice from the grass for you.

Yang: An excellent idea. (Exit and re-enter Su with juice. Yang begins to draw the picture.)

The leaves reveal the grass-green trace;

The flower looks like Beauty's face. (The picture is drawn.)

Su (Rejoicing over the picture): Excellent. It looks like a twig of peach blossoms.

Yang (Laughing and pointing to the fan): It is indeed a peach blossom fan!

Fragrant (Awakened, rising and saluting Yang and Su): Excuse me for my negligence at your arrival. Would you please take your seats? (They sit down.)

Yang: I have not come for a few days. And I am glad to find you recovered from the wound on your forehead. Here is a painted fan I would like to present to you for your dressing table. (Giving her the fan)

Fragrant (Taking the fan): This is my old fan stained with blood.

〔付旦扇介〕

〔旦接看介〕这是奴的旧扇，血迹腌臜，看他怎的。

〔入袖介〕

〔净〕扇头妙染，怎不赏鉴。

〔旦〕几时画的?

〔末〕得罪！得罪！方才点坏了。

〔旦看扇叹介〕咳！桃花薄命，扇底飘零。多谢杨老爷替奴写照了。

【锦上花】

一朵朵伤情，春风懒笑；
一片片消魂，流水愁漂。
摘的下娇色[11]，天然蘸好；
便妙手徐熙[12]，怎能画到。
樱唇上调朱，莲腮上临稿，
写意儿[13]几笔红桃。
补衬些翠枝青叶，
分外夭夭[14]，薄命人写了一幅桃花照。

〔末〕你有这柄桃花扇，少不得个顾曲周郎；难道青春守寡，竟做个入月嫦娥不成。

〔旦〕说那里话，那关盼盼也是烟花，何尝不在燕子楼中，关门到老。

〔净〕明日侯郎重到，你也不下楼么?

〔旦〕那时锦片前程，尽俺受用，何处不许游耍，岂但下楼。

What is there good for looking? (Putting it into her sleeve)

Su: The stain is beautified into a peach blossom. Why do you not appreciate the picture?

Fragrant (To Yang): When did you draw it?

Yang: I am sorry I have just vilified your fan.

Fragrant (Looking at the fan and sighing): You have vivified the poor peach blossom. It is a picture not only of the flower but also a portrait of myself. Thank you very much, dear Secretary Yang. (Singing to the tune of ***Flowers on Embroidered Brocade***):

The flowers grieved won't smile when spring winds blow
Or heart-broken petals on caressing waves flow.
Even when plucked up, they have natural charm;
Their beauty has outdone the most artful painter's arm.
The cherry-red lips seem to speak
And vie with blushing lotus cheek.
Is this a peach flower set off by green leaves
Or a picture of short-lived beauty who grieves?

Yang: Such a peach blossom fan must be accompanied by a beauty-lover. How can you live lonely as the Goddess of the Moon?

Fragrant: Do you not know the beautiful Panpan shut up in the Swallow's Bower all her life?

Su: But will you not go downstairs when Master Hou comes?

Fragrant: When he comes with a bright future, what is there I will not do? I will not only go downstairs, but also do whatever he wishes me to do and enjoy to the full.

〔末〕香君这段苦节，今世少有。

〔向净介〕昆老看师弟之情，寻着侯郎，将他送去，也省俺一番悬挂。

〔净〕是！是！一向留心访问，知他随任史公，住淮半载。自淮来京，自京到扬，今又同着高兵防河去了。晚生不日还乡，顺便找寻。

〔向旦介〕须得香君一书才好。

〔旦向末介〕奴家言出无文，求杨老爷代写罢。

〔末〕你的心事，叫俺如何写得出。

〔旦寻思介〕罢！罢！奴的千愁万苦，俱在扇头，就把这扇儿寄去罢。

〔净喜介〕这封家书，倒也新样。

〔旦〕待奴封他起来。

〔封扇介〕

【碧玉箫】

挥洒银毫[15]，
旧句他知道；
点染红么[16]，
新画你收着。
便面[17]小，
血心肠一万条；
手帕儿包，
头绳儿绕，

Yang: Such a faithful lover as you can hardly find an equal in the world. (To Su) As her teacher, you should try to find Master Hou and bring him back to her. Otherwise, how can he be worthy of her love?

Su: You are right. I will try my best to find him. It is said that he was in the service under Minister Shi and was defending the River with him. When I go there, I will inquire after him. (To Fragrant) Will you please write a letter for me to give him?

Fragrant: I am not good at writing. Secretary Yang, will you please write it for me?

Yang: I do not know what is in your heart. How can I write in your place?

Fragrant (Pondering): Well, all my sorrow and grief may be symbolized by this fan. So I had better send him this fan instead of a letter.

Su (Glad): This would be a wordless letter which says more than any word.

Fragrant: I'll put it in an envelope. (Wrapping it up)

(Singing to the tune of ***Green Jade Flute***):
If I write in words aglow,
What is there that he does not know?
If I dye red the dots in view,
Then he may keep the picture new.
Small is the surface plane,
But blood is carried from vein to vein.
Wrapped up and wound with strings, it would be better
Than an embroidered letter.

抵过锦字书多少。

〔净接扇介〕待我收好了，替你寄去。

〔旦〕师父几时起身?

〔净〕不日束装了。

〔旦〕只望早行一步。

〔净〕晓得。

〔末〕我们下楼罢。

〔向旦介〕香君保重。你这段苦节，说与侯郎，自然来娶你的。

〔净〕我也不再来别了。正是：新书远寄桃花扇。

〔末〕旧院常关燕子楼。

〔下〕

〔旦掩泪介〕妈妈不归，师父又去，妆楼独闭，益发凄凉了。

【鸳鸯煞】

莺喉歇了南北套[18]，

冰弦住了陈隋调[19]；

唇底罢吹箫，

笛儿丢，

笙儿坏，

板儿掠[20]。

(Giving the fan to Su)

Su: I will send this letter for you.

Fragrant: When will you set out?

Su: In the near future.

Fragrant: I wish you may start early.

Su: As early as possible.

Yang: Let us go downstairs.

(To Fragrant) Take good care of yourself. If Master Hou knew your grief and hardship, he would be sure to come and carry you away.

Su: Excuse me for not coming again to bid goodbye. (Singing)

I'll send afar the fan of newly-painted peach flower.

Yang: *The beauty is still shut up in the Swallow's Bower.*

(Exeunt.)

Fragrant (Hiding her tearful eyes under her sleeves):

My mother can't come back, my teacher will go away.
Shut up in my bower, how sad I stay.

(Singing to the tune of ***Love-birds' Song***):

The orioles' southern song I will no longer sing,
Nor shall I play my northern string.
My lips won't blow the flute,
My hands won't play on lute.
I'll send at once my peach blossom fan
By Master Su to my dearest man.

只愿扇儿寄去的速，
师父束装得早；
三月三刘郎到了[21]，
携手儿下妆楼，
桃花粥[22]吃个饱。

书到梁园[23]雪未消，
青溪一道阻春潮；
桃根桃叶无人问[24]，
丁字帘前[25]是断桥。

【注释】

[1] 料峭：形容风的寒冷、尖锐。
[2] 胭脂红让娇：意说胭脂一样的鲜红，也比不上她眉梢血痕的娇。
[3] 栏杆低雁字：意说望到栏杆外低低的雁行。
[4] 雪狸：白猫。
[5] “榴裙裂破舞风腰”二句：这两句是撕破了舞裙，剪碎了舞靴，结束歌舞生涯的意思。
[6] 转饶：更多。
[7] 蘸：沾染。
[8] “不是杜鹃抛”二句：传说杜鹃的啼声很凄苦，甚至啼到口里流出血来。
[9] 银镜里朱霞残照：形容脸上血痕。
[10] 鲛绡：鲛人所织的绡。传说有鲛人从海中来，寄居人家，每日织绡出卖，这里指丝巾。
[11] 摘的下娇色：意说扇上桃花颜色的娇鲜，像摘得下来似的。

In spring he will come to this land,
Then we'll go downstairs hand in hand.
We'll drink our fill the vernal breeze
Under the blooming peach trees.

(Singing the ***Epilogue of the Scene***)
Snow is not melt when my letter comes to his side.
How can the clear blue stream bar the rising vernal tide!
No one would care for the peach tree's root nor its leaves;
Before my window screen only a broken bridge grieves.

(Exeunt.)

[12] 徐熙：南唐画家，擅画花树竹木之类，尤擅长画花果。
[13] 写意儿：写意是中国画法的一派，用笔求神似而不求形似。儿，这里是词尾。
[14] 分外夭夭：特别美好的样子。
[15] 银毫：笔。
[16] 红么：么是骰子的一点，红色，故称红么，这里指扇上桃花。
[17] 便面：面，即团扇，因便于遮面，所以叫作便面。
[18] 南北套：南北曲，是中国歌曲的两种主要流派。一般说，北曲字多而调促，风格比较豪放；南曲字少而调缓，风格比较婉弱。
[19] 陈隋调：指陈隋时所流行的曲调。
[20] 板儿掠：板儿即拍板，掠，抛弃。
[21] 刘郎到了：疑借用刘晨在天台山遇仙女的故事。
[22] 桃花粥：过去洛阳一带的风俗，寒食节煮桃花粥吃。
[23] 梁园：本是西汉时梁孝王的兔园，这里借指侯方域的家乡中州归德。
[24] 桃根、桃叶：桃叶是东晋王献之的爱妾，桃根是桃叶妹。
[25] 丁字帘前：地名，在南京市利涉桥畔，明时为妓女聚居的地方。

第五本　歌舞声中花泣血

·
·
·

ACT V　Songs and Tears

第一出　骂筵

【缕缕金】〔副净扮阮大铖吉服上〕

风流代，
又遭逢，
六朝金粉样，
我偏通。
管领烟花，
衔名供奉[1]。
簇新新帽乌衬袍红，
皂皮靴绿缝，
皂皮靴绿缝。

〔笑介〕我阮大铖，亏了贵阳相公破格提挈，又取在内庭供奉；今日到任回来，好不荣耀。且喜今上性喜文墨，把王铎补了内阁大学士，钱谦益[2]补了礼部尚书。区区不才，同在文学侍从之班；天颜日近，知无不言。前日进了四种传奇，圣心大悦；立刻传旨，命礼部采选宫人，要将《燕子笺》被之声歌，为中兴一代之乐。我想这本传奇，精深奥妙，倘被俗手教坏，岂不损我文名。因而乘机启奏："生口不如熟口，清客强似教

Scene 1 The Banquet

(Enter Ruan Dacheng in ceremonial dress.)

Ruan (Singing to the tune of ***Golden Wreath***):

In times of gallantry,
We see the Six-Dynasties grace
Of golden dress and powdered face.
I am Secretary
In charge of ceremony of the capital town,
Wearing my new hat and black gown
And my leather shoes green or brown,
And my leather shoes green or brown.

(Smiling) I am exceptionally promoted to be Secretary in charge of ceremony through the influence of Prime Minister Ma. I am further honored to be imperial secretary in literary service. The other day I had the honor of presenting four musical plays to His Majesty who was so much delighted that orders were given to select actors and songstresses to sing and perform my *Swallow's Billet* as musical drama to glorify his succession to the throne. I am afraid my drama might be spoiled by unskilled

手。”圣上从谏如流，就命广搜旧院，大罗秦淮，拿了清客妓女数十余人，交与礼部拣选。前日验他色艺，都只平常；还有几个有名的，都是杨龙友旧交，求情免选，下官只得勾去。昨见贵阳相公说道：“教演新戏是圣上心事，难道不选好的，倒选坏的不成。”只得又去传他，尚未到来。今乃乙酉新年人日[3]佳节，下官约同龙友，移樽赏心亭[4]；邀俺贵阳师相，饮酒看雪。早已吩咐把新选的妓女，带到席前验看。正是：

花柳笙歌隋事业，

诙谐裙屐晋风流。

〔下〕

【黄莺儿】〔老旦扮卞玉京道妆背包急上〕

家住蕊珠宫[5]，

恨无端业海风[6]，

把人轻向烟花送。

喉尖唱肿，

裙腰舞松，

一生魂在巫山洞[7]。

actors and songstresses, so I requested that experienced and skillful performers and amateurs might be selected. His Majesty granted my request and dozens of actors and songstresses are selected by the Ministry of Ceremony. But during the rehearsal, their performance has left much to be desired. Some well-known songstresses and amateurs are old acquaintances of Secretary Yang Longyou, and at his request I exempted their service in the palatial theatre. Yesterday the prime minister told me that His Majesty was much concerned with the performance, so the most skillful actors and songstresses should be selected. Today is the lunar Spring Festival. I have invited Secretary Yang to the Delightful Pavilion to drink and enjoy the snow scene and see if the performance would please the prime minister. So the newly selected actors, songstresses and amateurs are ordered to come for rehearsal.

We shall hear songs and flutes under the willow trees

And see if the new actors' performance will please. (Exit.)

(Enter Jade Bian in Taoist dress.)

Bian (Singing to the tune of ***Orioles' Song***):

I lived in Pistil Bower,

But an ill wind blows me into a sing-song flower.

My throat is strained,

And my waist pained.

My soul longs for the cloud to quench my thirst with shower.

I am Jade Bian. Why should a smile-selling songstress be clad

俺下玉京，今日为何这般打扮，只因朝廷搜拿歌妓；逼俺断了尘心。昨夜别过姊妹，换上道妆，飘然出院，但不知那里好去投师。

望城东云山满眼，
仙界路无穷。

〔飘飖下〕

〔副净、外、净扮丁继之、沈公宪、张燕筑三清客上〕

【皂罗袍】〔副净〕

正把秦淮箫弄，
看名花好月，
乱上帘栊。
凤纸[8]签名唤乐工，
南朝天子春心动。
我丁继之年过六旬，
歌板久抛；
前日托过杨老爷，
免我前往，
怎的今日又传起来了。

〔外、净〕俺两个也都是免过的，不知又传，有何话说。

〔副净拱介〕两位老弟，大家商量，我们一班清客，感动皇爷，召去教歌，也不是容易的。

〔外、净〕正是。

in a Taoist dress? Since the songstresses are forced to sing and dance on the palatial stage, we cannot be paid as before. So I said goodbye to my sisters and left them for a fairy bower. But where can I find it?

Gazing eastward, I see but clouds and hills appear.

How can I know where is the celestial sphere?

(Exit with sleeves spread like wings.)

(Enter three amateurs: Ding Jizhi, Shen Gongxian and Zhang Yanzhu.)

Ding (Singing to the tune of ***Silk Robe***):

I play on flute in riverside bowers,

Viewing through window screen the moon and flowers.

Musicians are summoned to the palace to sing

For the imperial heart is stirred in spring.

I am Ding Jizhi, amateur musician of over sixty years old who has not sung to the rhythm of the clappers for a long time. The day before yesterday, I asked Secretary Yang's favor to be exempt from palatial service and won his approval. But unexpectedly I am still summoned to the palatial theatre today.

Shen & Zhang: We were also exempt from service and are summoned today, too. And we do not know what for either.

Ding (Saluting them with clasped hands): My fellow amateurs, it is not easy for us to be summoned to teach in the palatial theatre.

Shen & Zhang: Indeed it is not easy.

〔副净〕二位青年上进，该去走走，我老汉多病年衰，也不望甚么际遇[9]了。今日我要躲过，求二位遮盖一二。

〔外〕这有何妨，太公钓鱼，愿者上钩[10]。

〔净〕是！是！难道你犯了王法，定要拿去审问不成。

〔副净〕既然如此，我老汉就回去了。

〔回行介〕

急忙回首，青青远峰；

逍遥寻路，森森乱松。

〔顿足介〕

若不离了尘埃，

怎能免得牵绊。

〔袖出道巾，黄绦换介〕

〔转头呼介〕二位看俺打扮罢，道人醒了扬州梦[11]。

〔摇摆下〕

〔外〕咦！他竟出家去了，好狠心也。

〔净〕我们且坐廊下晒暖，待他姊妹到来，同去礼部过堂。

〔坐地介〕

〔小旦扮寇白门，丑扮郑妥娘，杂扮差役跟上〕

〔小旦〕桃片随风不结子。

Ding: You are young and have a bright future while I am old and ill, having no chance for advancement. So I wish not to go to answer the summon. Do you think it possible?

Shen: You may do as you will. The equality of unequals are inequality. How could the unequals be forced to be equal?

Zhang: You have committed no crime against the palatial theatre. Why should you be forced to teach actors on the stage?

Ding: What you say is right. Then I will not go to the palatial theatre. (Going back)

(Singing):

Turning my head, I see green peaks afar.

Going back, how lush the pine trees are!

(Stamping the feet)

If I do not take off my dusty dress,

How can I get free from the mess?

(Taking Taoist dress out from his sleeves and put it on, then turning back and calling):

Do you not find I seem

A Taoist awake from his dream? (Exit.)

Shen: Ah! How can he be determined to become a Taoist?

Zhang: Let us sit down and warm ourselves in the sunshine and wait for our fellow sisters to go together to the Ministry of Ceremony. (Sitting on the ground)

(Enter White Kou and Safe Zheng with a Man of Service.)

Kou: *The peach petals without fruit will fly with speed.*

〔丑〕柳绵浮水又成萍[12]。

〔望介〕你看老沈老张不约俺一声儿，先到廊下向暖，我们走去，打他个耳刮子。

〔相见，诨介〕

〔外问杂介〕又传我们到那里去？

〔杂〕传你们到礼部过堂，送入内庭教戏。

〔外〕前日免过俺们了。

〔杂〕内阁大老爷不依，定要借重你们几个老清客哩。

〔净〕是那几个？

〔杂〕待我瞧瞧票子。

〔取票看介〕丁继之、沈公宪、张燕筑。

〔问介〕那姓丁的如何不见？

〔外〕他出家去了。

〔杂〕既出了家，没处寻他，待我回官罢！

〔向净、外介〕你们到了的，竟往礼部过堂去。

〔净〕等他姊妹们到齐着。

〔杂〕今日老爷们秦淮赏雪，吩咐带着女客，席上验看哩。

〔外、净〕既是这等，我们先去了。正是：

Zheng: *The willow down floating on water becomes duckweed.*

(Gazing at Shen and Zhang) They have gone to warm themselves in the sunshine without calling us. Let us go and box them on the ear.

(Saluting them and making fun)

Shen (To Man of Service): Do you know where we are summoned?

Man of Service: You are summoned by the Ministry of Ceremony to teach in the theatre.

Shen: Last time we were exempt from the service.

Man of Service: The exemption is not approved by the prime minister, so you are again summoned to the palatial theatre.

Zhang: Do you know the names of those who are summoned?

Man of Service: Let me see the list.

(Reading the list) Ding Jizhi, Shen Gongxian, Zhang Yanzhu.

(Asking) Why is Ding Jizhi not here?

Shen: He is no longer an amateur musician but a roving Taoist.

Man of Service: Where can I find a roving Taoist? I shall report to my superior.

(To Shen & Zhang) You may go to the Ministry of Ceremony now.

Zhang: We shall wait for our fellow sisters to go together.

Man of Service: High officials will enjoy the snow scene on the riverside and songstresses are requested to take part in the performance.

Shen & Zhang: If so, we shall go now.

传歌留乐府，

拆笛傍宫墙[13]。

〔下〕

〔杂看票问小旦介〕你是寇白门么？

〔小旦〕是。

〔杂问丑介〕你是卞玉京么？

〔丑〕不是，我是老妥。

〔杂〕是郑妥娘了。

〔问介〕那卞玉京呢？

〔丑〕他出家去了。

〔杂〕咦！怎么出家的都配成对儿。

〔问介〕后边还有一个脚小走不上来的，想是李贞丽了？

〔小旦〕不是，李贞丽从良去了！

〔杂〕我方才拉他下楼，他说是李贞丽，怎的又不是？

〔丑〕想是他女儿顶名替来的。

〔杂〕母子总是一般，只少不了数儿就好了。

〔望介〕他早赶上来也。

【忒忒令】〔旦〕

下红楼残腊雪浓，

过紫陌早春泥冻；

不惯行走，

脚儿十分痛。

We shall sing in the music hall.

And play on flute by palace wall.

(Exeunt.)

Man of Service (Reading the list and asking Kou): Are you White Kou?

Kou: Yes, I am.

Man of Service (Asking Zheng): Are you Jade Bian?

Zheng: No, I am Safe Zheng.

Man of Service: So you are safe. But where is Bian?

Zheng: She has also become a roving Taoist.

Man of Service: Ah! Will the Taoists rove in pair? Who is the one with lotus feet lagging behind? Is she Chaste Lee?

Kou: No, Chaste Lee is married to a high official.

Man of Service: When I pulled her downstairs, she said she was Chaste Lee. How can it be otherwise?

Zheng: Perhaps her daughter has come in her place.

Man of Service: I do not care if it be mother or daughter, provided that we have not lessened the number of songstresses. (Turning back) She will soon overtake us.

(Enter Fragrant.)

Fragrant (Singing to the tune of ***A Tootoo Song***) :

Downstairs I go

In winter late in piled-up snow.

I pass the way

With early spring on frozen clay.

传凤诏，
选蛾眉，
把丝鞭，
骑骄马；
催花使乱拥。
奴家香君，被捉下楼，
叫去学歌，是俺烟花本等，
只有这点志气，就死不磨。

〔杂喊介〕快些走动！
〔旦到介〕
〔小旦〕你也下楼了，屈尊，屈尊。
〔丑〕我们造化，就得服侍皇帝了。
〔旦〕情愿奉让罢。
〔同行介〕
〔杂〕前面是赏心亭了，内阁马老爷，光禄阮老爷，兵部杨老爷，少刻即到。你们各人整理伺候。
〔杂同小旦、丑下〕
〔旦私语介〕难得他们凑来一处，正好吐俺胸中之气。

【前腔】

赵文华陪着严嵩，
抹粉脸席前趋奉；
丑腔恶态，演出真鸣凤[14]。

Unused to walking, my feet feel sore;

Songstresses are called to the palace door.

On a proud steed I may flip

My silken whip.

How can I hasten flowers

To run riot in royal bowers!

I am hastened downstairs to learn to perform on the palatial stage, that is a songstress' duty. But it is not my duty to marry again, and my determination will not change even at the price of death.

Man of Service (Calling her): Be quick!

(Fragrant comes.)

Kou: You condescend to come down.

Zhang: We have the good luck to serve His Majesty.

Fragrant: I wish the good luck will not fall on me.

(They walk together.)

Man of Service: Ahead is the Delightful Pavilion. The prime minister and secretaries will be there soon. You may get ready for the performance. (Exit with Kou and Zhang.)

Fragrant: I do not know they should come together with me. Then it would be a chance for me to give vent to my discontent before them.

(Singing to ***the previous tune***):

An evil-doer and his flatterers base,

How could they talk with grace?

俺做个女祢衡，挝渔阳，

声声骂；看他懂不懂。

〔净扮马士英，副净扮阮大铖，末扮杨文骢，外、小生扮从人喝道上〕

〔旦避下〕

〔副净〕琼瑶楼阁朱微抹。

〔末〕金碧峰峦粉细勾。

〔净〕好一派雪景也。

〔副净〕这座赏心亭，原是看雪之所。

〔末〕请酒！

〔同举杯介〕

〔副净问外介〕选的妓女，可曾叫到了么？

〔外禀介〕叫到了。

〔杂领众妓叩头介〕

〔净细看介〕

〔吩咐介〕今日雅集，用不着他们，叫他礼部过堂去罢。

〔副净〕特令到此伺候酒席的。

〔净〕留下那个年小的罢。

〔众下〕

〔净问介〕他唤什么名字？

〔杂禀介〕李贞丽。

〔净笑介〕丽而未必贞也。

〔笑向副净介〕我们扮过陶学士了，再扮一折党太尉何如？

〔副净〕妙！妙！

〔唤介〕贞丽过来斟酒唱曲。

Beating the drum with my two hands,

I'll blame him and see if he understands.

(Enter Prime Minister Ma and Secretaries Ruan and Yang, followed by attendants.)

(Exit Fragrant.)

Ruan: *The crimson mansions are adorned with jasper bright,*

Yang: *The green mountains are covered in powder white.*

Ma: What a beautiful snow scene!

Ruan: The Delightful Pavilion is built for the enjoyment of beautiful scenes.

Yang: Let us drink.

(They hold up their cups and drink.)

Ruan (To Attendants): Have the selected songstresses come here?

Attendant: Here they are.

(Another attendant leads the songstresses in and they kowtow to the high officials.)

Ma: We need no songstresses in our feast. Tell them to withdraw.

Ruan: They are summoned for the performance.

Ma: Then leave the youngest here.

(Exeunt all songstresses but Fragrant.)

What is her name?

Attendant: Chaste Lee.

Ma (Laughing): How can she be chaste?

Ruan (To Fragrant): Come here to serve wine and sing!

(Fragrant waves her head.)

〔旦摇头介〕〔净〕为何摇头?

〔旦〕不会。

〔净〕呵呀！样样不会，怎称名妓。

〔旦〕原非名妓。〔掩泪介〕

〔净〕你有甚心事，容你说来。

【江儿水】〔旦〕

妾的心中事，
乱似蓬，
几番要向君王控。
拆散夫妻惊魂迸，
割开母子鲜血涌，
比那流贼还猛。
作哑装聋，
骂着不知惶恐。

〔净〕原来有这些心事。

〔副净〕这个女子却也苦了。

〔末〕今日老爷们在此行乐，不必只是诉冤了。

〔旦〕杨老爷知道的，奴家冤苦，也值当不的[15]一诉。

【五供养】

堂堂列公，
半边南朝，
望你峥嵘[16]。
出身希贵宠，

Ma: Why are you waving your head?

Fragrant: I do not know how to serve.

Ma: If you do not know how to serve, how can you be a songstress?

Fragrant: I am not a service songstress. (Hiding her face with her sleeves)

Ma: What do you have in your mind? You may tell us.

Fragrant (Singing to the tune of ***Water in the River***):

My mind is in pell-mell.
It is His Majesty I'd like to tell.
My lord from me is torn apart;
My mother left me with broken heart.
You are more cruel than the foe
And harder than the rebels' blow.
You pretend not to hear the blame;
You feel nor fear nor shame.

Ma: Is that all in your mind?

Ruan: She has suffered indeed.

Yang: Do not let her grievance disturb our pleasure.

Fragrant: Secretary Yang knows my grievance. Why should I give vent to it?

(Singing to the tune of ***Five Provisions***):

You are officials high.
On you the Southern Dynasty would rely.
You do not do your duty,
But seek to enjoy beauty.

创业选声容，

后庭花[17]又添几种。

把俺胡撮弄[18]，

对寒风雪海冰山，

苦陪觞咏[19]。

〔净怒介〕哇！这妮子胡言乱道，该打嘴了。

〔副净〕闻得李贞丽，原是张天如、夏彝仲辈品题之妓，自然是放肆的。该打！该打！

〔末〕看他年纪甚小，未必是那个李贞丽。

〔旦恨介〕便是他待怎的！

【玉交枝】

东林伯仲[20]，

俺青楼皆知敬重。

干儿义子从新用，

绝不了魏家种。

〔副净〕好大胆，骂的是那个，快快采去丢在雪中。

〔外采旦推倒介〕

〔旦〕冰肌雪肠原自同，铁心石腹何愁冻。

〔副净〕这奴才，当着内阁大老爷，这般放肆，叫我们都开罪了。可恨！可恨！

〔下席踢旦介〕

〔末起拉介〕

〔净〕罢！罢！这样奴才，何难处死，只怕妨了俺宰相之度。

〔末〕是！是！丞相之尊，娼女之贱，天地悬绝，何足介意。

You sing the song of conquered land with glee,
And make light of poor me.
You order me to sing in biting breeze,
Of snowy sea and icy mountain as you please.

Ma (Angered)**:** What is she singing? She should be given a box on the ear or on the mouth.

Ruan: As a renowned songstress, she should be given more boxes.

Yang: But she looks so young. Maybe she is not Chaste Lee.

Fragrant (Resentfully)**:** What if I am?

(Singing to the tune of ***Entwined Branches***):

We songstresses respect those who do no wrong,
But not those who to Eunuch Wei's party belong.

Ruan: How dare she blame high officials! Push her down in snow! (Attendants push her.)

Fragrant: *Pure heart and icy skin since days of old,*
Like stone or iron, I fear no cold.

Ruan: How dare a servile songstress insult the prime minister! Nor are we exempt from her insult. How hateful! (Going down from the table to kick her, but stopped by Yang.)

Ma: It would be easy to put to death such a servile songstress, but it might not become my premiership's dignity.

Yang: Yes, yes, your dignity and her servility are as far apart as heaven

〔副净〕也罢！启过老师相，送入内庭，拣着极苦的脚色，叫他去当。

〔净〕这也该的。

〔末〕着人拉去罢！

〔杂拉旦介〕

〔旦〕奴家已拼一死。

吐不尽鹃血[21]满胸，

吐不尽鹃血满胸。

〔拉旦下〕〔净〕好好一个雅集，被这奴才搅乱坏了。可笑，可笑！

〔副净、末连三揖介〕得罪，得罪！望乞海涵[22]，另日竭诚罢。

〔净〕兴尽宜回春雪棹[23]。

〔副净〕客羞应斩美人头。

〔净、副净从人喝道下〕

〔末吊场介〕可笑香君才下楼来，偏撞两个冤对[24]，这场是非免不了的；若无下官遮盖，香君性命也有些不妥哩。罢！罢！选入内庭，倒也省了几日悬挂；只是媚香楼无人看守，如何是好？

〔想介〕有了，画友蓝瑛托俺寻寓，就接他暂住楼上；待香君出来，再作商量。

from earth. So your premiership might not mind such trifles.

Ruan: If your premiership will, send her to be punished in the palatial theatre.

Ma: That would be her due.

Yang: Then send her to the palatial theatre!

(Attendants come to pull Fragrant out.)

Fragrant: I am not afraid of death.

Could I care for the cuckoo's bloody breath?

Could I care for the cuckoo's bloody breath?

Ma: A joyful feast is spoiled by this servile songstress. How regrettable!

Ruan and Yang (With clasped hands): Excuse us. We shall remedy our fault by putting on a new performance.

Ma: *We may go back when we feel no more pleasure.*

Ruan: *We're sorry not to have punished her at leisure.*

(Exeunt with attendants.)

Yang: It is regrettable that Fragrant has offended two adversary high officials. It would seem inevitable for her to lose her life without my poor excuse. Now she is sent to the palatial theatre. It might take a load off my mind for sometime. But who shall take care of her bower, where nobody dwells now?

(Thinking over) Well, my friend Lan Ying is looking for an artist's atelier. I may ask him to live in it before her return.

赏心亭上雪初融，
煮鹤烧琴宴钜公[25]；
恼杀秦淮歌舞伴，
不同西子入吴宫。

【注释】

[1] 衔名供奉：供奉是指以文学、技艺供奉内庭的官。

[2] 王铎：字觉斯，孟津（今河南孟县）人，书法名家。钱谦益，字受之，号牧斋，常熟人。

[3] 乙酉新年人日：乙酉为南明弘光二年，即公元 1645 年。人日是阴历正月初七日。

[4] 赏心亭：在江苏江宁县西，下水城门上，下临秦淮。

[5] 家住蕊珠宫：意说她本与神仙有缘，表现她这时要出家入道的心情。蕊珠宫，神仙居住的地方。

[6] 业海风：业海是佛经上的话，意说世人造成种种罪业，无量无边，有如大海。业海风指从业海吹来的风。

[7] 一生魂在巫山洞：这里是卞玉京自怨一生过着娼妓的生活。

[8] 凤纸：凤诏，皇帝的诏书。

[9] 际遇：机遇。

[10] “太公钓鱼”二句：相传姜太公（吕望）曾在渭水边用无饵的直钩钓鱼，说“负命者上钩来”。

[11] 道人醒了扬州梦：意说他已从歌舞繁华中清醒过来。唐朝杜牧《遣怀》诗：“十年一觉扬州梦，赢得青楼薄倖名。”

[12] 柳绵浮水又成萍：我国古时传说，以为浮萍是柳绵入水所化的。

Epilogue of the Scene

When snow begins to melt in the delightful bower,
A sumptuous feast is spread for officials in power.
The riverside songstress is angry with the guest;
Another Beauty enters the palace in the west.

(Exeunt.)

[13] 擫（yè）笛傍宫墙：这引用唐李謩的故事。李謩爱好音乐，唐玄宗在宫里奏乐时，他拿笛子在宫墙外偷听，把曲调都记回来了。擫笛，用手指按笛子。

[14] 鸣凤：《鸣凤记》，相传是明朝王世贞撰的。

[15] 值当不的：值不得。

[16] 峥嵘：强盛、振作之意。

[17] 后庭花：歌曲名，陈后主所作。后人一般以《后庭花》指亡国之音。

[18] 胡撮弄：任意摆布玩弄。

[19] 觞咏：饮酒赋诗。

[20] 伯仲：本指兄弟，这里意指朋党。

[21] 鹃血：传说杜鹃的啼声很凄苦，甚至啼到口里流出血来。

[22] 海涵：海量包涵。

[23] 兴尽宜回春雪棹：东晋时，王子猷在雪夜乘船到剡溪访问戴安道，船将要到时，他忽然又叫船夫把船开回去。船夫问他，他说："乘兴而来，兴尽而返。"

[24] 冤对：冤家对头。

[25] 煮鹤烧琴宴钜公：煮鹤烧琴指杀风景的事情。钜公指大官。

第二出　选优

〔场上正中悬一匾，书“薰风殿”，两旁悬联，书“万事无如杯在手，百年几见月当头”。款书“东阁大学士臣王铎奉敕书”〕

〔外扮沈公宪，净扮张燕筑，小旦扮寇白门，丑扮郑妥娘同上〕

〔外〕天子多情爱沈郎[1]。

〔净〕当年也是画眉张[2]。

〔小旦〕可怜一树白门柳。

〔丑〕让我风流郑妥娘。

〔外〕我们被选入宫，伺候两日，怎么还不见动静。

〔净仰看介〕此处是薰风殿，乃奏乐之所；闻得圣驾将到，选定脚色，就叫串戏哩。

〔外〕如何名薰风殿？

〔净〕你不晓得，琴曲里有一句：“南风之薰兮”[3]，取这个

Scene 2 Selection of Songstresses

(Scene: A palace hall with a horizontal signboard on the background inscribed with three golden words: *Summer Breeze Hall*, and two perpendicular boards on the left and right pillars inscribed with the following couplet:

(Left) *Nothing is better than a cup of wine.*

(Right) *How often can we see the full moon shine?*

(Enter two amateurs, Shen Gongxian and Zhang Yanzhu, and two songstresses, White Kou and Safe Zheng.)

Sheng: *My sire was loved by the king in his life.*

Zhang: *And mine pencilled the eyebrows of his wife.*

Kou: *Who pities at White Gate the willow tree?*

Zheng: *No one is so coquette and safe as me.*

Shen: We were summoned to the palatial theatre, but two days have passed with nothing for us to do.

Zhang (Looking at the signboard): This is the Summer Breeze Hall where His Majesty is entertained with music and performance. It is said we are summoned to perform a musical drama here.

Zheng: Why is the hall called Summer Breeze?

Zhang: Summer Breeze means some men please.

意思。

〔丑〕呸！你们男风兴头，要我们女客何用。

〔小旦〕我们女客得了宠眷，做个大嫔妃，还强如他男风哩。

〔丑〕正是，他男风得了宠眷，到底是个小兄弟。

〔净〕好徒弟，骂及师父来了。

〔外〕咱们掌了班时，不要饶他。

〔净〕谁肯饶他。明日教动戏，叫老妥试试我的鼓槌子罢。

〔丑嗤笑，指介〕你老张的鼓槌子，我曾试过，没相干的。

〔众笑介〕

〔副净冠带扮阮大铖上〕

【绕地游】

汉宫如画，

春晓珠帘挂，

待粉蝶黄莺打。

歌舞西施，

文章司马[4]，

厮混了红袖乌纱。

〔见介〕你们俱已在此，怎的不见李贞丽？

〔小旦〕他从雪中一跌，至今忍痛，还卧在廊下哩。

〔副净〕圣驾将到，选定脚色，就要串戏；怎么由得他的性儿。

〔众〕是，是，俺们拉他过来。〔同下〕

Zheng: If some men please each other, is it homosexual love?

Kou: If a woman pleases the king, she may become the queen, far better than a homosexual lover.

Zheng: A homosexual lover is at best a younger brother.

Zhang: How dare you jeer at your master?

Shen: When we become her master, we shall spare her no pain to learn.

Zhang: Then I shall press her, squeeze her, beat her like a drum and teach her to obey.

Zheng (Sneering): I have been the drum you beat and I know how strong you are.

(All burst in laughter.)

(Enter Ruan Dacheng in official dress.)

Ruan (Singing to the tune of ***Around the Earth***):

On spring morning in picturesque palace high,
On pearl screen flutter oriole and butterfly.
Songstress' dancing feet and poet's head
Blend his black crown and her sleeves red.

(Saluting them) You are all here. But where is Chaste Lee?

Kou: She lies still painful at a corner of the hall as a result of her fall in snow on that day.

Ruan: His Majesty will soon come to select songstresses for the perfor-mance. How can she stay apart?

All: We shall try to bring her here. (Exeunt.)

〔副净自语介〕李贞丽这个奴才，如此可恶，今日净、丑脚色，一定借重他了。

〔杂扮二内监执龙扇前引，小生扮弘光帝，又扮二监提壶捧盒，随上〕

〔小生〕满城烟树间梁陈，高下楼台望不真；原是洛阳花里客[5]，偏来管领秣陵春。

〔坐介〕寡人登极御宇，将近一年，幸亏四镇阻当，流贼不能南下；虽有叛臣倡议欲立潞藩[6]，昨已捕拿下狱。目今外侮不来，内患不生，正在采选淑女，册立正宫，这也都算小事；只是朕独享帝王之尊，无有声色[7]之奉，端居高拱[8]，好不闷也。

〔副净跪介〕光禄寺卿臣阮大铖恭请万安。

〔小生〕平身。

〔副净起介〕

【掉角儿】〔小生〕

看阳春残雪早花，

蹙愁眉慵游倦耍。

〔副净〕圣上安享太平，正宜及时行乐；慵游倦耍，却是为何？

Ruan (Aside): Chaste Lee is so disagreeable that I must assign her an obscure role.

(Enter Emperor Hong Guang— i.e. Blissful Prince—preceeded by eunuchs holding imperial dragon fans and followed by two eunuchs with pot or box in hand.)

Emperor: Mist-veiled trees in the capital loom left and right,

High and low dimly appear palace bowers bright.

Of flowers in West Capital I loved to sing,

But now I come to reign over the Southern spring.

(Sitting) One year has nearly passed since I succeeded to the throne. Thanks to the four generals defending the empire, the rebels cannot drive to the south and rival princes are put in prison. Now there is no danger within nor aggression from without, and we may enjoy peace for the time being. An emperor should gratify his sensuous pleasure, or how can we drive away daily annoyance?

(Enter Ruan Dacheng.)

Ruan (Kneeling): Long live Your Majesty!

Emperor: You may rise.

(Ruan rises.)

(Singing to the tune of ***A Corner Song***):

Early spring snow begins to melt,

On my eyebrows worry is felt.

Ruan: In time of peace Your Majesty should enjoy pleasure. Why should you feel worried?

〔小生〕朕有一桩心事，料你也应晓得。

〔副净〕想怕流贼南犯？

〔小生〕非也。阻隔着黄河雪浪，

那怕他天汉浮槎[9]。

〔副净〕想愁兵弱粮少？

〔小生〕也不是。俺有那镇淮阴诸猛将[10]，

转江陵大粮艘，有甚争差。

〔副净〕既不为内外兵马，想是正宫未立，配德无人？

〔小生〕也不为此。那礼部钱谦益，采选淑女，不日册立。

有三妃九嫔，教国宜家。

〔副净〕又不为此，臣晓得了。

〔私奏介〕想因叛臣周镳、雷缜祚，倡造邪谋，欲迎立潞王耳。

〔小生〕益发说错了。那奸人倡言惑众，久已搜拿。

〔副净低头沉吟介〕却是为何？

〔小生〕卿供奉内庭，乃朕心腹之臣，怎不晓得朕的心事。

〔副净跪介〕圣虑高深，臣衷愚昧，其实不能窥测。伏望明白宣示，以便分忧。

〔小生〕朕谕你知道罢，朕贵为天子，何求不遂。只因你所

Emperor: I have something on my mind that you should know as imperial attendant.

Ruan: Could Your Majesty be worried about the rebels' invasion?

Emperor: No. *The Yellow River bars the rebels' southern way.*

They have no ships to cross it night or day.

Ruan: Are you worried for lack of food and supply for the armed forces?

Emperor: No. *We have so many generals in spirits high,*

And so many ships loaded with food supply.

Ruan: If it is neither worry within nor without, then can it be the enthronement of the queen?

Emperor: *No. We have selected so many maidens fair,*

Their beauty would do good to state affair.

Ruan: If it is not the worry within the palace, can it be that without about the rival princes who plot to succeed to the throne?

Emperor: *Do you not know that all the plotters are arrested and put in prison?*

Ruan (Meditating with bowed head): Then your humble servant is at his wit's end.

Emperor: The imperial attendant is nearer to us than other high officials. If you do not know what is in my mind, who else can?

Ruan (Kneeling): Your humble servant is near to Your Majesty as your clothes, but not so near as your skin. Would Your Majesty tell me what is near to your heart?

Emperor: I shall tell you what is in my heart. An emperor may have

献《燕子笺》，乃中兴一代之乐，点缀太平，第一要事；今日正月初九，脚色尚未选定，万一误了灯节，岂不可恼。

〔指介〕你看阁学王铎书的对联道："万事无如杯在手，百年几见月当头"。一年能有几个元宵，故此日夜踌蹰，饮膳俱减耳。

〔副净〕原来为此，巴里之曲[11]，有廑[12]圣怀，皆微臣之罪也。

〔叩头介〕臣敢不鞠躬尽瘁，以报主知。

〔起唱介〕

【前腔】

忝卿僚填词辨挝[13]，

备供奉诙谐风雅。

恨不能腮描粉墨，

也情愿怀抱琵琶。

但博得歌筵前垂一顾，

舞裀边受寸赏[14]，

御酒龙茶，

三生侥幸，

all he wishes. I wish to have a musical drama to glorify my reign, so I would like to have your *Swallow's Billet* to be performed on the palatial stage on the Vernal Moon Festival, which will arrive in a few days, but the actors and songstresses are not yet selected, so I am worried if the play can be performed in time.

(Pointing to the couplet on the left and right pillars and reading)

Nothing is better than a cup of wine.
How often can we see the full moon shine?

As there is only one Vernal Moon Festival in a year, so we are so much worried about the performance as to neglect my meals and disturb my sleep.

Ruan: If that is Your Majesty's worry, as the author your humble servant is the first to blame.

(Kowtowing) What would I not do to show my gratitude to Your Majesty? (Rising)

(Singing to ***the previous tune***):

As writer of the musical play,
I would set all my wits on display.
Though I can't act with powdered face,
I would play on the lute with grace.
If you should favor with a glance
The songstresses and performers of the dance
Or give them a cup of wine or tea,
They would receive the gifts with highest glee.

万世荣华。

这便是为臣经济，

报主功阀[15]。

〔前问介〕但不知内庭女乐，少何脚色？

〔小生〕别样脚色，都还将就得过，只有生、旦、小丑不惬朕意。

〔副净〕这也容易，礼部送到清客、歌妓，现在外厢，听候拣选。

〔小生〕传他进来。

〔副净〕领旨。

〔急入领外、净、旦、小旦、丑上〕

〔俱跪介〕

〔小生问外、净介〕你二人是串戏清客么？

〔外、净〕不敢，小民串戏为生。

〔小生〕既会串戏，新出传奇也曾串过么？

〔外、净〕新出的《牡丹亭》《燕子笺》《西楼记》[16]，都曾串过。

〔小生〕既会《燕子笺》，就做了内庭教习[17]罢。

〔外、净叩头介〕

〔小生问介〕那三个歌妓，也会《燕子笺》么？

〔小旦、丑〕也曾学过。

I'd think it an honor all my life long.

Which should be glorified with wine and song.

That is my only desire strong.

May I know if the selected actors and songstresses are satisfactory?

Emperor: Actors are more or less satisfactory, but the hero, the heroine and the clown leave much to be desired.

Ruan: It would not be difficult to solve this question. The Ministry of Ceremony has sent amateurs and songstresses who are waiting outside for selection.

Emperor: Tell them to come in.

Ruan: I will call them.

(Enter Shen Gongxian, Zhang Yanzhu, White Kou, Safe Zheng and Fragrant Lee, kneeling before the emperor.)

Emperor (To Shen and Zhang): Are you amateur performers?

Shen & Zhang: We are unqualified amateurs living on performance.

Emperor: Have you performed new drama?

Shen & Zhang: We have been actors in *Dream in Peony Pavilion, Swallow's Billet* and *Romance of the Western Bower*.

Emperor: Since you have performed *Swallow's Billet*, you may teach the actors in the palatial theatre.

Shen & Zhang (Kowtowing): Long live Your Majesty!

Emperor (Asking the three songstresses): Can you sing the songs in *Swallow's Billet*?

Kou & Zheng: We have learned our part.

〔小生喜介〕益发妙了。

〔问旦介〕这个年小的，怎不答应？

〔旦〕没学。

〔副净跪介〕臣启圣上，那两个学过的，例应派做生、旦。这一个没学的，例应派做丑脚。

〔小生〕既有定例，依卿所奏。

〔小旦、丑、旦叩头介〕

〔小生〕俱着起来，伺候串戏。

〔俱起介〕

〔丑背喜介〕还是我老妥做了天下第一个正旦。

〔小生向副净介〕卿把《燕子笺》摘出一曲，叫他串来，当面指点。

〔外、净、小旦、丑随意演《燕子笺》一曲，副净作态指点介〕

〔小生喜介〕有趣，有趣！都是熟口，不愁扮演了。

〔唤介〕长侍斟酒，庆贺三杯。

〔杂进酒，小生饮介〕

〔小生起介〕我们君臣同乐，打一回十番何如？

〔副净〕领旨。

〔小生〕寡人善于打鼓，你们各认乐器。

Emperor (Glad): Well. Why does the youngest songstress say nothing?

Fragrant: I have not learned my part in the drama.

Ruan: Will Your Majesty select the learned to play the roles of hero and heroine, and the unlearned to play the clown?

Emperor: Your suggestion is approved.

(Kou, Zheng and Fragrant kowtow.)

You may rise and get ready for the performance.

(They rise.)

Zheng (Aside): I am glad to play the most important role of heroine.

Emperor (To Ruan): You may select songs from *Swallow's Billet* for them to sing and play, and see if they are qualified for their roles.

(Shen, Zhang, Kou and Zheng sing their songs and perform as if on the stage. Ruan gives his instruction.)

Emperor (Glad): The performance is interesting. Since they are experienced actors and songstresses, I need not worry about the success of the performance. (Calling) Attendants, pour wine in the cup and let us congratulate the performance with three cups of wine. (Wine is served.)

Emperor (Drinking and then rising): Let us enjoy the pleasure of playing on ten musical instruments.

Ruan: Very well, Your Majesty.

Emperor: I am good at beating the drum. You may choose your instrument you like.

〔众打雨夹雪一套，完介〕
〔小生大笑介〕十分忧愁消去九分了。
〔唤介〕长侍斟酒，再庆三杯。
〔杂进酒，小生饮介〕
【前腔】

旧吴宫重开馆娃[18]，
新扬州初教瘦马[19]。
淮阳鼓昆山弦索，
无锡口姑苏娇娃。
一件件闹春风，
吹暖响，
斗晴烟，
飘冷袖，
宫女如麻。
红楼翠殿，
景美天佳。
都奉俺无愁天子[20]，
语笑喧哗。

〔看旦介〕那个年小歌妓，美丽非常，派做丑脚，太屈他了。
〔问介〕你这个年小歌妓，既没学《燕子笺》，可曾学些别的么？

〔旦〕学过《牡丹亭》。
〔小生〕这也好了，你便唱来。
〔旦羞不唱介〕

(All play to the tune of ***Rain and Snow***.)

Emperor (Laughing): Nine-tenths of my sorrow are gone. Attendants, let us congratulate the success with three more cups of wine.

(Drinking and singing to ***the previous tune***):

Ancient palace halls reopen for ladies fair;
The riverside town begins to drill horses bare.
Let us beat sunny drum and play on hillside string,
And hear how beautiful Southern songstresses sing.
How blows spring breeze,
Warms blooming trees.
Melts mist away,
Makes cold sleeves sway
And beauties shine all day.
Palace halls red and green,
What splendid scene!
All worship the son under the sky,
And burst in laughter far and nigh.

(Seeing Fragrant) How beautiful is the young songstress! How can she stoop to play the role of a clown? (To Fragrant) You do not know any part of *Swallow's Billet*, but have you learned to play any other drama?

Fragrant: I have learned *Dream in Peony Pavilion.*

Emperor: Then you may sing any song from it.

(Fragrant feels shy and will not sing.)

〔小生〕看他粉面发红，像是腼腆，赏他一柄桃花宫扇，遮掩春色。

〔杂掷红扇与旦介〕

〔旦持扇唱介〕

【懒画眉】[21]

为甚的玉真重溯武陵源，
也只为水点花飞在眼前。
是他天公不费买花钱，
则咱人心上有啼红怨。
咳！辜负了春三二月天。

〔小生喜介〕妙绝，妙绝！长侍斟酒，再庆三杯。

〔杂进酒，小生饮介〕

〔指旦介〕看此歌妓，声容俱佳，岂可长材短用；还派做正旦罢。

〔指丑介〕那个黑色的，倒该做丑脚。

〔副净〕领旨。

〔丑撅嘴介〕我老妥又不妥了。

〔小生向副净介〕你把生、丑二脚，领去入班；就叫清客二名，用心教习，你也不时指点。

〔副净跪应介〕是，此乃微臣之专责，岂敢辞劳。

〔急领外、净、小旦、丑下〕

〔小生向旦介〕你就在这薰风殿中，把《燕子笺》脚本，三日念会，好去入班。

〔旦〕念会不难，只是没有脚本。

Emperor: She seems timid with her rosy face blushed. Attendant, give her a fan to veil her face. (Attendant gives her a palatial fan.)

Fragrant (Singing with fan in hand to the tune of ***Idly Pencilled Eyebrows***):

Why should the beauty come back where peach petals fly,
For water sprinkled on the flowers before the eye?
To buy the flowers Heaven need not pay,
It cares not for my bloody tears shed on the way,
Nor for the vernal month in vain passed away.

Emperor: Bravo. Let us congratulate her song with three cups of wine again! (Drinking and pointing to Fragrant) Such a beautiful songstress should play the leading role.

(Pointing to Zheng) That songstress may play the role of the clown.

Ruan: Yes, Your Majesty.

Zheng (With pursed lips) Safe Zheng is no longer safe now.

Emperor (To Ruan): You may lead the songstress, actors and the clown to the theatre and ask the two amateurs to teach them under your direction.

Ruan (Kneeling): It is the duty of your humble servant.

(Exit with Shen, Zhang, Kou and Zheng.)

Emperor (To Fragrant): You may stay in the Summer Breeze Hall to learn how to perform *Swallow's Billet* for three days and then go to the theatre.

Fragrant: It is not difficult to perform, but I have got no script.

〔小生唤介〕长侍，你把王铎抄的楷字脚本，赏与此旦。

〔杂取脚本付旦，跪接介〕

〔小生〕千年只有歌场乐，万事何须酒国愁。

〔杂引下〕

〔旦掩泪介〕罢了，罢了！已入深宫，那有出头之日。

【前腔】

锁重门垂杨暮鸦，
映疏帘苍松碧瓦。
凉飕飕风吹罗袖，
乱纷纷梅落宫髽[22]。
想起那拆鸳鸯，
离魂惨，
隔云山，
相思苦，
会期难拿。
倩人寄扇，
擦损桃花。
到今日情丝割断，
芳草天涯。

〔叹介〕没奈何，且去念会脚本；或者天恩见怜，放奴出宫，再会侯郎一面，亦未可知。

【尾声】

从此后入骨髓愁根难拔，

Emperor: Attendant, give her the script.

(Attendant gives her the script and she receives it on her knees.)

Emperor: Only the pleasure of music lasts from year to year.

Wine cup in hand, how can sorrow appear?

Fragrant (Hiding her face with her sleeves): What can I do, shut up deep in the palace? When can I come out?

(Singing to ***the previous tune***)

The door is locked up, the sun on the decline,
Before my window screen crows fly over the pine.
My silken sleeves waft in the chilling breeze,
Mume petals fall in pell-mell from the trees.
I still remember we were torn apart
With broken heart.
Clouds and hills bar the way.
How lovesick I'm from day to day!
We long in vain
To meet again.
I have sent my peach blossom fan
To my dearest and nearest man.
But now we are cut far apart, alas!
Like spring and autumn grass.

(Sighing) What can I do but read the script! I only wish Heaven would set me free and let me see my dearest lord once more.

(Singing ***the Epilogue***):

How to remove my sorrow rooted in my bone?

真个是广寒宫姮娥守寡[23]。
只这两日呵！
瘦损宫腰剩一把。

曲终人散日西斜，
殿角凄凉自一家；
纵有春风无路入，
长门关住碧桃花。

【注释】

[1] 沈郎：古曲戏曲中凡称沈郎，一般系指梁尚书令沈约，这里沈公宪引以自比。
[2] 画眉张：汉代张敞，他曾替妻子画眉。
[3] 南风之薰兮：琴曲《南风歌》："南风之薰兮，可以解吾民之愠兮。"相传是虞舜所作的。
[4] 文章司马：汉代文学家司马相如，剧中阮大铖引他自比。
[5] 原是洛阳花里客：福王原封在洛阳。
[6] 潞藩：指朱常淓，是潞简王翊镠的嗣子，袭封潞王。
[7] 声色：音乐女色等。
[8] 端居高拱：端居而高拱双手，形容帝王的清静无事。
[9] 那怕他天汉浮槎：天汉即天河，槎是水中的浮木。那怕他天汉浮槎，意说不怕他从天河上乘槎飞渡。
[10] 镇淮阴诸猛将：指江北四镇。
[11] 巴里之曲："下里巴人"之曲，即俚俗的歌曲。
[12] 厘：少，这里应解作损。

I'm lonely as the Goddess in moon palace alone.

Only in these two days

My waist turns more slender as the breeze sways.

Epilogue of the Scene

The songs are sung and men go away,

At a corner of the hall sad and dreary I stay.

The spring breeze can find no way to enter the bower;

In Long Gate Palace is shut up the green peach flower.

(Exeunt.)

[13] 忝卿僚填词辨挝：意说自己惭愧地列在大臣里面，能够填词奏乐。挝，这里指击鼓的音节。

[14] 舞裀边受寸赏：舞裀是供舞蹈的地毯，寸赏，指极微小的奖赏。

[15] 功阀：阀即阀阅，挂在门上记载功劳的榜，挂在左门叫阀，右门叫阅。功阀意功劳。

[16]《西楼记》：剧曲名，明末袁于令撰，演于鹃和妓女木素徽的故事。

[17] 内庭教习：宫内的歌舞教师。

[18] 旧吴宫重开馆娃：馆娃即馆娃宫，是吴王夫差建筑给西施住的地方。

[19] 新扬州初教瘦马：扬州风俗称妓女作瘦马。

[20] 无愁天子：北齐后主作《无愁曲》，自弹琵琶而唱。民间因称无愁天子。

[21] 懒画眉：这是汤显祖《牡丹亭·寻梦》中的一支曲文。

[22] 宫髽（zhuā）：髽本是妇女的丧髻，这里指一般宫女的髻子。

[23] 广寒宫姮娥守寡：广寒宫即月宫。姮娥即嫦娥，本是羿的妻子。传说羿在西王母处得了不死的药，姮娥把它偷吃了，奔到月中去。

第三出　题画

〔小生扮山人蓝瑛上〕美人香冷绣床[1]闲，

一院桃开独闭关，

无限浓春烟雨里，

南朝留得画中山。

自家武林[2]蓝瑛，表字田叔，自幼驰声画苑[3]。与贵筑杨龙友笔砚至交，闻他新转兵科，买舟来望，下榻这媚香楼上。此楼乃名妓香君梳妆之所，美人一去，庭院寂寥，正好点染云烟[4]，应酬画债。不免将文房画具，整理起来。

〔作洗砚、涤笔、调色、揩盏介〕没有净水怎处？

〔想介〕有了，那花梢晓露，最是清洁，用他调丹濡粉，鲜秀非常。待我下楼，向后园收取。

〔手持色盏暂下〕

【破齐阵】〔生新衣上〕

地北天南蓬转，

巫云楚雨丝牵[5]。

Scene 3 Lee's Bower Revisited

(Enter Painter Lan Ying.)

Lan: The beauty's gone, her fragrant bed unoccupied,
The courtyard shut up, by peach blossoms beautified.
The boundless spring in bloom is veiled in mist and rain,
The Southern mountains left in the picture in vain.

I am Lan Ying, a prodigy painter. My fellow artist Yang Longyou, recently appointed Secretary of Defence, confided Lee's bower to me, where lived the beautiful Fragrant, but which is deserted after her departure for the palatial theatre. The bower, though lonely, is good to paint pictures of beautiful scenery. But where can I find pure water for painting? Well, the morning dew on the peach petals is the purest water which will make the picture glitter with fresh color. I shall go down to the back garden to take some dewdrops.

(Exit with a vase in hand.)

(Enter Hou Chaozong in new dress.)

Hou (Singing to the tune of ***Cavalier's Song***):
I go from north to south between the earth and sky;
The cloud brings showers for flowers in mountains high.

巷滚杨花，
墙翻[6]燕子，
认得红楼旧院。
触起闲情柔如草，
搅动新愁乱似烟，
伤春人正眠。

小生在黄河舟中，遇着苏昆生，一路同行，心忙步急，不觉来到南京。昨晚旅店一宿，天明早起，留下昆生看守行李；俺独自来寻香君，且喜已到院门之外。

【刷子序犯】

只见黄莺乱啭，
人踪悄悄，
芳草芊芊[7]。
粉坏楼墙，
苔痕绿上花砖。
应有娇羞人面，
映着他桃树红妍；
重来浑似阮刘仙[8]，
借东风引入洞中天。

〔作推门介〕原来双门虚掩，不免侧身潜入，看有何人在内。

〔入介〕

【朱奴儿犯】

呀，惊飞了满树雀喧，
踏破了一墀苍藓。
这泥落空堂帘半卷，

The willow down wafts to the hall,
The swallows fly over the wall.
They know the rosy bower in the mansion red,
My heart is stirred like tender grass wide spread.
My sorrow is running riot.
How could her sleeping mind keep quiet!

I met Su Kunsheng in a boat on the Yellow River and we came to Nanjing together. Last night we stayed in a hotel and I got up early at dawn to find Fragrant. Here is her bower.

(Singing to the tune of ***Prelude to the Brush***):

I only hear the golden orioles' warbling song;
No human voice but silence reigns on grass for long.
The white-washed walls no longer clean,
The bricks are covered with moss green.
Does her rosy face still feel shy?
Why with peach blossoms in beauty will she not vie?
Coming again, I seem to be in fairy land.
Would the east wind lead me there with a helping hand?

(Pushing open the door) The door is not well closed. I may slip in to see if she is there.

(Singing to the tune of ***Rosy Maid***):

Ah! Startled chirping birds fly pell-mell from the trees;
I tread on moss as biting breeze.
The clods of clay fallen in half-screened empty hall,

受用煞双栖紫燕。
闲庭院，
没个人传，
蹑踪儿[9]回廊一遍，
直步到小楼前。

〔上指介〕这是媚香楼了。你看寂寂寥寥，湘帘[10]昼卷，想是香君春眠未起。俺且不要唤他，慢慢的上了妆楼，悄立帐边；等他自己醒来，转睛一看，认得出是小生，不知如何惊喜哩！〔作上楼介〕

【普天乐】

手拽起翠生生罗襟软，
袖拨开绿杨线。
一层层栏坏梯偏，
一桩桩尘封网罥[11]。
艳浓浓楼外春不浅，
帐里人儿腼腆。

〔看几介〕从几时收拾起银拨冰弦[12]；
摆列着描春容脂箱粉盏，
待做个女山人画叉乞钱[13]。

〔惊介〕怎的歌楼舞榭，改成个画院书轩，这也奇了。

〔想介〕想是香君替我守节，不肯做那青楼旧态，故此留心丹青，聊以消遣春愁耳。

Only a pair of violet swallows enjoy all.
In the courtyard I see,
There is no one to announce me.
On tiptoe in the corridor I walk around,
At last I come to her bower's foreground.

(Pointing upward) Here is her bower, with curtain drawn down by day. She cannot have risen from her bed and should not be awakened from sleep. I shall go up on tiptoe to her curtained bed. What would not be her surprise to find me standing before her!

(Going upstairs and singing to the tune of ***Universal Joy***):

Caressing the soft green silk robe with my sleeves
And pulling apart the branches of willow leaves,
I find the balustrade in decay
And dusty railings seem to stray.
In the garden spring is in full bloom.
Why is she in her curtained bed in deep gloom?

(Seeing the tea table)

When did she no longer play on the string
But begin to paint the beauty of spring?
Would she live as artist in painting?

(Surprised) How could a dancing hall change
Into a painter's atelier? How strange!

(Thinking over) Perhaps Fragrant is unwilling to be a songstress in the green mansion, so she finds new pleasure in painting so as to pass her time.

〔指介〕这是香君卧室，待我轻轻推开。

〔推介〕呀！怎么封锁严密，倒像久不开的；这又奇了，难道也没个人看守。

〔作背手徬徨介〕

【雁过声】

萧然，
美人去远，
重门锁，
云山万千，
知情只有闲莺燕。
尽着狂，
尽着颠，
问着他一双双不会传言。
熬煎，
才待转，
嫩花枝靠着疏篱颤。

〔下听介〕帘栊响，似有个人略喘。

(Pointing to the bedroom) This is her bedroom. Let me push and open the door lightly.

(Pushing) Ah! Why is it locked tight as if no one had entered for a long time? How strange! Is there no one taking care of the bower?

(Loitering with his fingers crossed behind his back.)

(Singing to the tune of ***Wild Geese's Song***):

Lonely,
The beauty's gone far, far away;
Only
The locked doors and cloud-veiled mountains bar my way.
Who knows
But orioles and swallows at leisure
Where she goes?
They may look mild,
But they run wild,
And wild beyond measure.
Wordless, they fly in pair,
How could they bring word there?
In pain
They remain
With fenceside flower
Shivering before her bower. (Listening)
I hear the curtain's flapping sound.
Someone must be coming around.

〔瞧介〕待我看是谁来。

〔小生持盏上楼，惊见介〕你是何人，上我寓楼？

〔生〕这是俺香君妆楼，你为何寓此？

〔小生〕我乃画士蓝瑛。兵科杨龙友先生送俺来寓的。

〔生〕原来是蓝田老，一向久仰。

〔小生问介〕台兄尊号？

〔生〕小生河南侯朝宗，亦是龙友旧交。

〔小生惊介〕呵呀！文名震耳，才得会面。请坐！请坐！

〔坐介〕

〔生〕我且问你，俺那香君那里去了？

〔小生〕听说被选入宫了。

〔生惊介〕怎……怎的被选入宫了！几时去的？

〔小生〕这倒不知。

〔生起，掩泪介〕

【倾杯序】

寻遍，

立东风渐午天，

那一去人难见。

〔瞧介〕看纸破窗棂，

纱裂帘幔。

裹残罗帕，

戴过花钿，

(Looking out) Let me see who is coming?

Lan (Coming upstairs with a vase in hand and startled): Who are you coming up uninvited?

Hou: This is my Fragrant's bower. How can you come to live here?

Lan: I am painter Lan Ying. My friend Yang Longyou asked me to take care of this bower.

Hou: Glad to make your acquaintance, dear artist.

Lan (Asking): May I know who you are?

Hou: I am Hou Chaozong, also an old acquaintance of Yang Longyou.

Lan: Ah! You are a well-known man of letters. What good luck to make your acquaintance! Please take a seat.

(Both sit down.)

Hou: May I ask you where Fragrant is?

Lan: It is said she was selected by the palatial theatre.

Hou (Startled): How...how could she be selected? When did she go to the palace?

Lan: That is what I do not know.

Hou (Rising in tears and singing to the tune of ***Filling the Cup***):

I seek and stay
In the eastern breeze till noonday.
But she is gone, (Gazing)
I find but the paper of the window torn,
While the silk screen,
Her handkerchief and hairpin are not seen.

旧笙箫无一件。

红鸳衾尽卷，

翠菱花放扁[14]，

锁寒烟，

好花枝不照丽人眠。

想起小生定情之日，桃花盛开，映着簇新新一座妆楼；不料美人一去，零落至此。今日小生重来，又值桃花盛开，对景触情，怎能忍住一双眼泪。

〔掩泪坐介〕

【玉芙蓉】

春风上巳[15]天，

桃瓣轻如剪，

正飞绵作雪，

落红成霰[16]。

不免取开画扇，

对着桃花赏玩一番。

〔取扇看介〕

溅血点作桃花扇，

比着枝头分外鲜。

这都是为着小生来。

携上妆楼展，

对遗迹宛然，

为桃花结下了死生冤。

Does she no longer play on the lute
Nor on the flute?
I see her mirror unused and rolled up her quilt red,
The incense burned no longer spread.
Even flowers would weep
To find no beauty here asleep.

I still remember our wedding day in the new bower when peach flowers were in full bloom. How could I know it would be deserted like this? Now I come again to see the blooming peach flowers. How can I refrain my tears when the scene reminds me of the bygone days?

(Singing to the tune of ***Jade Lotus***):

The vernal breeze blows in the the sky;
Light as snowflakes, peach petals fly.
They remind me of my peach blossom fan,
I will enjoy its beauty when I can.

(Taking out the fan and looking about)

Bloodstains turned to peach flowers as you see,
Look fresher than those on the tree.
I'll bring the fan up to her boudoir high
To find the trace
Of her rosy face.
The peach blossoms will unite us, live or die.

〔生〕重到红楼意惘然，
〔末〕闲评诗画晚春天；
〔生〕美人公子飘零尽，
〔末〕一树桃花似往年。

【注释】

[1] 绣床：妇女刺绣用的架子。
[2] 武林：山名，在浙江省杭州城西，杭州因此也别称武林。
[3] 驰声画苑：在画坛上出名。
[4] 点染云烟：指画风景画。
[5] "地北天南蓬转"二句：蓬转比喻一个人到处飘荡。巫云楚雨即巫山云雨，用来形容男女之间的爱情。
[6] 翻：翻飞。
[7] 芊芊：草很茂盛的样子。
[8] 重来浑似阮刘仙：阮、刘，即阮肇、刘晨。

Epilogue of the Scene

Hou: *I come again to her bower, but what to say?*

Lan: *We'll talk of verse and painting on this late spring day.*

Hou: *Where is the roving beauty dear?*

Lan: *Only the peach blooms as last year.*

(Exeunt.)

[9] 蹑（niè）踪儿：小步、轻步。

[10] 湘帘：指用湘妃竹编成的帘子。

[11] 尘封网罥（juàn）：为灰尘所封，蛛网所罥。罥，缠结意。

[12] 银拨冰弦：指琵琶。银拨是弹琵琶用的银片，冰弦是琵琶的弦。

[13] 待做个女山人画叉乞钱：山人，见第二本第二出注释 15。画叉是挂画用的铁叉。整句的意思是说，要做个女山人靠画画来谋生。

[14] 翠菱花放扁：意指镜奁掩盖。

[15] 上巳：阴历三月上旬的巳日。

[16] 霰（xiàn）：雪珠。

第四出　余韵

〔净扮樵子挑担上，丑扮渔翁摇船上，副末扮老赞礼上〕

〔净〕不瞒二位说，我三年没到南京，忽然高兴，进城卖柴。路过孝陵，见那宝城享殿，成了刍牧之场。

〔丑〕呵呀呀！那皇城如何？

〔净〕那皇城墙倒宫塌，满地蒿莱了。

〔副末掩泪介〕不料光景至此。

〔净〕俺又一直走到秦淮，立了半晌，竟没一个人影儿。

〔丑〕那长桥旧院，是咱们熟游之地，你也该去瞧瞧。

〔净〕怎的没瞧，长桥已无片板，旧院剩了一堆瓦砾。

〔丑捶胸介〕咳！恸死俺也。

〔净〕那时疾忙回首，一路伤心；编成一套北曲，名为“哀

Scene 4 Epilogue

(Enter Su as Woodcutter, Liu as Fisherman and an Old Man.)

Su: I had not been in the ancient capital for three long years. Suddenly it dawned on me to sell fuel downtown. When I passed by the Imperial Tomb of the Ming, I found the sacrificial hall turned into a pasture.

Liu: Alas! How about the ancient palaces?

Su: In the town I only found ruined palace walls and brambles and briars here and there.

Old Man (Wiping away his tears): How could we have anticipated such a scene!

Su: I went straight to the River Qinhuai and stood by the riverside for a long while without seeing a single human soul.

Liu: How about the bridgeside bower where we used to visit? Did you go there this time?

Su: How could I not have gone there? But there is no longer any red board on the bridge and I found only piles of broken bricks and tiles in the ruined bower.

Liu (Beating the breast): Alas! It breaks my heart to hear that.

Su: I made haste to come back with a broken heart and composed

江南”。待我唱来！

〔敲板唱弋阳腔[1]介〕俺樵夫呵！

【哀江南】[2]

【北新水令】

山松野草带花挑，
猛抬头秣陵重到。
残军留废垒，
瘦马卧空壕；
村郭萧条，
城对着夕阳道。

【驻马听】

野火频烧，
护墓长楸多半焦。
山羊群跑，
守陵阿监几时逃。
鸽翎蝠粪满堂抛，
枯枝败叶当阶罩；
谁祭扫，
牧儿打碎龙碑帽。

【沉醉东风】

横白玉八根柱倒，
堕红泥半堵墙高，
碎琉璃瓦片多，
烂翡翠窗棂少，

songs entitled *Elegies on the Southern Rivershore*. I will sing them for you if you like.

(Striking sandal clappers) Oh, we woodcutters!

(Singing to the tune of ***Elegies on Southern Rivershore***:

(1) ***New Northern Stream***):

I carry with wild flowers branches of pine tree.

Looking up, I find the ancient town before me.

In ruined fortress left by remnant forces

And empty dykes lie carcasses of lean horses.

Villages look desolate,

The town is drowned in setting sunlight when it's late.

(Singing to the tune of **(2)** ***Listening on Horseback***):

Wild fire wide spread now and again,

In the graveyard most tall trees scorched remain.

A herd of goats and sheep there stay.

When did the guardsmen and eunuchs run away?

Pigeon's plumes and bats' dung spread over the hall;

By withered branches and leaves the steps are covered all.

Who would now offer sacrifice?

The shepherds have broken royal monuments nice.

(Singing to the tune of **(3)** ***Intoxicated in the Eastern Breeze***):

Eight pillars of white jade are fallen in the hall;

Seared petals are piled up half as high as the wall.

Most glazed tiles are broken,

Jadeite window lattice unawoken.

舞丹墀燕雀常朝，
直入宫门一路蒿，
住几个乞儿饿殍。

【折桂令】

问秦淮旧日窗寮，
破纸迎风，
坏槛当潮，
目断魂消。
当年粉黛，
何处笙箫。
罢灯船端阳不闹，
收酒旗重九无聊。
白鸟飘飘，
绿水滔滔，
嫩黄花有些蝶飞，
新红叶无个人瞧。

【沽美酒】

你记得跨青溪半里桥，
旧红板没一条。
秋水长天人过少，
冷清清的落照，
剩一树柳弯腰。

Only swallows and sparrows dance o'er
Brambles and briars overgrown all the way
To the palace door;
Here I see only hungry beggars stay.
(Singing to the tune of **(4)** ***Plucking Laurel Twigs***):
I revisit our former bower by riverside
The torn-off window paper flutters in the breeze.
The window sill welcomes the rising tide.
How could my eyes and soul not freeze?
Oh, rosy face of bygone years with gloomy brow,
Where are you playing on the flute now?
No dragon boats contest on the Double Fifth Day,
On Double Ninth no wineshop streamers on the way.
White birds fly on high;
Green waves flow below.
Over yellow blooms there're some butterflies in flight;
Of newly red leaves no one would enjoy the sight.

(Singing to the tune of **(5)** ***Buying Good Wine***):
Remember the Half-Mile-Long Bridge over the Blue Stream?
Now, not a single red board is left there, even in dream.
The boundless sky sees the running brook,
Where but few people go.
Dreary is the parting sun's cold look;

【太平令】

行到那旧院门，
何用轻敲，
也不怕小犬哰哰。
无非是枯井颓巢，
不过些砖苔砌草。
手种的花条柳梢，
尽意儿采樵；
这黑灰是谁家厨灶？

【离亭宴带歇指煞】

俺曾见金陵玉殿莺啼晓，
秦淮水榭花开早，
谁知道容易冰消。
眼看他起朱楼，
眼看他宴宾客，
眼看他楼塌了。
这青苔碧瓦堆，
俺曾睡风流觉，
将五十年兴亡看饱。
那乌衣巷不姓王，
莫愁湖鬼夜哭，
凤凰台栖枭鸟。
残山梦最真，

The willow tree is bending low.

(Singing to the tune of (6) ***Song of Peace***):

When I come to our former bower by riverside,
I need not knock at the door.
I hear dogs bark no more.
What I see is only the wall dried,
The overturned nest,
The stone and steps which moss and grass infest;
Where are the willow trees I planted, where are they?
Even the oven is reduced to ashes grey.

(Singing to the tune of (7) ***Feast at Farewell Pavilion***):

I have seen in the ancient capital
Or in the palace of jade at least
At daybreak sing golden orioles all,
And open early flowers
by the riverside bowers.
Who knows as easy as ice they melt away?
I have seen the red mansion rise
And guests come to the feast,
But now in ruins the mansion lies.
Amid green moss and emerald tiles broken
Was the place where I slept with beauties unawoken.
I've seen the rise and fall in fifty years,
The mansions no longer belong to the peers.

旧境丢难掉，
不信这舆图换稿。
诌一套哀江南，
放悲声唱到老。

【注释】

[1]弋阳腔：是我国戏曲歌腔的一种，以最初流行于江西省弋阳江一带而得名。

[2]〔哀江南〕曲：此曲引自贾应宠的《贾凫西木皮词》中《历代史略鼓词·哀江南》。原曲的每支曲子有一标题，如〔北新水令〕标题为“总起”,〔驻马听〕标题为“吊金陵”,〔沉醉东风〕标题为“吊故宫”,〔折桂令〕标题为“吊秦淮”。

I have heard the weeping ghost break
The silence of the Griefless Lake;
On Phoenix Terrace the owl sings its evil song.
The dream of the conquered land has come true.
The past will come along.
Though empires change, and maps too.
I will sing the elegies of the South
Till I grow old with empty mouth.

图书在版编目（CIP）数据

许渊冲译桃花扇 ：汉文、英文 / （清）孔尚任著 ；许渊冲，许明译． -- 北京 ：中译出版社，2021.1（2021.7重印）

（许渊冲英译作品）

ISBN 978-7-5001-6457-9

Ⅰ. ①许… Ⅱ. ①孔… ②许… ③许… Ⅲ. ①传奇剧（戏曲）－剧本－中国－清代－汉、英 Ⅳ. ①I237.2

中国版本图书馆CIP数据核字（2020）第242943号

出版发行　中译出版社
地　　址　北京市西城区车公庄大街甲4号物华大厦6层
电　　话　（010）68359719
邮　　编　100044
电子邮箱　book@ctph.com.cn
网　　址　http://www.ctph.com.cn

出 版 人　乔卫兵
总 策 划　刘永淳
责任编辑　刘香玲　张　旭
文字编辑　王秋璎　张莞嘉　赵浠彤
营销编辑　毕竞方　顾　问

封面制作　黄　浩
内文制作　北京竹页文化传媒有限公司
印　　刷　山东临沂新华印刷物流集团有限责任公司
经　　销　新华书店

规　　格　840mm×1092mm　1/32
印　　张　10.75
字　　数　320千
版　　次　2021年1月第1版
印　　次　2021年7月第2次

ISBN 978-7-5001-6457-9　定价：59. 00元